GOOD GIRL GONE BADD

A BADD BROTHERS NOVEL

Jasinda Wilder

GOOD GIRL
GONE BADD

ONE

Baxter

DUDE. THIS CHICK, MAN. SHE'S FINE AS FUCK. BUT THE East Coast, old money, wealthy kind of classy fine. Not, like, bar honey, ring bunny sexy, or even model hot, or movie star gorgeous, or porn star fuckable. She's…one in a million. An actual factual motherfuckin' angel from heaven.

Evangeline du Maurier is…god, I don't have the words. She's a lady. Not a chick, not a honey, not a babe, or a dame, or any of that vaguely condescending, objectifying terminology. She's a goddamn *lady*.

I suppose a thorough description is in order.

Five-eight, five-seven. A true hourglass shape, as in she probably has a literal set of 36-24-36 measurements—I feel compelled, for the sake of honesty, to point out here that measurements and sizes and whatever else don't define a woman to me. I'm just saying, those are Evangeline's measurements by my estimation, and she fuckin' rocks the look so hard it makes me dizzy. Her hair is jet black, so black it shimmers and glints and gleams, thick and long and loose, pulled around the back of her neck to hang down her left shoulder. Green eyes, the shade of a maple leaf in the summer sun. Tanned skin, but naturally tan, not fake or spray tan. A combination of a lot of time in the sun and a natural caramel hint to her skin.

Sharp, exotic, symmetrical facial features, plump lips in a perfect cupid's bow. Not a lot of makeup as far as I can tell, nor a lot of jewelry. A pair of round diamond studs in her ears, a full carat at least, a bracelet with little charms and shit dangling from it, and a fine platinum chain with a tiny key pendant, a single chocolate diamond in the center of the head of the key. Her clothes look expensive, and I'm pretty sure her purse and shoes should be insured.

Money.

But understated money, not flashy *look how rich I am* money.

And right now, she's just barely on her feet, leaned

back against the wall of a closed bakery a block from the bar, gasping for breath, hyperventilating. She's got blood spattered across her face and clumping in her hair, there's blood dotting her forehead and hairline and down across her nose and chin. It's all a result of that punch I threw to lay out McDermott. An asshole move, I admit; I punched the fucker that way on purpose, knowing the splatter would hit her. I mean, it was obvious she'd wandered into the wrong end of town by accident, but she was staring at me like she'd never seen a real man before, and looked disgusted at what she'd probably term a *vulgar display of brutality* or some fancy, *Hah-vahd* educated highfalutin bullshit like that. She's got a bit of an East Coast lilt to her voice. Arch, crisp, educated, and formal.

She's a good girl.

A virgin even, maybe.

But then again, the way she looked at me? Maybe not. I don't know. I can usually sniff out and avoid virgins as if I'm a bloodhound, but this woman is so far outside my realm of understanding that I don't even know how to read her.

Her shirt is all bloody. It's ivory or cream colored—words for not-quite white, but almost, in my understanding—and it's sexy as fuck. Figure-hugging silk, a deep V-neck exposing a good bit of cleavage, sleeveless. Again, classy and sexy, expensive looking without being in-your-face. Her hands are shaking, trembling like crazy. There are dirty handprints on her shirt, from those fuckin' assholes. I really do hope brother Zane takes care of them properly, as they deserve.

I still have her hand in mine. I just kissed the back of her hand, like a storybook knight. Felt stupid doing it, but it got her eyes on mine, and her teeth caught at her lower lip, and her struggle to breathe seemed to intensify momentarily, and then she sucked in a sharp breath and yanked her eyes away from mine.

She'd said she trusted me; time to make good on that. I take her other hand in mine and lift her to her feet. "Come on. Let's get you that drink."

She nodded, and let me guide her into a walk. Not quite a full block later, we arrived at the front door of Badd's Bar and Grill. At one in the morning it was still crowded with people spilling out the door, which was propped open by a chair, on which sat Bast, my oldest brother. His burly, tattooed forearms crossed over his chest as he closely scrutinized the IDs of a quartet of college-age girls waiting to be admitted. He jerked his head toward the interior of the bar, indicating the girls could go in, and then his eyes cut to mine, and Evangeline.

"Jesus, Bax. The fuck did you do now?" He left the chair and took a step toward us. "Honey, is this ugly gorilla bothering you? Say the word and I'll break his legs for you."

Evangeline shrank away from Bast, which was understandable. He's taller than any of us at six-four, and he's built like a brick shithouse. He's covered in tattoos, and he's a surly, intimidating bastard. I may be big and beefy and scary looking, but I make up for it by having a winning personality, a show-stopping, panty-melting grin, and enough charm to knock an entire sorority house on their collective, PINK sweat-pants-clad asses. Bast is just scary, because he comes across pretty much like the surly, intimidating bastard that he is—unless you're his wife Dru, around whom he melts into this tail-wagging, golden retriever puppy dog-eyed soppy mush basket.

"I didn't do anything, you oversized cock waffle," I snap. "I *helped,* as a matter of fact."

"You're telling me you're not responsible for the blood all over her?" Bast asked, an eyebrow wryly arched.

I rolled my eyes and sighed. "That's irrelevant." I shoved him away. "Your wifey awake?"

He nodded "Probably. Why?"

I shrug. "Evangeline needs to clean up and change."

Bast waved. "Yeah, she's up there. You're gonna catch hell for this, though. You know that, right?"

"For what? I'm helping a damsel in distress."

Bast snorted. "Okay, Sir Galahad." He addressed Evangeline. "If he gets out of hand, let me know. Okay? I'm serious."

Evangeline just stared at Bast with an unreadable, blank expression on her face, and then she looked at me. "You promised me a drink, a shower, and some clean clothes, not amusing banter."

"She means a shower *alone*, Bax," Bast said, smirking. "Keep that in mind, yeah?"

"No shit, you ugly oaf. I *am* capable of chivalry, you know." I made sure that comment was the last word between us and then led Evangeline through the crowded bar, keeping a tight grip on her hand as we wove between clumps and clusters of sweaty, boozing, dancing customers.

The twins were on stage tonight, doing an acoustic set, with Canaan playing an acoustic guitar and Corin sitting on one of those box-drum things, which he slapped with his hands to create a rolling percussive rhythm. They were both singing, doing that eerily perfect harmony only those two can manage.

Evangeline tugged at my hand to slow me down just as we were reaching the locked doorway behind which was the stairs to the apartment over the bar.

"I recognize those guys," she said into my ear. "Either it's an amazing cover act, or that's actually

Bishop's Pawn."

I laughed. "That's actually Bishop's Pawn," I answered.

She eyed me in amazement. "No way! I saw them in Germany last year. They're amazing! What are they doing playing in this dingy dive bar?"

Apparently she hadn't put two and two together yet. "Well, sweetheart, that's a kind of complicated question to answer."

I dug into my hoodie pocket and produced my keys, unlocked the door, which was marked "private access only" as a joke. Usually doors like that say something like "No access," or just "Private" or "employee access only", but Cane and Cor apparently thought it would be funny to put "private access only" on the door, and so there it is. I led her up the stairs and into the apartment, letting go of her hand reluctantly as we entered. I say reluctantly, because I'd been holding her hand for ten or fifteen minutes at that point and her hand in mine felt really nice. Like, just holding her hand felt tingly and exciting. Made me feel like a twelve-year-old kid again, sitting at the high school football game with my crush, having just gotten up the courage to grab her hand. Now, as then, I didn't want to let go.

Which was stupid.

For a lot of reasons, none of which I was quite

ready to examine.

Dru was on the couch watching TV, a fleece throw blanket on her legs, a giant glass of red wine in one hand, a bowl of popcorn on her lap. Copper hair currently in a sloppy, frizzy braid, bright cornflower-blue eyes, creamy skin, and a fierce Irish temper, Dru was the closest in build to Evangeline of any of my brothers' women. They were similar in height, and they both had mouthwatering hourglass figures. Yeah, I don't mind admitting Bast's wife is hot as fuck, but she's my brother's wife and my sister-in-law, and all I'll ever do is appreciate what God made. Point is, their similar builds means Dru probably had clothes that will fit Evangeline. Which is why I'm bringing her here as opposed to the apartment over the twins' music studio a few doors down, where I actually live.

She shot a cursory glance at me as I entered; Evangeline was still hidden behind me. "Hey, Bax. Win your fight?"

"Obviously. McDermott is a puny little bitch. He didn't stand a snowball's chance in hell."

"What are you doing up here?" Dru asked, her eyes on the TV. "I'm not cooking for you."

"Can I borrow a change of clothes from you?" I asked, setting down my gear bag.

She turned her head toward me, exaggeratedly slowly. "Even if you did take up cross-dressing, I don't think my clothes are going to—HOLY SHIT." She shot to her feet when Evangeline appeared from behind me, tossing her blanket aside and setting the popcorn and wine on the coffee table as she hurried over to us. "What the hell did you do to this poor girl, Bax?"

I slapped my forehead with a snarl of irritation. "Why does everyone always assume the worst about me? Jesus." I gestured at Evangeline. "Dru, this is Evangeline. Evangeline, this is my sister-in-law, Dru. Now. Dru—would it be possible for Evangeline to clean up and get a change of clean clothes from you?"

"Of course! Come on." Dru took Evangeline by the arm and dragged her through the living room and into the hall bathroom, where she sat the shell-shocked and confused Evangeline down onto the closed toilet lid. "Sit. Relax. Let me get this blood off you. Are you hurt? What did Bax do?"

I remained in the kitchen, where I fixed Evangeline a vodka cranberry. "I DIDN'T DO ANYTHING TO HER!" I hollered.

"Then whose blood is this?" Dru shouted back. "And shut up. Claire is sleeping."

A door opened. "Not anymore, assholes." Claire shuffled out of her and Brock's room, blinking sleepily, wearing a T-shirt of Brock's and probably nothing else. "Who's this?—who are you? And why are we shouting at Bax?"

"We're *not* shouting at Bax," I said, bringing the drink to the bathroom.

I squeezed past Claire and into the bathroom, then slid behind Dru and sat on the lip of the tub, handing Evangeline the drink. "You seemed like a vodka cranberry type."

She took it and sipped at it. "Whoa. Heavy on the vodka, much?"

I shrugged. "That was a shitty situation. Figured if I promised you a stiff drink I'd better make it hella stiff."

"Does anyone actually even say 'hella' anymore?" Claire asked, from the hall outside the bathroom. "And will someone please explain to me what's going on?"

Dru—who had a package of makeup wipes in her hand was gingerly wiping at the blood on Evangeline's face—shot me a meaningful glare. "Bax? Care to explain?"

I sighed. "Well, Evangeline here wandered by mistake into the warehouse where my fight was happening. I noticed her but she seemed out of place, and then she left. On the way home I happened to walk past an alley near the warehouse. I saw these four fucking asswipes with their hands all over Evangeline, so I stopped them, and I brought her here to get her cleaned up."

Evangeline snorted, a somehow ladylike sound of derisive disbelief. She stood up, taking a wipe from the package in Dru's hand, and faced the mirror, wiping at her face vigorously. "You're leaving out a few things, I believe." She plucked at a strand of her hair, peeling away a clump of dried blood with her fingernails, grimacing in disgust. "Such as, for example, the way you punched that guy in the ring so hard his blood sprayed all over me—and I'm fairly certain you did it on purpose."

"You distracted me. What can I say?" I shrugged and crossed my arms over my chest. "But you're right, I did do that on purpose. It was kind of a dick move, and I apologize."

She eyed me sidelong, glaring. "I...*distracted* you? You demolished that poor man in a matter of seconds."

"Exactly!" I said. "I was planning on drawing it out a little bit, giving the audience a bit more of a show. Then you strutted in looking as lost as a poodle at a pit bull fight, and I forgot."

Evangeline stopped what she was doing entirely. "There are so many things wrong with that statement I don't even know where to start." She took a drink from her vodka cranberry and then ticked off items on her fingers as she listed them. "First, what do you mean by *more of a show*? Letting him rough you up a little before beating him half to death? Toying with him like a cat with a mouse? Secondly, a poodle? Of all the dogs you could compare me to, you choose a *poodle*? A yipping, obnoxious, useless little lapdog? Is that what you think I am, too? And third, pit bull fighting is vile and despicable. Those poor animals have no choice in those brutal fights. *You* have a choice. You *choose* to fight for money. All they get is hurt and abused."

I held up both hands. "Whoa there, Eva, slow your roll, honey." I stood up and moved a little closer, ignoring the way both Claire and Dru were following this conversation with unabashed interest. "First, yeah, I meant toy with him like a cat with a mouse—let him hit me a few times, make him and the audience think he's got half a chance against me. And also, I didn't beat him half to death. Even those fuckin' dickless cunt-holes who tried to rape you got off easy. I hurt 'em pretty bad, yeah, but not anywhere near as bad as they deserved, and not half to death. If you've never seen someone literally beaten so badly they're in danger of dying, then you can't possibly understand the difference."

I leveled her a look with all the hardened, world-weary bitterness I had inside me, just so she knew I wasn't kidding. "Second, I wasn't comparing you to a poodle. It was...a situational comparison. You, wandering into an illegal underground MMA fight is *relatable* to an innocent little mini poodle trotting unaware into the ring with a pair of pit bulls. If I was going to compare you to an animal, it sure as fuck wouldn't be an ugly-ass, stupid little goddamn poodle—more like a swan or something elegant like that. Third, you're right, pit bull fighting is bullshit and I hate it. I once beat the shit out of a guy for kicking his dog, so we're in agreement there. I choose to fight, because I'm good at it and I enjoy it."

She poked me in the chest with a manicured finger. "I've told you several times already, my name is Evangeline, not *Eva*. Get it right, you muscle-bound meathead." She went back to wiping at her face, scraping a dot of blood off her perfect little chin. "Now. If it's still all right with whomever lives here, I would be very grateful if I could take a quick shower."

Dru grabbed my wrist, digging her thumbnail into a pressure point, and hauled me out of the bathroom. "Out, Bax. Out. Let the girl get cleaned up." To Evangeline, then. "You're welcome here for as long as you need. Give me ten seconds and I'll have a change of clothes for you. Take as long a shower as you want."

Dru vanished and then reappeared with a pair of sweatpants and a T-shirt, and a pair of pink Gap flip flops, setting everything on the counter, and then I was shoved out of the bathroom and down the hallway into the living room, Claire following behind us.

Dru did some kind of twist and pivot move on me, and my right arm and wrist were bent wrong, so one false move on my part would have me eating left handed for a few months—just goes to show that even the biggest and baddest aren't invincible. I mean, I could power through the pain, chop out a kick, and have Dru on her ass in half a second...probably. But number one, she's my sister-in-law and I love her, because she's good for Bast and she's just a cool-ass chick, and number two, I'm not *entirely* certain I could take her. She's a bad bitch, and I mean that with every ounce of respect I've got.

"What the fuck, Dru?" I held still and didn't fight against the hold.

"*You* tell *me* what the fuck, Bax. She's wearing earrings that have to be at *least* fifteen thousand dollars, and I'm pretty sure that's a Hermes blouse, thousand dollar Manolo flats, and a Prada purse."

"I don't know what any of that means." I tested her hold, and she let go. "And so what if she's got money? What does that have anything to do with fuckin' anything, Dru?"

"Not to be mean, Bax, but women like her don't really tend to go for guys like you." She moved to take the opposite end of the couch from me, where she'd been curled up when we arrived.

I snort. "Well no shit, sis. Think I don't know that?" I shrugged out of my hoodie, leaving me bare-chested with my bloodstained tape on my hands and wrists; I sat on the couch and started peeling the tape off. "This ain't that, Dru. I told the truth, okay? She wandered into the fight by accident, I still don't know how or why. She got right up against the barrier, and sort of got a little blood on her. And yeah, I hit the guy on purpose so she'd get sprayed.

"She was staring at me, looking all disgusted and fascinated at the same time, and it pissed me off and made me all...I dunno...crazy, I guess. I've never been looked at like that before. Like I was...like I was a lion in a cage at the zoo, and she was fascinated by me but wasn't sure she wanted to get too close. So I hit McDermott and she got splattered. Dick move, my bad, what-the-fuck-ever. Thought that was that."

I tossed the tape from my right hand in a pile on the coffee table, and started on my left hand. "Then I take my cash and head out, pass an alley, and I hear noises. Guys talking shit, a girl's voice sounding upset. Peeked into the alley, and saw four guys holding down one girl, and having trouble with her. One guy had a knife and was talkin' mean. They were gonna rape her, all four of 'em, and that shit does *not* fly with me. So I kicked the motherfuckin' shit out of all four of 'em. And, let me add, I would have done the same for any woman, rich as hell or not."

The door opened, then, and Zane swaggered in. He was meticulously clean, except for a spray of blood down one cheek. "Bax, bro, we gotta talk."

"I *am* talkin', Zane. Filling the girls in on what happened."

"Well, there's more filling in to do, if you know what I mean." He sat down on the love seat kitty corner to the couch where I was perched.

Dru and Claire both stared at Zane suspiciously, and then I saw concern flicker across Dru's face.

"No. No—tell me you didn't, Zane," Dru murmured.

He kept his face admirably blank. "Didn't what, Dru?"

She eyed me, then him. "The fight Bax got in tonight, in the alley. Were you there?"

Zane's gaze didn't waver. "At the end, yeah. I wasn't in on the fun part, though."

"The *fun* part?" Dru flicked an eyebrow up. "Would that be the part where four guys almost raped a woman? Or the part where Bax put the hurt on them?"

He held up his hands palms out. "It's just an expression, Jesus."

The door opened again, and a massively pregnant Mara stormed in. "Zane, you fucking asshole! It's two thirty in the fucking morning and I expected you home forty-five minutes ago! I've texted you sixteen times, called you four, and you're sitting here with your brother like it's no big deal?"

I surged off the couch and moved to intercept. "Mara, babe, cool off. It's not his fault. He was helping me."

"Don't tell me to cool off, Baxter, you fucking cave troll!" She halted, her gaze going from me to Zane, to the pile of bloody tape, to the girls, and then to the unfamiliar Prada purse sitting on the half wall separating the kitchen from the living room, and then to the sound of the shower in the bathroom. "Wait. Helping you with what? Whose pimp-ass Prada purse is that? Who's in the shower? Because if Brock comes out buck naked again with that dick of his swinging around and I gotta see it again, I'm gonna be *pissed*."

Claire snickered. "We should all be so lucky. But no, he's downstairs behind the bar. You'd have seen him had you not been storming through on the warpath."

"When Zane ignores me, I get pissed. I'm about to have a baby any day, and he needs to answer me if I'm trying to get a hold of him."

Zane was off the couch and grabbing Mara,

holding her tight against him. "I'm sorry, babe. I wasn't ignoring you. I just...couldn't answer right then."

"And why is that, Zane, pray tell?" Dru asked, her voice heavily inflected with sarcasm.

I eyed my brother. "This may not be the best moment for this discussion."

Zane shook his head incrementally. "It's...not like that. Not like you're thinking."

We certainly didn't need the trouble, so just for that reason I hoped I was reading him right. "It's not?"

"Nope."

"You two macho fucksticks need to quit talking in riddles and start coming out with explanations," Dru snapped. "*Now.*"

Zane sighed, and sat back down, pulling Mara onto his lap. "Okay, here's the truth. Those four assholes who tried to rape that girl in the fancy clothes—what was her name? Eve? Eva? Something like that. Well...I felt like they needed to be taught more of a lesson than Bax put on them. I didn't personally do anything to them, though. All I did was make a phone call to a buddy who happens to be in the area on...ah...vacation, let's say. This buddy of mine specializes in teaching what you might call unforgettable lessons, and in such a way as to make sure none of it ever comes back to any of us." He waved a hand. "And

that's all any of you need to know, or ever *will* know."
He said this last part with a finality none of us dared
to challenge, even Mara.

"That girl in the fancy clothes is named
Evangeline," I put in. "And she's here, in the shower."

A fact I've been trying like hell not to think about.
Unsuccessfully. I mean, that body? God*damn.* I'd sell
a kidney for a single glimpse at that body of hers naked and dripping wet. Her long black hair, soaked and
sticking to her tan skin? Those tits and that ass, with
water sliding over her lush curves? Those eyes, wide
and green and staring up at me as I—

Fuck. No, no, no, nope. Can't go there.

Down boy, Baxter.

I don't think Zane missed the way my eyes glazed
over, just then.

"*Is* she, now?" he drawled, smirking. "Interesting."

"Shut the fuck up, Zane," I snarled.

"Testy much, Bax?" He chuckled. "Sorry to say,
kid, but I think she's out of your league."

"There's no league. It's not like that," I insisted.
"She needed help, and I helped her. That's it. Quit riding my dick about it."

The bathroom door opened, and Evangeline
wandered out. Her hair was damp, and blacker than
ever, reflecting the light. She had a brush in one hand,
and was running it through her hair. I clenched my

jaw and curled my hands into fists, because I was about to moan out loud from raw, unbridled lust.

The sweatpants were faded gray, tight around her hips and butt, loose through the legs, and tight around her calves, tugged up to just beneath her knees. The T-shirt was a green, white, and blue Seahawks raglan shirt, and it was cut to fit snug, but it was too small for her, and she wasn't wearing a bra and this apartment was a little chilly at the moment, and she had tits for fuckin' days, and I couldn't breathe because all the blood was flowing to my cock.

Because…

Jesus tits.

Girl had Jesus Tits. Capital letters. Wait, that's not good enough. All caps: JESUS TITS.

I mean…*damn*. The Hermes shirt and whatever bullshit bra she'd been wearing before did NOT do her rack justice. I could see them perfectly behind the cotton, their beautiful teardrop shape, heavy and natural and jiggling tantalizingly with each step she took, and her nipples were so hard and sharp they could just about poke straight through the thin cotton. It was an old shirt, well worn, and the cotton was so thin I could almost see the color of her skin, and the pink of her nips…

I was staring like a hormonal teenager at a titty club for the first time. I wrenched my eyes away, but not before meeting hers, and I realized she'd caught me staring. She shifted uncomfortably, pivoting away, her shoulders curling in, as if she was self-conscious, and then she straightened in defiance, her chin lifting, and she turned back to face the room, and me. It took a supreme effort of will to keep my eyes firmly fixed on her eyes as I addressed her.

"Hey, Evangeline. Feeling any better?" I asked.

She nodded, leaning against the wall in the entry of the hallway. "A shower does work wonders." She eyed the crowd in the living room, which had grown substantially since she got in the shower, now that Mara and Zane had joined Claire, Dru, and me. "What's...what's going on?"

"This is an intervention," I joked. "We're all here because we're concerned about you, Evangeline. This is a circle of trust, okay? You can talk to us without judgment."

She smirked. "I wish I could laugh, but I've been on the receiving end of an intervention that started almost verbatim like that."

I guffawed. "You? Hell, nah. What could you have been into that you needed an intervention?"

She shrugged, keeping a straight face. "You'd be surprised. What if I'm not as straight-laced and fancy as you assume?"

"Ohhhhh-kay, *sure*. Whatever you say, honey." I

heaped sarcasm into the words.

She couldn't keep the straight face. "Okay, fine. It was to do with my friends in high school. I was hanging out with some kids from a different group, and my friends held an intervention to remind me of the importance and responsibility of my social standing. It wasn't seemly for me to be associating with…the unsavory sort."

"Bet you wish they could get a load of me, then, huh? We could really shock 'em."

She laughed. "Oh my, they would faint dead away, I think. I doubt they've changed much since high school. They still flit around the same town they all grew up in, driving their husband's cars instead of Daddy's, spending money and judging people."

"Sounds like a wonderful bunch of bitches."

"God, they're awful. They all nearly fainted the first time I told them I'd refused Thomas's proposal—" she cut herself off, blushing. "But that's not important." She glanced around the room. "I'm Evangeline du Maurier."

Claire, perched on the arm of the couch near me, slapped my arm. "You're a mannerless barbarian, Baxter. Seriously. Introductions, maybe?"

I whacked her shoulder back, but gently and playfully, because Claire was all of five feet five inches and weighed *maybe* one-ten, one-twenty fully clothed and soaking wet and holding a ten-pound bowling ball, and if I smacked her too hard she might go flying through the wall and into the bay, the tiny, svelte, slender little thing that she was. Delicate looking, but fierce and ferocious in personality.

"Yep, mannerless barbarian. That's me." I gestured at Evangeline. "Well, like she said, her name is Evangeline du Maurier. Eva, you've met Dru, and I *know* I introduced you properly. The little blonde pixie here by my arm is Claire. Zane is the ugly fucker you've already met, back in the alley, my brother. The angry pregnant lady is Mara.

"For reference, Dru is married to Sebastian, the surly cock waffle with all the tats who was guarding the door when we came in. He's the oldest Badd brother. Zane and Mara are together, and thank god because he knocked her fine ass up *real* good. Claire is with Brock, who you may or may not have noticed slinging drinks behind the bar, he was the pretty, GQ-looking motherfucker. He's the next brother older than me, after Zane, who's in between Brock and Bast—which is short for Sebastian."

Evangeline looked like her head was spinning. "Wait. There are *four* of you? And you all look like... *that*?"

Dru laughed, a genuine belly laugh. "Oh god, Evangeline, honey: there's *eight* of them, and yes, they all look like that."

Evangeline boggled, her mouth opening and closing, no sound coming out. "No way. Nuh-uh. Not possible."

Dru tugged a slim silver cell phone out of her bra, opened it, tapped a few times, and then handed Evangeline the phone.

Evangeline eyed me, then the phone, and then moved to sit beside me, squishing in between Dru and me. "Who's who?" she asked, addressing me.

The photo was of the eight of us brothers standing in a line abreast by age with Bast on the far left and Xavier on the far right, our arms around each other from end to end. We'd closed the bar down on a Monday a month or so ago, rented a boat and took a trip to some island or another that Brock and Claire knew about, and we horsed around on the beach and swam in the ball-shrivelingly cold water and made a bonfire. And at some point, the girls had insisted we get a picture of all of us brothers together.

I ignored the way my whole right side was tingling from where her body was brushed up against mine, and tried to keep my eyes on the phone and off her tits; I started on the left and pointed at each of us in turn. "In order from oldest to youngest you've got Bast, Zane, Brock, me, Canaan, Corin, Lucian, and Xavier."

Evangeline just stared for a moment. And then I saw the penny drop. "Wait. Canaan and Corin—Bishop's Pawn...they're your brothers?"

I nodded, grinning. "Yep. Talented boys, ain't they?"

She glanced around the apartment, and then at the door to the downstairs. "So the, um, dingy dive bar they're playing in?"

"Badd's Bar and Grill. Family owned and operated since nineteen eighty...um...four? Five? Hell if I know." I winked at her expression. "We're the Badd brothers, spelled B-A-double-D."

"Oh." Evangeline just shook her head and handed the phone back to Dru. "Well that's just ridiculous. Nobody needs that much male perfection in one family."

Claire giggled. "Honey, you ain't seen male perfection until you've seen a Badd boy's big ol'—"

SMACK.

That would be the sound of an issue of *ELLE* magazine flying through the air, courtesy of Mara, and hitting Claire straight in the face.

"CLAIRE. SHUT—THE FUCK—UP," Mara said, managing to snap the phrase through grinding teeth. "We just met poor Evangeline. Let's not shock her all at once, shall we?"

Evangeline was blushing so hard it was a wonder

she had any blood left in her body, her cheeks were so red. "I, um. Wow. Okay."

"Awww, she's blushing." Claire grinned, a predatory gleam of her teeth. "I like her. I can have fun with this."

Mara sighed. "No, Claire. Just...no. Don't go there. Do *not* scare the new girl."

Evangeline eyed them both, and then looked to me for an answer. "What are they talking about?"

I winked at her. "Penises."

Claire threw the magazine at me, catching me on the jaw with the spine. "Baxter! Don't shock the new girl! She blushes easily."

And, indeed, Evangeline was blushing even harder, if that was possible. "This conversation has devolved rather swiftly, I must say."

I just laughed. "Babe, this conversation hasn't even gotten started."

Her perfectly arched eyebrows lifted. "That sounds...worrisome."

I laughed even harder, because it didn't seem as if she was trying to be funny, but rather she really was just that...conservative, shall we say. "You have no idea. We're not very politically correct around here. We're wildly inappropriate as a rule, we drop F-bombs with horrifying frequency, we drink a shit-load of booze on the regular, and we make fun of each other as a lifestyle. If you're easily embarrassed or shocked…well, babe…you're in for a hell of wild ride if you're gonna hang with us."

"I just…I wasn't trying to impose or…" she trailed off. "Become the new girl, or anything. It all just happened so fast. I don't even remember where the B and B I'm staying at is located. It's been a heck of a long day, and I'm still a little shaken up by what happened, and…"

Dru poured a healthy measure of red wine into the glass she'd been drinking from when we arrived. "The Badd brothers have a way of sucking us poor, innocent, unsuspecting good girls into their dark and dirty orbit. Just how they are. You're here, you've had our booze, you're wearing my clothes—you're in the gang now, babe. Better buckle up." She handed the glass to Evangeline and gently nudged her back down onto the couch. "Don't worry, between Mara, Claire, and me, we'll take care of you."

Evangeline took a big sip from the wine. "This is overwhelming."

"Isn't it? And this isn't even everyone. Bast, Brock, the twins, Luce, and Xavier are all still downstairs working the bar." Claire reached across me and stole the glass of wine from Evangeline, took a sip, and handed it back. "So. Evangeline. What brings you to Ketchikan?"

She tipped her head to one side. "Well…honestly, I needed to get away from…ah…everything, I guess. Ketchikan was recommended to me by one of my father's drivers as a remote but nice getaway, and it's certainly far away from anywhere my father or Thomas might look, so…" She shrugged. "Here I am. As far away from Father and Thomas as I can get, on short notice."

"So you're running away?" Claire asked.

Evangeline blinked, hesitating. "Sort of?"

"Fair enough," Claire said. "Can we go back to you turning down some kind of proposal from this guy Thomas? That sounded like a fun story."

Evangeline let out a breath. "It's really not."

"That sigh says differently," Claire says. "I'll trade you stories, if you want. How Brock and I met, for the dish on you and Thomas."

Another of those sighs, during which Evangeline stared into the ruby liquid in the glass. "Fine. But you go first. I need more wine if I'm going to talk about Thomas."

Dru tipped the rest of the bottle into the glass, and then glanced at Claire. "There's another bottle over the fridge. And some whiskey for the boys. Since we're having an impromptu party in my living room, we might as well make it a proper party."

In short order, glasses of wine and whiskey were

passed around, except for Mara, who sipped on sparkling water.

Evangeline kicked her feet up on the coffee table, crossed her arms over her breasts, keeping her wine clutched in one hand as if holding on to it for dear life. Her thigh and hip were touching mine, and she was slowly leaning into me, letting her shoulder rest against mine. I held still and let her decide on contact, because I didn't want to read into anything, and I sure as fuck wasn't going to try anything so soon after what she'd been through. I did like the way it felt to have her this close, though. She smelled amazing, like vanilla and flowers and shampoo; she smelled fuckin' delicious, is how she smelled, and I wanted to take a little taste of her. Start at the luscious, tanned column of her throat and devour my way downward, inch by inch, until I was between her thighs, and had her screaming my name.

And...fuck—I just gave myself a hard-on. Wonderful. She was sitting right next to me, with my sister-in-law on the other side, and I had a hard-on trying to unfurl behind my fighting trunks, which didn't do much to hide anything, especially since I'd taken off my cup and jockstrap and was rocking my junk commando.

I tried to casually rest my hands with my glass of whiskey over myself to hide things, but judging by the way Evangeline was blushing and studiously staring into her wine and not looking at me, I think it's safe to say she noticed.

Claire was talking, and I was mostly listening. I shot a sideways glance at Evangeline, and noticed her gaze sliding, inching, and creeping from her wineglass over to me. I moved my hands away, just a little bit, letting the outline of my cock show, just a hint. And yep, her gaze went right to it. Her knuckles whitened as she gripped her wineglass with one hand and her own forearm with the other.

Her eyes flicked away and up to mine, as if realizing she was staring—which she had been—and I caught and held her gaze.

And then I winked, and her breath stuttered.

This could be fun. I'd have to be cautious, but my interested-female radar was pinging like crazy. Didn't have to mean anything, and wouldn't, but it could be fun. If there's anything I'm good at besides fighting and football, it's corrupting good girls.

And Evangeline du Maurier seemed like the hottest, sweetest, and most innocent of all good girls.

TWO

Evangeline

WHAT WAS I DOING? WHY WAS I SITTING HERE WITH these strangers, getting tipsy, and thinking about talking about Thomas? I *never* talk about Thomas. Not with anyone. I mean, my friends at Yale knew about him, knew his limo, knew who he was, but they also knew I didn't talk about him. They just didn't get it—they couldn't understand why I would avoid a wealthy, influential, educated, handsome man like Thomas. If they'd known about his marriage proposals, they would have wet their pants with envy. A lot of those girls, as smart as they were,

were suckers for a good-looking man with a fat bank account, robust investment portfolio, and impressive resumé. A man like Thomas? Most of the girls I hung out with would sell their souls to be his wife.

But these people, though? The Badd brothers and the women in their lives? They were…like no one I had ever met in my life. I didn't have the words to properly describe them.

And Baxter was like no man I'd ever encountered. I was having trouble breathing properly, sitting next to him. I know, I know—I should be more shaken up by what had happened, what had *almost* happened, but Baxter had stopped them before they could do anything to me, aside from scare me and paw at me a little—and I'd been groped worse the one time I decided to try and brave a club with a couple girls from my poli-sci program. I mean, yes, I was shaken up. And, no, I wouldn't be walking down any more dark streets alone at night. But for some reason, Baxter's very presence just made me feel…safe.

And also he scared the absolute sense right out of me. Literally.

I was drinking wine, and feeling the vodka cranberry he'd made me. I didn't drink all that much or that frequently, so it didn't take much to get me tipsy. Getting drunk around a man like Baxter might be troublesome, I knew. Not because I thought he would do anything untoward while I was intoxicated—I had no way of knowing for sure, but I just got the feeling that he wouldn't take advantage of me like that. No, the danger was from myself. I might do something embarrassing and forward and stupid, if I got too drunk around him.

Because I was attracted to him.

I'd gotten caught staring at his...um...*member.* Which, as Claire's interrupted insinuation had hinted at, was...well, a LOT. The couple of times I'd slept with Thomas, it had always been quick and in the dark, and Thomas had been in control, which meant I hadn't had an opportunity to...explore, shall we say. So even though I wasn't a virgin, I wasn't exactly familiar, in a personal experience sort of way, with a man's, errr, tackle. At all.

But, from what I'd seen—which had only been the outline behind his trunks, Baxter was...ah...well-endowed. It had looked big enough to make my hands involuntarily tighten, and my mouth go dry, and my knees press together.

I realized abruptly that Claire was talking and that I was meant to be listening. I forced my attention to Claire's story.

"...And I was like, hell, why not, right? I had all this vacation time saved up, and it sounded like fun, so I booked an Alaskan cruise. Which was a sweet vacation, let me tell you. I spent the whole time on the deck, in a teeny bikini, drinking wine and catching up on my TBR list. Literally, that was all I did. Well, except for one of the bellboys, once. And the first mate, in exchange for a secret tour of the cockpit."

Mara shrieked. "What? You never told me this!" She threw another magazine at Claire. "You fucked a bellboy *and* the first mate on that cruise?"

I blinked in surprise, and assumed Claire had been joking. But she just shrugged. "Mara, diddly-dinkums, it's not like I've told you about every single dude I've ever fucked or messed around with. Only *most* of them."

"But the first mate of an Alaskan cruise line? That's kinda major news to keep to yourself, hooker."

Claire snickered. "Not if you'd seen him. He wasn't anything to write home about. Nice cock on him, though, and I'd rate him six out of ten on technique." I choked on my wine, and spluttered; Claire chortled at me in amusement. "What? Six out of ten is actually a decent score. I've fucked threes and fours. A two, once. Brock is a ten, obviously. Or, like, eleven or twelve. Maybe even a twenty. He does this thing where he—"

"CLAIRE!" Mara bellowed. "Overshare, babe. Even for me."

I blinked. "I'm sorry, but is this…for real? Or are

you joking? I know I might be a tiny bit naive, but your sense of humor is a bit dry, so it's hard to tell."

"My sense of humor is dry-ice dry, babe," Claire said. "It's a rare humor style called 'sick burn'. And no, I'm not joking. I'm telling the real story as it actually happened."

I looked to Mara for confirmation, and she just nodded. "Yes, she really was that much of a ho, until she met Brock."

"I really was. Brock has changed me, however. He has converted me from my sluttiness into a one-man woman." Claire glanced at the door to the stairs, which opened to admit a line of men each more handsome and sexy than the last. "Speaking of whom... hey there, snookums. How was work? Come throat-fuck me with your tongue."

The first man through the door strode immediately and with purpose across the room and straight to Claire, took her in his brawny arms, and, indeed, kissed her so thoroughly I began to grow uncomfortable. When the kiss ended, he straightened, brushed Claire's pixie-cut blonde hair aside and kissed her nose, and then her forehead, and then tweaked her nipple.

"Hey you," he said to her. "Work was fine. Why are you up?" He shot a look at Bax. "Scoot over, would you?"

"What, like your tubby ass is gonna fit on this couch? I don't think so, GQ." Bax crossed his enormous arms over his bare chest and shook his head. "Nope. Not scooting. Take your midget woman and go sit somewhere else."

I looked over the man I was assuming, based on Bax's introductions and previous description, was Brock, the next oldest Badd brother. And he was, indeed, GQ-model gorgeous. Clean cut, with wavy brown hair combed neatly back and to one side, with the perfect amount of stubble on his jaw, eyes a golden-brown to match Baxter's, and a lean but powerful build. His face, though, was what set him apart. He was just...beautiful. Not many men can claim that word as an accurate descriptor, but this man? Oh my. Definitely. More than beautiful, it was almost beyond description how just absolutely carved-from-marble perfect his features were. He scooped Claire off the arm of the couch and settled with her on his lap in a deep leather armchair.

Zane, too, was stupidly good looking, but in a deadly sort of way. Looking at Zane was like being three feet away from a wild, hungry Jaguar, seeing its eyes fixed on you and knowing it could pounce at any second and you wouldn't stand a chance. He just exuded lethality in a way I've never encountered before, even among Father's private security, and the

Secret Service members I'd met. He was gorgeous, but he was so outright terrifying in his presence that he made my bladder weaken, just a little; yes, he was pee-your-pants scary. Which reminded me, I had to ask him what he'd done to my erstwhile rapists.

The next man through the door was Sebastian, the bouncer I'd met earlier. Six-four, easily, towering over everyone else in the room, he was somewhere in between Zane and Brock in terms of dangerous bad boy attitude and raw masculine beauty. He had tattoos in what I think are called full sleeves on both arms, going from wrist to up under the sleeves of his T-shirt, short, messy brown hair, and the same liquid chocolate brown eyes as the other men. Handsome as the others, in a rugged, intimidating, intense sort of way. Big, burly, with fierce eyes scanning the room to find Dru. He stomped over to her, kissed her as intensely as Brock had kissed Claire, and then physically picked her up and sat in her place, settling her on his lap, where she curled up against him as if she were a cat. It was adorable and it made my heart ache, seeing the way these big, scary, intense, handsome men treated their wives and girlfriends.

The next two through the door, almost side by side, were Canaan and Corin, from Bishop's Pawn. Completely identical, differentiated only by their apparel and their hair, they looked every bit the rock stars they were. Nearly as tall as Sebastian and lean and hard, they both wore skinny jeans that were almost but not quite too tight, the cuffs tucked into slouched-open combat boots on one twin and well-worn, Sharpie-decorated Chucks on the other, tight graphic print T-shirts featuring the names of obscure bands on both, full-sleeve tattoos on both, piercings, leather belts with studs and iron crosses, leather bracelets and friendship bracelets and thick leather bands on both arms of both of the twins.

One of the twins had shoulder length hair left loose and messy, drifting across his face and sticking to the stubble on his jaw, and the other had a severe undercut, the sides buzzed and the top left long enough to tie back into a ponytail, with the last two or so inches dyed a bright pink—according to the photo, Canaan was the long-haired one, and Corin had the undercut.

After the twins came another brother, tall and lean and razor-sharp in build and facial features. His hair was easily the longest of any of them, bound low on the nape of his neck, with the end trailing down to mid spine in a thick, wavy, brown ponytail. Like the other brothers, he had dark brown eyes, and was absurdly good looking. This one, though, was...hard to encapsulate in mere words. Not GQ, male model beautiful like Brock, nor rugged and intimidating like

Sebastian or the other older brothers, he was…elfin. He reminded me of Tolkien's description of the elves in *Lord of the Rings*. Definitively masculine, exuding a calm, quiet sense of inner strength and confidence. Sharp featured, exotic looking, with a gaze that flitted around the room and missed nothing. From the photo Dru showed me, and Baxter's identification, I knew this brother was Lucian.

Lastly, Xavier, the youngest. Like Baxter and Canaan, the long-haired twin, Xavier sported a hipster undercut, but the top of his hair wasn't as long, instead was just long enough to be messy, wavy, and effortlessly attractive. His hair was by far the darkest brown of any of them, and he was the only one to have green eyes, rather than what seemed to be the Badd brother signature puppies-and-chocolate brown. He had tattoos on his forearms, a complex web of higher math symbols and interlocking geometric shapes, and three small gold rings through each ear, and he was built like the twins and Lucian, meaning tall and rangy and lean. And like all the brothers, he was breathtakingly gorgeous, coming across as a little nerdy and completely unaware of how good looking he was.

And now I had all eight brothers in one space, and it was seriously overwhelming.

I leaned close to Dru and whispered in her ear.

"How do you do it?"

"Do what?" she whispered back.

"Deal with…" I tilted my head to indicate the room in general. "This amount of macho, testosterone, hot guy intensity all in one place."

She snorted, choking on restrained laughter. "Honestly, you never really get used to it. They're all so fucking gorgeous it's just stupid. What's worse is, no matter which order you look at them in, they're each hotter than the last. It's a problem. And when they're all in one room like this, my ovaries tend to go a bit haywire."

Sebastian—whom everyone else seemed to call Bast—heard this exchange, since he was right there with Dru on his lap. "Did you know we have our own secret fan page on Facebook?" His voice was so deep I felt it vibrating my stomach, yet it was smooth and rumbly, reminding me of nothing so much as the warning snarl of a grizzly bear.

Dru twisted on his lap and eyed him skeptically. "Bullshit."

Sebastian glanced at Xavier, who had slid to a spot on the floor with his back against the wall, a bit separated from the rest of the group. "That Facebook fan page you stumbled across, Xavier—Dru doesn't believe it exists."

Xavier lifted up, snagged a tablet computer off

the island counter, and sat back down, flipping the device open and tapping and swiping so fast his finger was a blur. In seconds, he had something pulled up, and passed the tablet to the nearest person, Lucian, who was sitting on a stool. Lucian scrolled, frowning slightly, and then snorted a soft breath out of his nostrils.

"Crazy. There really is a fan page. Who knew?" His voice was quiet, soft, and smooth. "How'd you find it, if it's a secret, invite-only page?"

Xavier shrugged, a little too casually. "You know. Just...one of those things."

Sebastian laughed. "Meaning you hacked in?"

"More or less," Xavier answered, shrugging, but not quite able to suppress a mischievous grin.

Lucian handed the tablet to Canaan, who shared it with Corin, both of them taking turns swiping and tapping in eerily perfect synch.

Corin passed it off to Baxter, and I glanced over his shoulder.

"Dude, some of those chicks are seriously thirsty. Some of the shit they post would make even Claire would blush."

The name of the page was *Badd's Bar and Grill in Ketchikan, Alaska: home of the eight most sinfully gorgeous brothers on the planet*. A bit of a long and wordy title for a Facebook Page, but it conveyed the content clearly. And as Baxter scrolled through the page, tapping on a post or a photo here and there, it became obvious what Corin was talking about. Most of the posts were photos of the brothers taken by patrons of the bar. Some were candid, and others were selfies of the patron with one or two of the brothers. These guys were like small-scale local celebrities, it seemed, judging by the sheer number of photos posted to the page. And, as Corin had said, the posts were almost uniformly libidinous. Indeed, reading some of the posts, I did blush. They mentioned in explicit detail what they wanted to do, and to whom, and for how long, and in some cases, in which position. Others just featured suggestive use of emojis, and some were an open invitation addressed to the brother in the photo; one such was a photo of a buxom blonde cozied up to Baxter, grinning ear to ear, who had added a caption to the photo: *bax, if you're ever in D.C. hit me up and I'll suck your cock until you can't walk straight*—and then she included in a comment beneath the photo her phone number and a photo of herself, naked in front of a mirror, with stars added by a filter to cover her nipples.

Bax left the photo and the comment up, and passed it to Sebastian, laughing. "Seriously, though, check out that shit. I mean *damn*... that's forward. Just straight up find me in D.C. and I'll blow you? Not even asking for a howdy-doo first or anything. And she leaves her phone number? I mean sure, it's a private, invite-only, all-female group, but still. That shit is *bold*, man."

"And would you?" I asked, unsure what answer I was hoping for. "Find her in Washington for a free blowjob? And, by the way, the phrase is actually *without so much as a how-do-you-do*."

Bax winked at me. "Eva, sweetheart, I'll be straight with you. Yes, I would, in a New York second. But—and this is the shit you gotta hear—not if I've got someone else around I'm interested in. I don't play mind games or bullshit like that. If I'm into someone, straight up, my interest is locked and loaded and I will not be distracted by anyone or anything, not even a free BJ from a bottle blonde with silicone tits. Naw'm'sayin'?" He slurred the final phrase so badly that I wasn't sure, at first, what he'd said.

"They were rather obviously fake, weren't they?" I said.

"Nobody is born with tits that firm and that perfectly round. That shit is silicone or I'm Freddy Mercury." He eyed me, and his gaze deliberately slid down to my breasts, and then back up to my eyes. "And lemme just point out that while I'm not, like, against it, that look ain't really my aesthetic. I prefer things…natural."

I felt my nipples harden under his scrutiny. "I see. Good to know."

"How did my story about meeting Brock get hijacked into a conversation about Evangeline's luscious mounds?" Claire demanded.

I blushed yet again, and crossed my arms over my chest. I was naturally well-endowed, a fact which I was beginning to think, clearly, had not escaped the notice of, well, anyone in the room. I half-wished I'd left my bra on, but it had just felt far too good to take it off and let the girls breathe a little, and I hadn't been expecting…well, any of this.

"Luscious means delicious, succulent, lush, and juicy, Baxter. Just so you don't miss the context of the comment," Brock said.

Baxter glared at Brock. "Shut your vapid shithole mouth, you waifish bitch of a man. I *did* go to fucking college, you know." He glanced at me, addressing his next comment to me. "I graduated high school at seventeen, got a full athletic scholarship to Penn State, started varsity all four years, and carried a three-six GPA, graduating with *cum laude* with a degree in Special Education. Just so you know."

I blinked at him. "You have a degree in Special Ed?"

He shrugged. "I had some experience with it in high school. Never did anything with it, since I got drafted by the CFL after I graduated."

"The Canadian Football League?" I specified.

He nodded. "It was that or try out at the combine, and it seemed like playing ball in a pro league would be a better experience than playing some shitty farm team somewhere in Butt-Fuck Illinois or wherever. The NFL drafting process is complicated, and I just wanted to play ball." He shrugged. "I had the Bears, the Patriots, and Seattle all put down offers to sign me earlier this year, but then I got word that I was needed back here, so...here I am."

Sebastian leaned forward to look at Bax. "You had actual offers?"

Bax shrugged. "Yeah. I was talking through the best options with my agent when that shitstick attorney called me—what was his name?"

"Richard Ames Borroughs," Sebastian answered.

"Yeah, him. God, what an obnoxious asshole. He called me and filled me in on Dad's fucked-up will, and, well, that was that. Bros before ball, you know? And besides, I was good, but NFL good? I dunno. Those guys are *good*."

I was trying to keep up, but they were skipping large chunks of information, since they were both familiar enough with the subject to use shorthand.

"Wait," I cut in, "you gave up a chance to play football in the NFL to come back home?"

Bax shrugged, picking at a scabbed-over scar on one of his knuckles. "Uh…yeah."

"Why?"

He was quiet a moment, and the whole room was silent. "Um. Our dad died, leaving a pretty specific will. All of us had to come back to help out at the bar for a year before any of the inheritance he'd left could be distributed to any of us. It was his way of bringing us all back together. We'd sort of scattered to the four winds, and I guess he wanted us to reunite as brothers."

"Wow. I—that's—"

"I want to hear the rest of Claire's story," he interrupted, clearly not wanting to talk about it any further.

Claire jumped at her name. "Oh. Um. Well, when the cruise put in here, I went out to find a decent dive bar to drink at, which happened to be Badd's, and I met Brock, and we spent a rather, um, *memorable*… night together. Which led to a day together, and then another night, and then somehow we just forgot to stop sleeping together, because like I said, sex with Brock is a twenty on a one-to-ten scale, and how am I gonna quit the best sex of my life? And then his stupid ass fell in love with me and begged me to keep fucking him, and I'm super generous, so I agreed."

"Hate to break it to you, babe," Brock put in,

amused, "but *your* stupid ass fell in love with *me*."

"Um, no. I'm pretty sure you fell first."

"Pretty sure I didn't," Brock argued. "And I also wasn't the one who ran off like a scared little puppy at the first sign of real emotions."

Claire elbowed him in the diaphragm. "No reason to bring ridiculous shit like the truth into this."

It seemed a bit odd to me, how they were arguing about who fell in love first. And Brock's statement about running? That had sounded pretty brutal to me, yet Claire literally acknowledged it as truth without flinching, and even made a joke out of it.

I did *not* understand these people.

Claire looked at me. "He's right, you know. I totally did run away like a pussy. Being in love with a Badd brother is no joke." She looked at Dru and then Mara. "Am I right, ladies?"

"Word," Dru and Mara said, in unison.

I just blinked, because what was I supposed to say? "Um. Okay. I suppose I can see how that might be, um…"

Claire just laughed. "So. Thomas. Dish."

I sighed. "Well, you'll probably need a little backstory. He's ten years older than me, and works for my father. He started out working as an intern during college, and stayed on until he graduated with a double major from Harvard, in business and politics.

"He's the only son of Richard and Elaine Haverton, which, unless you're well-versed in the who's who of the East Coast business and politics scene, won't mean anything to you. They're a wealthy family, powerful and influential. Richard Haverton and my father, Lawrence du Maurier, were both senators, and now they're two of the most influential men on the East Coast, my father as a political consultant and Richard as a lobbyist for several of the big energy companies. They've been friends for thirty years, and our families have been vacationing together to the same estate in Mallorca for twenty-five years, longer than I've even been alive, mind you.

"And if you're not familiar, all these wealthy East Coast business and politics families are the modern American version of the Old World aristocracy, meaning marriages are pretty much arranged from birth, and you don't marry outside certain circles, and you go to the right schools and you intern at the right firms and you take residencies at the right hospitals with the right physicians, and everything is…just so. Stuffy, pretentious, conceited, materialistic, and stupid. But it's what I was born into.

"And Thomas, as my father's best friend's son, has been pushed at me my whole life. Meaning, they assume I'm going to marry him because that's what's expected, and arranged. He's wealthy in his own right as well as coming from the Haverton's money, having worked for my father's firm since he graduated from Harvard, and invested well, and all that.

"Father has, quite literally and in so many words, promised Thomas that I *will* marry him someday, even though no one ever asked me what I wanted, or if I even *liked* him. Which I don't. I despise him. Yet he shows up everywhere I am, and he corners me on family vacations with these elaborate marriage proposals. He's purchased at least three different engagement rings that I know of, each more expensive than the last, and he just keeps proposing. He shows up at Yale and whisks me away on these ridiculous dates and expects me to…well, you can imagine—and then gets mad when I won't, and gets mad when I refuse his proposals, and never takes a hint."

I blew out a long breath, because I'd never said so much about Thomas all at once to anyone.

"Sounds horrible," Claire said, frowning.

"You have no idea," I said, waving a hand. "Everyone at Yale thinks I'm crazy for turning him down. But they all think I'm crazy anyway because Father set up an internship for me at this lobbyist firm in Boston, and it's one of the most prestigious firms on the whole East Coast, so getting internships there is practically a gladiatorial process, and I refused to go because I hate politics.

"But Father is paying, and he has the ear of the dean since he's a major benefactor, so he can basically get whatever he wants, which is me with a degree in political science even though I have absolutely *no* intention whatsoever of ever going anywhere near politics, which means I'm double majoring in poli-sci and fine arts, because I'm an artist and that's my dream and my passion, but the only way I'll get the degree and thus the opportunities the degree will provide is if I keep Father happy.

"But really, I barely attend the political science classes and only do enough work to pass, focusing the majority of my attention on my art studies. Which makes Father furious, of course, because art is a waste of time and not a worthy profession for his daughter. Mainly because he wishes I'd been born male so I could follow in his footsteps. Which is the stupidest thing ever, because why couldn't I follow in his steps as a politician if I wanted to? I mean, hello, Hillary? Elizabeth Warren? Maxine Waters? Kamala Harris? But it's just not what I want.

"And Thomas...*god*, he's such an insufferable bore, and so conceited, and entitled, and just assumes I'll marry him because Father said so, and hasn't ever even stopped to wonder what I think about him, despite my having *told* him I'd never marry him and that I can't stand to even look at his stupid, handsome, arrogant face. He just doesn't care. He wants me, and that's all that matters. He feels he deserves me because he wants me, and thus he'll get me one way or another."

Everyone was staring at me, silent, and I realized I'd been ranting.

"And, um…that's the story of Thomas." I stood up, hands shaking, stomach churning. "I should go. It's late, and it's been a long day."

I hustled out of the room and retrieved from the bathroom the plastic bag with my clothing in it and my purse from the kitchen counter, and headed for the door.

"It was very nice to meet you all. Thank you so much for your kindness and hospitality, Dru. I'll bring your clothes by tomorrow." I had the door open and was halfway down the stairs when I heard feet behind me.

"Yo, Eva, hold up." Baxter, of course. He caught up to me as I reached the bottom of the stairs and the darkened bar, the stools and chairs all flipped up on the bar and the tables, the only light coming from an illuminated "EXIT" sign.

I turned. "Yes, Baxter?"

"Ain't you learned your lesson about walking around in the dark, alone?"

I stiffened because he was only inches away,

staring down at me in the darkness with his eyes shining bright and glittering and intense, and his body was warm and his chest was bare, and he was enormous and far too close.

"It's not far. I'll be fine."

He snorted. "It wasn't far from the fight to here, either, and look what happened."

I sighed. "Fine. Baxter, my knight in shining armor, would you please escort me back to my bed and breakfast?"

He winked down at me. "Sure thing, sexy." He offered me his arm. "Let's go. Which one you staying at?"

"Um. It's got a funny name. King's something? King's Abode?"

He laughed. "The Kingsley's Rest, owned and operated by John and Beverly Kingsley. Nice place, nice folks. Good choice."

"You know it?"

He shrugged, leading me out the door. "Eh, sure, of course. Never stayed there, obviously, since I grew up in this town. But I've...um...hung out with a few people who have stayed there, and they always rave about it, plus I know Tate and Aerie, John and Beverly's twin granddaughters. They spend a few weeks up here every summer."

I glanced at him as we strolled down the street. It

was something like three in the morning at this point, and it was pretty chilly out, yet he was clad in nothing but his red fighting trunks and a pair of bright yellow cross trainers, his feet shoved in barefoot. He didn't seem fazed by the cool air at all, yet I was fighting the urge to shiver.

"Aren't you cold?" I asked him.

He shrugged. "Nah, not really. I was born and raised here in Alaska and lived in Calgary for two years, so I'm plenty used to the cold." He glanced at me, his eyes going to my nipples, which had hardened into protruding spikes yet again. "Why, you gonna give me your shirt if I am? In which case, yeah, I'm freezing."

"You're ridiculous," I snapped.

"True. No way it'd fit me." He winked, grinning. "You could take it off and I could wrap it around my shoulders like a cape?"

I couldn't help a laugh. "You really will say anything, won't you?"

He nodded. "Pretty much. Never had a filter, and don't see the point."

"Well, in case it's not clear at this point, no, I'm not taking off my shirt for you."

He snapped his fingers. "Damn. You've been teasing me with these things"—and here he tapped the underside of my breast with two fingers, a gentle tap—"since the second you came out of that bath-room. I'm fuckin' dyin' for a peek."

I cradled my breast with one hand and turned away from him, putting space between us, glaring daggers at him. "HEY! You can't just…you can't do that! Keep your hands to yourself, Baxter. I'm serious."

I dropped my hand and tried not to feel self-conscious about how…out there…my breasts were, and also tried not to think about the fact that Baxter had just touched my breast and that I'd had to fake a certain amount of indignant anger, since I'd not minded as much as I should have.

"Oh, you're serious?" he asked, the picture of studied innocence. "Good thing you told me you're serious. Because if you weren't serious, I'd probably do something else, just for fun."

A step, another, and I was tense, expecting him to try something. Anticipating. Waiting.

And then, just when I began to lower my suspicious defenses, he reached around me and pinched my butt, his finger and thumb quickly and sharply squeezing a generous portion of flesh. It had stung but didn't hurt, and yet I squealed and trotted out of reach.

"Baxter! Stop."

He rounded a corner, and I followed, and we were on a side street lined with trees, the branches waving in a cool breeze, the stars bright overhead, the bay and the docks behind us, boats clunking against the posts, sails clinking against masts.

"Stop? Stop what?" He tapped the underside of my breast, like he had before. "Stop that?" Then he pinched my butt. "Or stop this?"

Instead of reacting, I pretended not to notice, which was even harder than faking an indignant reaction.

He sidled close, so close I could smell him, feel his body heat. His lips brushed my ear. "Not answering now, huh? See, I think you don't mind. Do you? If you did, if you *really* meant you wanted me to stop touching you, you wouldn't let me get this close. I mean shit, babe, I'm so close I could bite your earlobe." His breath was hot on my earlobe, and I tensed, my breath caught, and I quavered, anticipating. But he didn't do it.

"Or, I could even sneak a little kiss, if I really wanted to." His lips slid across my cheekbone, and I wasn't breathing at all, now, and then his mouth brushed mine, his lips sliding gently across mine.

My mouth parted instinctually, and his tongue grazed the underside of my upper lip, and then he backed away a couple inches, and I was left off-balance and gasping.

"See what I mean?" he whispered.

I'd stopped walking, and my back was up against a wrought iron fence, and he was in front of me, shielding me from the world, blocking out everything except his enormous body, his hard muscles and his heat and his fierce brown eyes.

"Baxter…"

He wasn't touching me, not at all. Yet I could *feel* him. My heart was thundering.

"What up, babe?"

"You're crowding me."

"Yeah, and you like it."

"Are you asking, or telling?"

"Which one is the right answer?"

I snorted in laughter again, shaking my head and finally looking up at him. "Seeing as all the other men in my life seem to think they can tell me what to do and think they know what's best for me and expect me to do what they say, I'll let you guess."

He nodded, absorbing my statement. "Ah. Well, in that case, I'm asking. Evangeline, does my proximity bother you?"

"A little," I answered. "You make me nervous."

He backed up a bit, giving me space. "That better?" He wrapped a gorilla-sized fist around a spindle of the fence, just beside my ear. "Why do I make you nervous?"

I shrugged. "Just…everything about you."

"The fight? That shit in the alley?" He frowned at me. "Hope you realize that just because I'm a fighter doesn't mean I'm always a violent guy. Around you, I'm a big ol' teddy bear, gentle as can be."

I shook my head. "No, I get that. I'm not *afraid* of you, in that sense. You just...make me nervous."

"Then I'm confused. You might have to explain that one." He tipped his head to one side, thinking. "And you said *in that sense*, meaning there are other senses you could be afraid of me, and that implies some of them might be true."

I inhaled deeply, and as if drawn down by a string, his eyes fixed on my breasts as my chest swelled with the breath.

"Good grief, Baxter," I snapped, and shoved a finger under his chin to tip his gaze up to mine. "My eyes are up here. And besides, they're just breasts. You act like you've never seen them before."

"Sorry. It's just...you don't see perfect tits every day, and yours happen to be kinda mesmerizing." He shrugged. "Plus, I like looking at tits, yours most of all."

"Could you keep your eyes on mine while we're talking, though? I am more than a pair of mammary glands, you know."

He met my gaze, now, intently. "I know that, Evangeline." He leaned a little closer, his face once again kiss-close. "Don't mistake lust for objectification, honey."

"L-lust?" I swallowed hard.

"Yep. Raw, unbridled lust." He shifted closer with his body, so we were almost but not quite pressed up against each other. "I take one look at you, and my balls ache and my cock goes hard, and I have to remind myself to behave."

"What—*ahem*. Behave? What would you—what would happen if you didn't behave?"

Why did I ask him that? God. It was like I was actively trying to set him up.

Maybe I was.

He laughed, a deep rumble of amusement, rife with incendiary insinuation. "Eva, sweet thing, I don't think you could handle knowing that."

"Don't tell me what I can't handle, Baxter Badd," I snapped. "I'm no fainting, innocent little daisy."

Yes, actually, I rather was. But I refused to be put into a box by this man, or told what I couldn't handle.

He now pressed his body up against mine, fully flush. And god, his whole body was hot to the touch despite the cool air, and he was just so…hard. I don't mean it like *that*, though. His muscles, his stomach, his chest, his thighs, he was just hard everywhere, his muscles thick and firm.

Although, he was, in fact, hard like *that*. I could

feel it. Feel him, pressed against my lower belly, just above my core. Thick, a hard ridge between us.

I couldn't breathe. My hands shook and my lungs wouldn't expand all the way, and I was frozen in place, because now all I could feel, all I could think of was *him*, his…his *thing*, hard and thick and huge and right there, pressed against me.

"Are you a virgin, Evangeline?" he murmured.

I shook my head. "No…no. I'm not."

Barely.

"Then you wouldn't be shocked if I tell you I'm *this* close to tugging those sweatpants down and seeing if I can make you scream loud enough to wake up the neighbors."

I swallowed hard. "You wouldn't."

My brain went fuzzy, shorting out. Feeding me images of him doing exactly that. I could only imagine, though, because that wasn't in Thomas's repertoire; such an act would require thinking about something beyond himself and his own pleasure.

"Is that a dare?" he demanded.

His finger hooked in the waistband of the sweatpants, just below my navel.

"No?" I breathed, and it sounded like a question, as if I doubted my own answer.

"You don't sound convinced."

I wasn't.

My imagination was running wild. I was feeling rebellious. Daring. Crazy. I was here, in a city I'd seen literally nothing of except a warehouse, a few streets, the interior of a bar, and an apartment; I was here on my own, alone, in defiance of my father's wishes, without a plan, without luggage; my phone was turned off, and likely dead now; I'd used my debit card to book the room, and that card drew off my personal, secret account which Father knew nothing about, so he couldn't easily track me that way.

And I was pressed up against this gorgeous, rugged, dangerous man, a man who had fought in an illegal underground boxing match, and had utterly destroyed his opponent with laughable ease, and then he'd saved me from being assaulted by four men, one of whom had been armed, and he'd destroyed them as well. And he was touching me. He was teasing me, toying with me. But when I said he was crowding me, he'd backed up to give me space. Yet he could read my reactions. He knew I was attracted to him. And I was, intensely.

It's not like this could...*be* anything, but why shouldn't I indulge in a bit of fun? Who would have to know? No one. Only me.

But...like this? Here? God, I was crazy for even hesitating. No: that was the easy, obvious answer.

"Evangeline, I need some words here, honey."

He was breathing hard, and when I peeked up at him, his jaw was clenching and his eyes were narrowed, as if focused and straining.

"Which words?"

He tugged at the waistband, and an inch of my belly was exposed. "I really, really wanna think I'm reading you correctly, here. I feel like you want this, but you're scared of it. That's okay. If you want to dabble at being naughty with a Badd boy, sweetheart, I'm your man. I can lead you into temptation and show you the time of your fuckin' life, and then when you're ready, you go back to Yale and you'll have some dirty memories of the time you had some fun with big ol' Bax in Ketchikan, Alaska." He tugged a little more. "But if you're really not sure, you say so, and you're safe from me. I won't try nothin', I'll just walk you the rest of the way to the Kingsley's and that'll be that. But I need to know what you want, either way."

What did I want? I wasn't sure. I had no idea.

That wasn't entirely true. I did want him. Or, at the very least, I felt something deep inside that I'd never felt before. With Thomas, I'd gone along with things because it felt adult and daring and I knew he expected it of me, and I'd liked it when he kissed me and I'd liked it when he groped under my shirt and laid me back on the bed and it had felt like I was getting lost in something. Even though it'd never amounted to more than a few brief and unsatisfying fumbles in the dark, little more than Thomas moving briefly and finishing and leaving, it had made me aware that there could be...more.

I wanted that *more*.

It was a sure bet that Bax could give me more.

But I was terrified.

Thomas and Father were going to find me, sooner or later. If they caught me dallying with a local, especially someone like Baxter...oh, there'd be hell to pay.

But wouldn't it be worth it? And couldn't I have my fun and then leave and act like nothing had happened, that I'd gone off to get some space and was done?

I had my own money. Well, Father's money, which I'd more or less stolen depending on how you looked at it, because even though he'd given it to me as an allowance, it was, technically, dependent on me obeying his rules. He tolerated me defying him in regard to Yale because he still hoped I'd change my mind, that I'd eventually end up toeing the line and marrying Thomas.

But god, Baxter made me feel...so much.

He was so different from anyone else, so big, so hard, so wild. He was totally free. He did what he wanted, said what he wanted, and he took what he wanted. But he wasn't a pig about it. He seemed to genuinely care that I really wanted this.

"I don't—I don't know."

"You don't know," he echoed.

I shook my head. "Unh-uh." I was uncharacteristically inarticulate, for some reason.

"What aren't you sure about?"

I stared up at him. "Everything. You. This. What I want. What I should do."

"Keeping me stuck in no-man's-land, huh, halfway between yes and no?"

I winced. "I'm sorry, Baxter. I just…I truly don't know what to do." I dared to touch him, to put my hands on his broad shoulders, feeling his warm skin and the rippling power of his muscles under my hands. "I…I *am* attracted to you. And there is a part of me that—that does want to—to let you lead me into temptation. Truth be told, I'm already there—I'm very tempted. But—I don't, I'm not—"

He laughed. "You don't do things like this," he filled in. "You're not that kind of girl."

I shook my head. "I don't, and I'm really not."

With one hand, he tugged at the waistband a little more, and now the line between my lower belly and bikini line was being teased, and with the other hand he reached up and tucked a lock of my hair away from my face and then brushed my cheekbone with the rough pad of his thumb. "Sweetheart? You couldn't be more obviously *not* that kind of girl."

"It's that obvious, is it?"

He laughed again and nodded. "Yeah, it kinda is." He stared down at me, and I wasn't sure if he was thinking, or assessing, or just looking at me. Deciding, maybe? "How about this: we'll operate on the assumption that I've got a hair trigger when it comes to you saying no. Okay? So I'm gonna keep going, and when you really, truly want me to stop, you tell me. But don't say it if you don't mean it, because I'm not gonna play around. So I'll keep on leading you into temptation, and you just follow my lead. Ask questions. Say what you want, if you figure that out. Or, just trust me and let me do things my way."

"Your way? What is your way?"

His lips brushed mine again, a teasing hint of a kiss. "Oh, you'll find out." He tugged the waistband lower yet, and now the elastic, taut around my waist from the pressure of his pull, inched down in the back, sliding down over the top of my butt, baring the upper few inches, and now the slightest amount of my privates were exposed and my heart thundered wildly. "One thing you should know about me doing things my way, though, Eva: I'm the kinda guy who gets off on a woman's pleasure. Meanin' the harder you get off, the harder I get off."

"I like the sound of that," I whispered, unsure where the bold words had even come from.

God knows there's been little enough pleasure in my life that didn't come with expectations, I thought.

Or…so I'd thought.

But the way Baxter stiffened, and the way his eyes fixed on mine told me I'd accidentally said it out loud. "Babe, you really gotta explain that comment."

"I just—" His eyes were fierce, fiery, and made me forget what I was saying, and then when I remembered, the unvarnished, unfiltered truth came out. "Everyone expects things of me. My father expects me to do everything his way, and do what he wants. Thomas expects me to marry him, to be his trophy wife, to go on his stupid dates and to sleep with him just because we have a history, and even my friends at Yale…they know who my father is, and they've all seen Thomas, and they want to be close to me because either they want a piece of my father's influence and connections, or they're hoping Thomas will notice them and forget about me, which would be fine by me, but they still just don't seem genuine, and if I go hang out with them I'm always wondering what their angle is."

I growled in frustration and anger, a snarl that'd been building up inside me for a long damn time. "And guys, god, don't get me started on guys. They either want to sleep with me, or—like the girls—they want to get close to Father for his political and business connections...and with men it's both: they try to sleep with me in hopes of getting close to Father. And when I don't play their games, they're gone. Like all I am to them is sex and networking. I'm not a virgin, but I haven't had as much experience as I might wish simply because there are literally zero men with the slightest ability to even *pretend* as if they like me for more than my cup size and their stupid fantasy of me putting out for them even when they put less than zero effort into wooing me. They think their daddy's bank account and their trust funds and their portfolios and their internships and their fancy cars are enough to impress me, like I'm going to see the stupid shiny Porsche their father bought them and I'm going to just...just fall onto my back with my legs open and beg them to sleep with me, because fancy cars just impress me *so* damn much."

Baxter blinked at me. "Wow. That's...a lot to unpack."

I thumped my head forward against his chest. "I'm sorry. I shouldn't have unloaded on you like that."

He brushed his thumb over my lower lip. "Nah, honey, don't apologize. You gotta unload that shit. You can't keep it buried inside forever, or it'll fester. I know I may not seem like it, but I am actually a good listener."

I frowned up at him. "Why wouldn't you seem like a good listener?"

He shrugged a big shoulder. "My size, my looks, the fact that I'm a football player and an MMA fighter…and the way I talk. People just assume I'm a stupid meathead. I don't exactly go out of my way to dispel that notion 'cause, for the most part, I don't really give a shit, and it's kinda useful to be underestimated. But sometimes, I do give a little bit of a shit about what people think."

"So far, Baxter, you seem to me like a rather more complex individual than you get credit for."

"I like to think so. And I also like to think at some point, the right person will see that, instead of just… assuming shit about me."

"Like when people assume that because I come from money and power, that I'm nothing but a spoiled rich bitch, like those ridiculous rich kids on Instagram?"

Our gazes were locked, and the intensity between us, a kind of unspoken understanding, sizzled and sparked. We couldn't come from more vastly different backgrounds, but we both knew what it was like to be misunderstood and underestimated and relegated to one particular and unfair little box.

He'd relaxed the pressure on the waistband of my borrowed sweatpants when I'd started venting, and now he increased it once more, slowly and inexorably dragging them downward, centimeter by centimeter.

I wasn't wearing any underwear. After the shower, it had felt too good to be clean after all that had gone on that I'd not wanted to put my old, dirty underwear on, and so I hadn't. I'd not been expecting... all of this.

"Pretty much," Baxter said. "And for the record, you're a hell of a lot more than just a set of body parts to me, Eva. You got spunk, and you're sassy, and you're smart. You put shit out there, take it or leave it, and I like that. Also, I got absolutely no use for connections of any kind. I got seven connections—my brothers—and that's all I need. So...just want you to know, my interest in you is all about *you*."

"And what exactly is the nature of your interest in me, Baxter?"

"Thought that much was fairly obvious," he said.

I kept my gaze on his, waiting for his answer. At some point, I'd dropped the plastic grocery bag containing my clothing, so my hands were free, and they were resting on his shoulders. Now, I skimmed my hands down his arms, cupping the bulge of his biceps, simply because I'd never been this close to biceps like his, the kind of muscles you typically only see on guys in the movies, or on a billboard.

He ran his thumb over my lower lip, tugging my mouth open, touching my chin, and then he dropped that hand to my waistband, and now his hands were at my hips, he was pushing the sweatpants down, down over my hips. The wrought iron fence was cold against my skin as my buttocks were exposed, and the air was cool against the dampness of my privates; I wasn't breathing at all, at all.

I was gasping past the throbbing lump that was my heart in my throat.

He lowered the sweatpants until I was completely exposed from the hem of the shirt sitting above my navel to the top of the sweatpants, riding at mid thigh. His eyes remained on mine, however, rather than on the delicate, private flesh now exposed for him.

"Eva, sweet thing…my interest is in making you feel things you've clearly never felt before. My interest is in touching you and making you scream, making you wriggle and writhe and beg me to do all the things you've never even dared to fantasize about." His gaze remained locked on mine, yet I felt his hand moving. Reaching. "My interest, Evangeline, is in getting you naked and fucking you six ways to Sunday, and then on Sunday, staying in bed with you from sunrise to sunset and listening to every last damn thing you have to say, about absolutely anything. My interest is in finding out how loud you can scream, and how many times in a row you can come."

"Baxter—"

"My interest is in throwing you onto your bed and spreading your legs apart and devouring this sweet wet pussy of yours"—and now, finally, he touched me as he mentioned the area by name, and his touch was delicate and gentle and slow, and I sizzled and I seared and I gasped—"until you can't take any more."

"And—oh. And then?" I was encouraging this?

What was wrong with me? I should be outraged that he'd dare touch me, I should be angry that he was taking such liberties with me even though we'd known each other less than three hours. I should…I should be squirming away from his touch because of what had happened earlier.

But I was none of those things.

I was letting him touch me, and I was *enjoying* it, and hoping for more.

He laughed. "That's not enough?"

He slipped a finger in; I couldn't believe this was happening. It didn't seem real, yet it was far too real all at once. It was a fantasy I was sure I was going to wake up from, yet for the time being I was blissfully content to play along with the dirty dream and let this man I'd obviously conjured up from the depths of my clearly depraved imagination do these wicked, dirty things to me, like finger my privates in public, at three in the morning on a quiet neighborhood street.

"And then, if you're still hungry for more," he continued, "the nature of my interest would be in seeing you on your knees, naked, with that sweet, sassy mouth I been tryin' not to kiss all damn night wrapped around my cock, takin' as much of me as you can."

I tried to swallow, my throat wouldn't work, and I was shaking all over, and his finger felt so thick and rough inside me, and I looked down because I wanted to see what this looked like, his finger inside me. God, even his forearm was powerful. He was barely touching me. Barely past the first knuckle of his middle finger, yet I felt absolutely split apart and filled by his touch. And he was curling, then swirling, and dragging it up and then down, and I realized he was just toying with me, letting me get used to his touch. His finger was so big, so dark and tanned and strong, and his knuckles were all so scarred from fighting, and this huge powerful hand was touching me, gently sliding inside me in a way I've never experienced, a touch that was sure and unhurried.

"I don't know if I could do that," I said, unsure why I was admitting it in the first place.

"Which part?" he asked.

"The last thing you said. About...me...with my

mouth on your…your…I've never—I haven't—"

"Not a shock. You don't wanna do it, no big deal. You want to, I'll let you." He dragged his finger up to my…up to the part of me that sent shocks and shivers thrilling through me when he touched it. "Anybody ever do this to you? I mean at all, I don't mean just… out here, like this."

I could only shake my head. "Aside from me, no."

"Then nobody's ever gone down on you," he stated.

"Oh my goodness, no way."

"But you one hundred percent *are not* a virgin?"

I nodded. "One hundred percent. But…if there's degrees of not-a-virgin, I would probably count as only barely not a virgin."

He laughed. "Yeah, I got that part."

"Are you laughing at me?"

He met my eyes as I stared up at him. "No, honey. Not laughing at you. Not in mockery or cruelty, at least."

"But you *are* laughing."

"A little." He touched that spot again, and I quivered. "Just because you're so damn sexy and erotic and gorgeous it's not even real, and you don't even understand how incredible you are. You, barely a virgin? It's crazy. I'd expect there to be a line of suitors a million miles long."

He was touching me, the tip of his finger swirling in small circles, just so, in one particular spot way up high, and he clearly knew exactly what it would do to me, that it would make me gasp and that my knees would tremble and that my stomach and back would tighten and heat would pool low and deep in my belly. He clearly knew that I would sag against the fence as lightning blasted through me at his touch. He knew I would be weak, and grow incapable of supporting myself—he wrapped a hand around my lower back, clinging to me, holding me upright against his body. I stared up at him and breathed shakily as he kept going, touching, performing his sorcery.

I'd done this to myself under the covers frequently enough in my life, but this was utterly unlike the way I touched myself. That was experimentation and release of tensions, this was…sorcery. Magic.

"Baxter…" I breathed.

"Yeah, honey."

I clung to his broad shoulders and let myself quiver and shake. "I'm…"

"Close?"

I nodded.

He grinned. "I know. I can feel it. I can see it." He pulled his finger down and slid it deep inside me, slowly filling me, gathering the moisture of my desire and the heat of my impending detonation, and returned his touch to where it had been. "You're squeezing. Clamping down."

"I am?"

He slid his finger back in, and now used his thumb to rub that spot, and I felt myself, as he'd said, clamping down around his finger, squeezing and pulsing as I neared the edge, brought closer and closer by his touch.

"Feel that?" he whispered. "The way you squeeze? That means you're close. And those little noises you're making? Whimpering, gasping, all that? Means you're getting even closer."

He was right. I hadn't been aware of it, but it was making all sorts of breathy little sounds.

God, this dream was crazy. I'd obviously fallen asleep on the plane, and my pent-up sexual frustration was making itself known. This was a dream—it *had* to be: there was no way I was really doing this, letting a complete stranger put his finger inside my vagina, on a public street, three in the morning or not. No way. I wasn't like that. With Thomas, the lights had always been off, and he'd only fumbled at my breasts for a moment, and we hadn't even gotten totally undressed except for that first time after prom, and it hadn't even really seemed real, just a quick few moments of feeling Thomas above me and feeling something inside me, a little too big, a little too much, and it had hurt a little but not terribly—just a quick, sharp pinch—and then it had started to feel not too unpleasant, and then there'd been a flurry of Thomas making noises and movements, and then it had been over. He'd gotten dressed and popped a bottle of champagne and given me a glass as I held the sheet against me.

That was sex, to me. That, even that, hadn't seemed real.

This, with Baxter, felt even less real.

Thus, it was a dream.

I would never, ever, in a million years, *ever* do this for real. I wasn't this daring, this rebellious. I was a good girl. I got good grades, I had the right friends, wore the right clothes. My only disobedience in my whole life was my major at Yale.

If anyone knew that I was even having this dream? God. And if, somehow, this was *real*? Oh god.

The wild manic frenetic pulsing pounding inside me felt real enough, though. The heat and the pooling pressure felt real. Baxter felt real. His touch felt *so* real. And now, god, oh god.

There—I was there, falling over the edge, crying out.

I was dizzy and limp and he was holding me up and my thighs were clenching and my belly was spasming and my whole body was going crazy, twisting and writhing and jackknifing in Baxter's hold as a crashing tsunami of raw intense pleasure shattered me into a million pieces, and only Baxter was there to hold me together, his arms were all that kept me in place, kept me from floating mindless and weightless to the moon.

I was vaguely aware of my voice, of the whimpers turning to a howl as I came utterly apart. And then Baxter was kissing me. Kissing me. God, the kiss. Like I'd seen his brothers give their women. Intense, possessive, wild. I drowned in it. I continued to shatter through the kiss, and came apart even harder for the kiss, and I was screaming and couldn't kiss him back because I was unable to function for the wracking bliss shaking me, possessing me.

I floated on the pleasure.

Drifted.

Ached.

Throbbed.

Gradually, I filtered back to awareness, and I was in Baxter's arms. My pants were around my knees, and my hair was in my face, and his arm was around my waist and his hand was cupping my head.

I blinked up at him. "Did...did I faint?"

His chuckle was an amused, aroused rumble. "Sure did, sweetheart."

"Oh god, that was incredible." I sighed, shivering

as aftershocks rippled through me. "I like this dream."

"Dream?" He sounded confused.

"Yes. I'm dreaming, obviously. I'd never do this in real life." I stood up, and Baxter's arms held me in place as I wobbled unsteadily, my knees trembling; his hands were gentle as he slid the sweatpants back into place. "I'm still on the jet. I don't know how my sub-conscious came up with someone as delicious as you, but I'm glad it did."

His thumb brushed across my cheek. "Eva, hon-ey. This ain't a dream. At least, I don't think it is." He frowned thoughtfully. "Although, how would I know if I was something you'd dreamed up?"

I straightened, backed out of his reach and caught up against the fence behind me. "No, no-no-no."

His grin was, complicatedly, somewhere be-tween predatory and comforting. "Yes, yes-yes-yes." He brought his fingers to his face, inhaled, and then stuck them into his mouth.

Holy…whoa. Did he just do that? Those fingers, they were just in my…and he just…

"I'm *dreaming*," I insisted.

He sidled closer to me, pressed his body up against mine. Bracketed my face with both hands, and then clutched my cheeks in his huge rough palms, closing in slowly, and I blinked and blinked and strug-gled to breathe, and then his lips were brushing mine and I was kissing him.

I was kissing *him*.

It lasted only a moment. Just his lips, warm and soft on mine.

"That feel real enough for you?" he murmured.

I shook my head. "No. I'd never kiss a complete stranger. Much less…what I just let you do."

He laughed. "Still in denial. I know I'm a lot to get used to, babe, but you gotta face it. This is real." He brought his fingers to my nose, and I smelled my own scent on him. "I fingered your pussy, right here on the street. You screamed into my mouth, sweetheart."

I whimpered. "It's not real. I'm dreaming. I'm on the jet to Mallorca. I want so badly to not be going on that stupid vacation that I'm dreaming about this adventure as a mental escape."

My ability to believe myself was fading, and panic was welling up inside me.

He teased the hem of the Seahawks shirt I was wearing with a fingertip. Then he slid that fingertip along my belly, his touch searing my skin. I kept my breathing slow and even, through sheer force of will, as he skated that single fingertip up the center-line of my torso, higher and higher, dragging the front of the shirt up with it, baring more and more and more skin. And then the curves of the bottoms of my breasts were bared, and I was utterly still, staring up at his molten brown gaze, wondering what he was going to do now. What I was going to *let* him do now. Because, since I was still clinging to the insistence that this whole business just *had* to be a dream, I might as well let myself do daring things. Let this big, brutal, beautiful, rugged, possessive, protective man do dirty and forbidden things to me.

He traced up between my breasts, and now they were almost completely bared. I wasn't breathing, and I had to remember to suck in a breath because my lungs were burning and I was getting dizzy.

His touch drew slowly across my torso, to the right side of my body, baring the whole of one heavy, aching breast. My nipple was thick, rigid, and hypersensitive, all but begging for his touch. Which...he gave me. Just not as I'd expected it. Instead of cupping the weight of my breast or caressing it or circling the nipple, or even bending to mouth it—all the actions men in love scenes in movies and books always did—he pinched my nipple. Suddenly, and *hard*.

I shrieked in surprise and pain, writhing out of his touch and tugging the shirt down into place. "What was that?" I demanded. "That hurt, Baxter!"

"Did it feel real, babe?"

I swallowed as realization of what he'd just proven rifled through me. "Yes," I whispered.

He kissed me again, briefly and softly. "Did *that* feel real?"

"Yes," I whispered.

"So...am I a dream?" He closed the space between us again, pressing his erection against my lower belly and core. "Is this whole thing a dream? Or is it real?"

I closed my eyes. *Wake up, wake up, wake up*, I told myself. *When I open my eyes, I'll be on the jet.*

I opened my eyes, carefully and slowly and warily; Baxter stood towering over me, hands grasping the fence spindles beside my face, grinning triumphantly.

"Crap," I breathed.

He laughed. "I'm as real as they come, Eva."

"Crap!" I repeated. "I'm such an idiot. I need—I need to go. I have to go. This was a mistake."

I could still feel his touch. I could still feel the delightful, shivery, erotic quaking of the orgasm, the gentle, skilled circles of his finger around my... around me. His kiss. His lips. His body, hard and powerful, blocking out the world beyond his massive frame. Even at that exact moment I could feel his manhood between us, as improbably massive and hard as the rest of him, and I felt my cheeks flaming from the knowledge that he was aroused because of me, for me.

"Did it feel like a mistake when you came apart

in my hands?" he murmured. He pressed against me, and then his lips darted against mine in a tease of a kiss. "Does *this* feel like a mistake?"

I whimpered again, panicking, overwhelmed, embarrassed, afraid, and most of all...aroused in a way I'd never felt before, and thus confused and terrified at the potency of my need and desire—at the way I wanted him to touch me and do things to me and teach me everything I'd been missing my whole life.

"Yes!" I said, whisper-shouting. "Yes, this whole thing is *crazy*. I must have been more drunk than I thought to let you...to do this."

I ducked under his arm and trotted away, flip-flops slapping noisily against my feet. I expected Baxter to chase me, but when I glanced back at him, he was leaning against the fence with his huge arms crossed over his chest, an amused grin on his lips.

"Eva?" he called, his voice pitched low.

I stopped, turned back to look at him. "What, Baxter?"

He jerked his thumb at a two-story Victorian house kitty-corner across the street, a house that I vaguely recognized. "That's you, babe."

Sure enough, a hand-carved and painted wooden sign in the yard announced the property as *The Kingsley's Rest*.

I sighed in frustration. "Crap."

I had to walk past him to get to it, and he knew it.

I tried to hustle past him, keeping as small a profile as possible, ignoring him completely. Baxter just laughed, a genuine bark of amusement.

"Seriously, Evangeline?" He slung an arm around my middle and hauled me up against him, my arms pinned between us, my hands flat on his chest. Which, admittedly was a very nice and masculine chest, and felt wonderful under my hands. "What's the problem, honey?"

"What's the *problem*?" I yanked away from him, snagging the bag with my things in it, which I'd forgotten. "Everything! You, partly, but mostly just me being an idiot and a reckless, wanton, irresponsible slut." I walked away, then.

He jogged few steps to catch up to me. "Whoa, hey now. Them's fighting' words, missy," he drawled in an exaggerated Old West accent.

"I don't know what that means."

"It means nothing about what just happened was bad or wrong, Evangeline. It was *good*. You enjoyed the fuck out of it, and you're allowed to do whatever the fuck you want to do with whoever the fuck you want to do it...unless you're married or in a serious relationship. Which you aren't, are you?"

"No, I'm not married! And I'm not with anyone,

although Thomas might have himself convinced otherwise."

"I don't give two shits what your boy Thomas thinks. If you say you ain't with him, that's all that matters."

"No, I'm not with him and never will be." I was nearly at the B and B, now—nearly safe from Baxter, and my own foolish impulses. "What does that have to do with anything?"

"It has everything to do with everything. You're a grown-ass woman, Evangeline. You wanna hang out and drink with some cool as fuck folks till ass o'clock in the morning, you can. You wanna get a little dirty, have some innocent, pleasurable, consensual, adult fun, you can. Your body, your life, your decision."

"But this...it's not—it's not *me*!" I whirled on him, shouting out loud now. "I don't *do* things like this. I've had sex exactly five times, all with Thomas, always in the dark, in a proper bedroom. I've never even been *kissed* in public! And now, suddenly, I'm letting you pull my pants down and touch me intimately, in public, on a sidewalk, where anyone could see? I should be checked into an asylum!"

"It's three in the damn morning, Eva. Who's gonna see? And who cares if they do? They don't know you, and it's not like you're a local who has to see any of these people again anyway. Not to mention, I was blocking anyone from being able to see anything anyway. In case you hadn't noticed, I kinda make a better door than a window."

"I don't know what that is supposed to mean," I muttered. "You and your odd phrases."

"It's not odd, it's—" he cut himself off with a laugh. "It just means I'm kinda big, and kinda hard to see past. I was in front of you. We were pushed up close. My body was blocking anyone's view of you, or what I was doing. Anyone who happened to even be awake to see us woulda just seen two people makin' out, gettin' a little cozy. They wouldn't have seen any of your bits, or what I was doing to you."

"Oh." I glared up at him. "Still. It's the principle of the thing. I don't *do* this sort of thing. I'm the daughter of a former United States Senator. I'm expected to behave a certain way. With decorum, and decency. I'm expected to dress conservatively and appropriately. I do not consort with—"

His gaze went hard and angry as he cut in over me. "With guys like me? Yeah, got it. Message received, princess."

"No, that's not—I just meant strangers, Baxter. It had nothing to do with what type of person you are."

"Suuuure, sweetheart," he said in a sarcastic drawl. "Keep telling yourself that. If your daddy and your precious Thomas caught you with me, something tells me they wouldn't be pleased."

"That's not my concern, and Thomas isn't my precious anything!" I stepped closer to him and poked his chest. "It's not *like* that. I am not, have not, nor will I ever judge you for who you are. It seems to me you're doing an excellent job of judging *yourself*, Baxter, and me."

"How the hell did this get turned around on me?" He poked my chest right back, directly between my breasts, which managed to be oddly non-erogenous, surprisingly. More...accusatory. "You're the one acting like you've committed a crime or some stupid shit. You got finger-banged, and you had a killer orgasm. And you're welcome, by the way—*that's* how that shit should feel. You should be proud of yourself. You're getting out of your fuckin' shell, experiencing new things. Living for yourself, instead'a for what your mom and dad think or want or expect."

"I do not have a shell."

"Say cock, then."

"No. Choosing to not engage in vulgar speech has nothing to do with whether or not I have a shell."

"Then touch me. Do something crazy. Kiss me. Invite me in. Flash me your tits. Something you, as you've been insisting, never do."

"What's that going to prove? You get touched or kissed or flashed, and all I get is embarrassed. A lopsided deal, if you ask me."

"Just body parts, princess. Nothing embarrassing about it." He untied the strings of his shorts. "I'll show you mine if you show me yours. How about that? I'll even go first. Just to show you there's nothing weird or embarrassing or crazy about it. When two people are attracted to each other, it's totally normal and natural for them look at and touch each other *intimately*, as you put it."

"Baxter, you don't need to do that. You're missing the point of what I'm—" I stopped talking abruptly, my breath leaving me in a shocked huff, as Baxter dragged down his shorts to bare his manhood. "Oh—oh my…wow. Um…*wow*."

He was massively erect. Thick, pink, and straining. *Enormous*. I felt faint just looking at it. And a little tempted to touch it, just to see what something like that felt like in my hand. Instead, I clenched my fists behind my back.

"Put it away, Baxter," I said.

"Why? Don't you like it? Don't like looking at it? It's a pretty nice one, I've been told."

I sucked in a deep breath, and tried to keep my eyes on his, but my gaze kept wandering back down to the absurdly big, absurdly straight, absurdly incredible monster between his legs. "That's not the point."

He inched closer. Too close. Within reach. My

hands shook and I clenched them even harder behind my back. "What *is* the point then, princess?"

"I don't—god, I don't know." I closed my eyes, the only way to stop seeing that *thing*. "You're confusing me."

" 'Cause you live in a shell. A box. A cage. Whatever you want to call it. You don't know how to get out there and take what you want out of life." He was whispering now, and he was so close I could smell him and feel his heat, and if I opened my eyes or let my hands unclench and move between us, I would be touching him. "Life is short, princess. You gotta just… reach out and take what you want."

"I'm not touching your…your—I'm not touching you, Baxter."

He chuckled, and I felt him move, letting his shorts snap back into place, covering him. "You want to, though."

We were in the middle of the street, dead center in the middle of an intersection, underneath a flashing yellow traffic light. All the lights in the windows of the buildings around us were dark, and the moon above was a bright waxing half-moon, and there were a countless million stars twinkling and gleaming. It was cool out, with a steady breeze ruffling my hair. A cricket chirped, somewhere.

"What I want is to sleep. I was up at six this

morning, and I've flown across the entire country. I ran away from my father and his bodyguards, and then I watched a brutal fight happen and I got blood sprayed all over me, *intentionally*, and then I was assaulted, and *then* I watched you brutalize the men assaulting me, and I think your brother murdered them…and then I met your entire family and they all know what happened to me, and your sisters-in-law seem to think I'm part of the *gang* now or something, and I don't even have any real girlfriends that I trust and I'm an only child so I don't know *how* to part of a group like your family even if I *wanted* to be, or could be. And then—and then you…I let you touch me in public and you kissed me and you showed me your… your *thing*, and I'm confused and overwhelmed and exhausted and I don't know what I want, except that I want to lay down and have it just stop being *today* for a little bit."

Baxter sighed, and brushed my cheekbone with his thumb, which seemed to be a favorite gesture of his. "Go sleep, babe." He then stepped back, dropping his hand to his side, and when I hesitated, he jerked his chin at the B and B behind me. "Go on. You'll see me tomorrow."

I sighed in amused irritation at his presumptuousness. "I will, will I?"

"You will, will you."

I laughed, despite my irritation. "Good night, Baxter."

"Good night, Eva."

I went inside, turning the knob as silently as I could, and made my way up the stairs to my room, stepping softly, and closed my door behind me. It wasn't until I'd climbed into the bed still clothed that I realized at some point I'd stopped insisting he stop calling me Eva. And then I realized I kind of liked his nickname for me, and all the terms of endearment he called me. Presumptuous, and a little sexist, perhaps, but for some reason, I didn't mind.

I'd expected to fall asleep immediately, but I didn't. My eyes were burning, but they wouldn't stay closed, and then when they did, all I saw was Baxter. His body, the lines of his muscles, the craggy perfection of his jawline. His manhood. His eyes, hot and chocolate brown and intense. Seeing me far too clearly.

When I fell asleep, I dreamed of him. Of touching him. The dream, when I woke up abruptly with my core throbbing and my breasts aching, only served to reinforce that what had happened had been real. Almost too real, maybe.

I did eventually fall asleep again, and Baxter was there once more.

THREE

Baxter

I WAS IN THE DINING ROOM OF THE KINGSLEY'S B AND B BY ten, which I felt wasn't too early or too late, given the lateness of the night before. It was empty, everyone else staying there having eaten and gotten on their tourist way by then. So, I sat and sipped coffee and chatted with John and Bev, discussing the changes to Ketchikan over the last few years, and sports, and the weather. Unlike most of my other brothers, I'm naturally garrulous and have no problem making small talk, and I can make it charming. When you're built like I am, and have my somewhat brutal-looking and rugged features—as women I've known in the past have thus described me, mind you—you have to fight against stereotypes; people tend to assume because I have twenty-inch biceps and I shave the sides of my head, and because of the scarring to my face and knuckles from all the fighting that I must be a meathead mouth-breather capable of only the most basic of verbiage, like "ugh" and "punch" and "Bax hungry."

This one time, in Calgary, after a game, I was in a bar hitting on this chick, buying her drinks and such, prepping to chat her up and see about taking her back to my place for a few hours. She gets her drink, gives me one up-and-down scrutinizing look-over, and then starts talking to me in a loud voice using small words, like I was a dog or a child, or like some assholes talk to people for whom English is a second language. I hadn't even spoken to her, only bought her a drink from across the bar and made my over after the bartender pointed me out as the buyer. I told her to go fuck herself in French first, to make a point, and then in English.

But by eleven a.m., even my ability to make small talk was waning, and Beverly clearly had other work to do and was getting antsy, so I told them I was content just waiting for Evangeline to wake up.

By noon, I was done waiting.

I made sure John and Bev were both elsewhere, and then I went up to her room—which I'd promised myself I wouldn't do, but hey, this is me we're talking about. Her door was unlocked, the silly, trusting girl; John and Beverly's house was an old one, restored to look as close to the original Victorian style as possible, so all the bedroom doors featured manual locks as opposed to the newfangled electronic keycard kind, which I figured Eva was used to and, being sleepy, just forgot to lock it behind her. So, after peeking in to make sure she was still in bed and that she wasn't, like, naked on top of the covers or anything, I left the B and B, zipped up to the local coffee shop for a couple cups of coffee and a nice toasted bagel with local lox and cream cheese.

When I returned, Eva was still sleeping. Still clothed, too, dammit. I let myself into her room and crouched on the floor beside her bed. She was fast asleep, and goddamned beautiful…just fuckin' lovely as hell. Made the pit of my stomach flip-flop, just looking her. She'd left her hair loose and it was all in her face in fine glossy black strands, and her face was at peace, her lips slightly parted. Her hand was curled into a loose fist under her chin, and she had the blankets tugged up to her shoulders, lying on her side facing the room.

I took off the top of one of the paper cups of

coffee and wafted it under her nose; she made a soft grumbling sound, and then wrinkled her nose, sighed, and stirred. I unwrapped the bagel and held it near her nose, and the freshly toasted scent had her stirring and moaning. The moan, though? That shit went straight to my dick, and I went hard as a rock in an instant, hearing her moan like that.

She stirred again, and I switched the bagel for the coffee. Another even more temptingly erotic moan, and I put the bagel up near her nose again.

Her eyelids flickered and fluttered. Emerald eyes peered at me, sleepy, confused. "Mmm...bagel?" I held half of the bagel up to her mouth, and she parted her lips and took a dainty, genteel bite. "Mmm. Mmmm-hmmm. 'S good."

"Local lox on a freshly baked bagel," I said. "Fit for a princess."

She blinked at me, and then took the bagel and rolled to her back, shimmying upward into a partially reclined position. "You show up in all the best dreams, Baxter."

I laughed. "Oh god, not that horseshit again."

She devoured half of the bagel in a few bites, and then licked the cream cheese off her fingers, at which gesture I may or may not have audibly groaned. "What?"

I eyed her. "What, what?"

"I'm confused."

"Me too," I said.

She rolled her eyes at me, spied the lidless cup of coffee on the nightstand, and snagged it, sipped carefully. "This coffee is amazing."

I winked at her. "Only the best for you, babe."

I was still holding the rest of the bagel in my hand, and she was eyeing it hungrily. "About that other half of the bagel…"

I laughed and handed it to her. "All yours." I stood up and perched on the edge of her bed. "You're so fuckin' cute when you sleep it should be illegal."

She froze with the bagel in her mouth. "You… watched me sleep?" she asked, delicately.

I nodded. "I mean, only long enough to wake you up with coffee and food. It's not like I sat in here staring at you as you snored all morning."

She tugged the blanket a little higher, self-consciously. "I do *not* snore."

"Do too."

She sipped the coffee and glared at me. "I do not." A hesitation. "Do I?"

I held out as long as I could, and then snorted in laughter. "No, Eva, you don't snore. Not even a cute little ladylike snore."

"While I'm grateful to be woken up with food and coffee, I'm a little creeped out that you're in my room." Eva took a bite, chewed, swallowed, and gestured at me with it. "Actually, a lot creeped out."

"I'm sorry, I just got impatient."

"Impatient?" she said, blowing across the top of the coffee.

"Well, yeah. I've been here since ten, and it's almost twelve thirty. I waited until noon, and then got fed up with waiting. Your door wasn't locked, and I made sure you were decent before I came in. Then I went and got the bagel and coffee."

Eva frowned at me. "Made sure I was decent... how? By looking to see if I was naked or not?"

I grinned and shrugged. "Pretty much, yeah."

"And if I had been less than fully clothed, what would you have done then?"

"Enjoyed the view," I said with a wink. "Kidding. Not really, but mostly. Honestly, I probably would have still come in, and I would have covered you up."

"And gotten a free peek while you were at it, too. Jerk."

I took a swallow of my own coffee. "Not gonna hear me deny that, Eva. You are, without a doubt, the most fine-ass woman I've ever met. If an accidental peek is all I'm ever gonna get, you bet your ass I'll take it." I eyed her across the rim of my coffee cup, letting her see the earnestness in my gaze. "A guy like me, a lady like you...yeah, that's all I'm gettin', and

I'm fine with it."

She finished the bagel in silence, brushed crumbs off her hands and the blanket, and sipped coffee, staring at me thoughtfully. "There are quite a few possible retorts to that, and I'm not sure where to start."

"Say what you gotta say, babe."

"How about I say what I have to say while you take me shopping for clothing."

"Sounds good to me." I stood up. "Do I get to watch you try on the outfits?"

She rolled her eyes and snorted derisively. "No, Baxter. You do not get to watch me change. Not now, not ever."

I snapped my fingers. "Damn. Worth a shot." I paused on my way to the door, reached down and snagged her bra out of the plastic bag containing her clothes, a full-coverage white lace number; I tossed it onto her lap. "Might want that." I deliberately let my gaze travel down to her breasts, and the outlines of her, ahhh, high beams, which were prominent and poking at the thin cotton, teasing me. "For my sake, if nothing else."

Eva glanced down at herself, blushed, and tugged the sheet up to cover herself. "God, that's embarrassing."

I shook my head. "Embarrassing? Hell nah. Hot as fuck." I gripped the doorknob to anchor myself on this side of the room. "Tempting as fuck, too. Every time I steal a little peek, I'm more and more tempted to just lean in and take a little nibble. Just to see if they taste as delicious as they look."

I watched her press her thighs together under the covers.

"You can't say things like that to me, Baxter," she murmured.

"Why not?"

"You're supposed to be taking me shopping, not trying to seduce me." She clutched the covers for dear life, holding them in front of her body as if they were a shield.

"Eva, sweetheart…that wasn't an attempt at seduction." My feet carried me back across the room, to her bed, and I leaned over her. Tugged the sheet out of her grip. "That was just me making a point."

She set her coffee aside, and I did the same with mine. "What point?"

I moved slowly, giving her plenty of opportunity to slap me silly. I traced a fingertip across her belly, over the narrow strip of tanned skin left exposed between the hem of her shirt and the waistband of the sweatpants, a deliberate echo of the way I'd touched her last night/this morning. She sucked in a breath, watching my hand with hawkish intensity. I sat on the edge of the bed again, this time pressed up against her legs. I slid both middle fingers along that strip of bared flesh. Teasing, teasing. Keeping her gaze locked on mine. Dragged the hem of her shirt up her torso, baring her navel, and then her diaphragm, halting when I started to see underboob.

She bit her lower lip between her teeth, blowing out the breath she'd sucked in moments ago. "Wha— what are you doing?"

"Not sure," I admitted. "What does it seem like I'm doing?"

"Taking my shirt off."

Still using only middle fingers, I traced around the undersides of her breasts and then grazed the outsides on my way up; it was my turn to catch my breath, now, as her tits were both exposed. My cock, already hard as a steel beam, started throbbing painfully, my balls pulsating, a groan escaping my lips involuntarily at the sight of the most perfect pair of breasts God ever put on a woman.

"Is that what I'm doing?" I asked, nudging the Seahawks shirt a little higher yet.

"Yeah, I am fairly certain that's what you're doing."

I finally took hold of the hem, preparing to lift it off entirely. "Don't hear you telling me to stop," I murmured, "so I'm gonna keep going."

I met her gaze, giving her yet another opportunity

to put an end to this; she remained silent. Better yet, she unfroze, just a little bit. Her hands, clutched into her thighs through the covers, released their death grip, and she lifted her hands over her head.

I searched her eyes, her face, looking for hints of...I wasn't sure. Panic? Fear? Excitement? Anticipation? I found the last three, at least. And maybe it was more nerves than fear.

I pulled the thin raglan T-shirt off her head and set it aside, letting myself fully soak up the incredible beauty of a topless Evangeline. "God*damn*, Eva."

"What?" she whispered.

"You." I reached out, and I wasn't at all embarrassed to note that my hands were trembling, just a little bit, a fact which I think she noticed. "You are... baby, you're *perfect*. Literally, the most perfect woman I've ever seen."

I cupped her left breast in my right hand, letting my thumb brush over her erect nipple; she gasped sharply, and her pupils dilated.

She shook her head. "I'm not."

I tipped my head to one side. "We can agree to disagree on that. I think you are." I transferred my touch to the right side, softly caressing the fullness of the heavy globe. "Why are you letting me do this, Eva?"

"I'm telling myself this is all still a dream." She

was breathless, watching my hand touching her as I explored the curves and weight and softness of her breasts. "Because otherwise I'd never have the courage to really do this, to let you—to let *anyone*—touch me like this. At all. Much less someone I don't know. Because I—I *want* this. It feels wrong, but it also feels right, and I want it, and no one in my life would approve of any of this which is why I'm doing it, partially."

"Tell yourself whatever you want, sweetheart, as long as you know I'm real, and that I'm in literal awe of you, and that the second you stop wanting any of this, all you gotta do is say so. Until you tell me to go fuck myself, I'm gonna keep pushing your boundaries, and I'll be considering myself the luckiest bastard on the planet in the meantime."

"I would never tell you...that."

"What if I tried something that was a hard limit?"

"Hard limit?" She crinkled her nose in adorable confusion.

How could anyone be hot as fuck, sexy as hell, beautiful and elegant and classy, and yet cute and adorable all at the same time? Didn't seem possible, yet Evangeline kept proving it was, in her case.

"Like, not just a 'no, I don't like that, Bax' kind of way, but in a '*hell* no, quit that before I break your nose' kind of way."

"Oh." Her eyelids fluttered closed as I grasped her by the waist and pulled her down into a laying position, leaned over her, and kept caressing her breasts, with both hands now, tweaking her nipples now and again, hefting their glorious weight, cupping their softness. "I, um. Well, for one, I wouldn't know how to break your nose even if I wanted to, and I couldn't even begin to imagine what you could possibly do to incite such a—oh, *ohhhhh!*—such a violent reaction from me."

The *oh—ohhh* was a reaction to pinching her nipples between fingers and thumbs and twisting sharply, testing her reaction to a little bit of a sting.

I took her hand in mine, tilted it back so her palm was face out in palm-strike position. "Watch." I brought the heel of her palm up to my septum in a gentle approximation of a strike. "Like that, as hard as you can, hitting kinda upward and inward at the same time. Like you're trying to push my nose backward into my skull." I redirected her palm into a side-on strike. "Or like this, trying to smash it right off my ugly face. Use your hand like this, though, open, like a slap. If you've never been taught to throw a punch, you're more likely to hurt yourself trying to hit me with a closed fist. Open-hand, like this, you can't really hurt yourself, as long as you keep your wrist braced back all the way."

"Won't it kill you? Like, drive the bone into your brain?"

I couldn't help an outright laugh. "Babe, that's Hollywood horseshit. It's so hard to do it's almost impossible. Takes a shitload of skill and practice to perfect. Most you'll accomplish is breaking my nose. Most guys, that'll stop 'em in their tracks. Gettin' your nose broke ain't no picnic."

"Would it stop you?"

I kept hold of her hand, brought it to my lips. Kissed her palm, and then the underside of her wrist. Up along her forearm, kissing my way toward her body. "Nah. I can shake that shit off easy enough. Nah babe, you wanna stop me, you gotta nut-shot me with all you've got. Otherwise, I'm pretty much un-stoppable. That's why they call me Basher in the ring, 'cause I can just bash my way through any amount of pain and get the win."

"Oh," she breathed.

Her eyes were wide, and her breathing was catching now and again, alternating between sucking in deep, shaking breaths—which did wonderful things to those big, natural, jiggly tits of hers—and not breathing at all. And then she would suck in a breath, suddenly and sharply, and she would jiggle and bounce all over again, and god, my dick was going to explode like a motherfuckin' pipe bomb in a second.

I kept kissing along her arm, my lips now pressing along the inside of her bicep, laying it down on the pillow, over her head. When I reached the transition point from arm to armpit, I took her other hand in mine and repeated the line of kisses from palm to armpit. And this time, keeping my eyes on hers for any hint of hesitation, I touched my lips to the outside of her breast. She sucked in a sharp breath at the contact, her lower lip caught between her teeth. Her eyes were on me, on my mouth, watching me. I met her gaze, sliding my lips along her silky flesh, closer and closer to her nipple.

"The point I was making," I murmured, "was that I take one look at *these* points"—and here I nibbled at the sweet, delicate, firmness of one erect nipple, and then the other—"and I'm just...fuckin' helpless. I *gotta* taste you. Taste this, and this, and this." At each repetition of *this*, I kissed her somewhere else on her breast, the insides, the underside, the nipples. "I don't know how else to put it, Eva. I'm normally pretty good at resisting temptation and keeping my shit in check, but you just...you fuckin' do somethin' to me, babe."

"What? What do I do to you?"

"Drive me crazy, that's what."

She gasped as I suckled her nipple, letting my

teeth graze and nip. "But I'm not—I'm not doing anything."

"Don't have to. That's the point. It's just…you."

I forced myself away, forced my hands and mouth away from the delicious perfection of her breasts, which was a monumental feat of self-control on my part.

I slid my hand under her neck and lifted her up.

"Bax? What are you—"

I answered her before she could finish the question: I kissed the ever-loving fuck out of her. Which, in terms of helping the achy-breaky, dick's-about-to-explode hard-on I was rocking, was a stupid move, since I had no intention of letting it go there between us just yet. Which meant suffering through it until it went away or I had a few minutes to rub one out…or two, or ten.

God, what a kiss. This time, I didn't hold back. I just fuckin' gave it to her, both barrels, full blast. Tongue searching the hot cavity of her mouth, lips scouring hers, teeth nipping at her lips, fingers buried in her thick black locks. I couldn't help myself. Once I got that kiss going, I was just lost. Gone. Buh-bye. Brain short-circuited, body going haywire. I leaned over her, pressed against her, moaning into her mouth as I felt the squish of her bare tits against my chest. She lifted up into the kiss, reaching around to cup the back of my head and slide against me eagerly, and her tongue slid against mine, and her lips sought mine with wild fervor. I knelt on the bed, and she shifted, accepting my weight above her, and she kicked the blankets and sheet away. Her bare toes slid along my calf, and her palms slid down to my shoulders, clinging to me, keeping me locked into the kiss, as if I'd ever give up a kiss like this.

More, more.

Fuck, this was dangerous. I was riding the razor-edge of my control, pushing the envelope. I knew I couldn't take her all the way yet, but I needed...fuck, just...*more*. I knew it was going to end, I knew she would come to her senses and ghost on me, and soon. Go back to her life, to her dad, to Thomas, to Yale, to her fancy life of luxury in which foul-mouthed, hard-fisted, blue-collar bruisers like me had no place. But shit, I *wanted* her. I wanted to hear her talk more, hear more about her, get her to open up, hear her scream, feel her lose control, watch her discover the wild thing living inside her.

For now, all I could do was kiss her.

I lifted up, bracing my weight on one hand, and let my other hand palm her tit, thumbing the nipple until she gasped into my mouth, and then I traced the bell of her waist and hip, teased the waistband of the sweatpants. Her hands sought the hem of my shirt and eagerly dug under it, palming the muscles of my back, my shoulders, and then my waist.

She was touching me greedily.

Kissing me just as greedily.

She shifted against me, tilted her hips, and I felt myself yanking at the sweatpants and hauling them down so I could palm her ass, kneading it, clawing the firm heft of it, pulling at her, tugging her closer. She moaned, murmured something unintelligible. Pushed at my shirt, trying to get it off.

Flexed her hips again.

God, she wanted it.

She wanted an orgasm. Wanted me to touch her. She may not have known or understood outright, in so many words, but that was what she was begging for, right then.

Kissing me, giving me access to get those pants down, even shimmying her hips and thighs so they were lower. Pressing against me. Devouring my tongue and exploring my back and shoulders with her hands, daring to reach down to the waistband of my shorts.

I wanted to bury myself in her. Make her scream. Haul those pants all the way off and taste the delight between her thighs. Get her to touch me. Really get her going.

I broke the kiss and rested my forehead against

hers. Slid my hand between us, teasing over her now-bare hip, the crease where thigh met hip bone, inches from her core. "You want to come again, don't you, honey?"

She hummed an affirmative, flexing her hips.

"Let me hear some words, honey." I nipped her lip as I slid the tip of my middle finger to the upper crest of her slit. "*I want it*—say that."

Her arms wrapped around my neck, and she whimpered. Clung to me, shook her head. "I can't."

"Try—'I want it, Bax.' Four little words." She shook her head, and I withdrew my touch.

She whimpered in desperation. "No! Wait." She cradled my cheek in her hand, pushed my face away so she could look me in the eyes. "Why? Why do I have to say it? You know that's what I want, so why do I have to say it?"

"Because I want to hear it," I admitted. "I want to watch that hot mouth of yours saying you want me to touch your pussy and make you come."

She actually laughed. "Good lord, Bax. I'm certainly not saying *that*."

"I think that's the closest to swearing you've come since we met," I remarked.

I gave her a light, teasing touch. Watched her eyelids go heavy and her mouth go slack as I delved my finger lower and deeper, and then her breathing stopped entirely as I slid my touch inside her and gathered her wetness—and holy *fuck* was she wet—and smeared it around her clit and she squirmed and ground against me.

"At least tell me you like that." I couldn't help bending to lap at her breast, suck her nipple into my mouth. "Tell me it feels good."

She moaned. "I like that, Baxter. What you're doing, it feels...*ohhhh*...it feels so good." Another moan. "Too good."

"*Too* good?" I pretended to sound alarmed, and moved my touch away. "Wouldn't want that. Better stop."

"NO!" she squealed. "No. Don't...please don't stop."

I laughed, and resumed touching her. Circling. Delving in, gathering, smearing. Bringing her to the edge in seconds. "Teasing, Eva. Just teasing."

"Jerk." She tried to glare at me, but her eyes fluttered closed and then were back open, ruining the glare. She gave up trying to glare, and just gave me a look of desperation and intense delight. Raw bliss. Unfiltered ecstasy—and all I was doing was fingering; holy *shit* would she be surprised when she discovered what I could do with my mouth...and other parts.

"Ask me nicely." I slowed my touch, right as she

was nearing the cusp of climax.

"For what?"

"If I'll let you come."

"Really, Baxter?" She managed to scold me even as she was writhing and gasping. "You expect me to *ask* you to do something you enjoy doing?"

I laughed. "It's the principle of the thing, babe. I like the sound of your voice. I like the reassurance that you're enjoying what I'm doing. I want to hear you say it because it turns me on to hear you beg."

"Beg?" She sounded dangerously close to angry at the sound of that word.

"Just a little bit." I kept her hovering on the edge, slowing when she got too close, and bringing her back again. "'Let me come, Bax.' That's all."

She was *so* close. *So* close. Her fingers were clawed into my back, and her hips were flexing. She was moaning, whimpering. A touch, one direct brush against her clit, my lips around her nipple, she would explode.

I kept her from it, though. Trying to coax a little verbal enjoyment from her.

"I'm not begging, Baxter." She had iron in her voice.

"No?"

She shook her head, trying to shut down on me even as I kept her riding the edge. "No. I'll never beg.

There's not much I can claim as all my own, only for me," her glare was fiery and firm, "but this... my body, what feels good, what I want, what I do...I *won't* beg. So...so then you should just stop, if that's what you're expecting of me."

I grinned fiercely, my heart swelling. "Goddamn, Eva. Now *that* was the right fuckin' answer, sweetheart."

I buried my face against her breast and sawed my teeth around her nipple and flicked the tip of it with my tongue and gave her the quick light rhythmic touch against her clit she needed to fall over the edge. She bit down on a scream, and I moved my mouth to hers, covering and devouring her scream, milking her through the orgasm until she was bridged upward, heels and shoulder blades digging into the mattress, core shoved into my touch.

When the climax faded, she collapsed onto the bed, sweat dotting her forehead and upper lip and the slopes of her breasts. She was gasping in a series of relieved, disbelieving, euphoric moans. "Wow. I mean—*wow*. Just...wow."

I felt pride ripple through me. I found her bra, took one of her hands and threaded it through the appropriate loop, then the other, and then lifted her to a sitting position. Hooked it behind her back on the loosest setting.

Leaning against my neck, she murmured, "One tighter."

So I tightened it, and she pushed away enough to stuff herself into place. And then I tugged her pants up and found her shirt, slid it over her head, and helped her fit her arms through.

"I can dress myself, you know," she remarked with a bemused smirk.

I shrugged. "I know. This was more fun." I stood up, trying to be at least somewhat subtle in my adjustment of my monster erection as I moved to the door and grabbed the crystal knob. "Meet you in the foyer when you're ready?"

She eyed me, and the obvious outline. "Where... where are you going?"

I jerked my head at the door. "We're going shopping. Also, it's time for lunch, thought maybe we could hit up my favorite burger joint."

She indicated me with a flick of her finger. "Like that?"

I shrugged. "It'll fade...eventually."

"Isn't it...I don't know...uncomfortable?"

"Hurts like a bitch, if you really wanna know." I shrugged again. "I'll live."

"Isn't there some way of..." she moved her hand in a vague, circular gesture, "...alleviating the discomfort?"

I grinned. "Yeah, but I'm not beating off in the bathroom of a bed and breakfast."

She blushed. "Oh. You mean…masturbating."

I laughed again. "Yeah, princess. I mean masturbating. Which is when I take my cock in my hand and stroke it until I come all over the place." I winked as she gulped. "That's the only option, other than letting it subside on its own."

"Oh."

Just to test her a little, I moseyed back across the room. "There is…*one* other option."

She was wide-eyed and innocent and lovely and intoxicating. "Oh—oh really?"

"You could help. Instead'a my hand, you could touch me." I stopped when I was just within touching distance. "The thought just occurred to me. Just, you know, as a possibility."

"I see." She was playing along with the game, keeping her expression wide-eyed and innocent and naive. "I suppose that *is* an option."

FOUR

Evangeline

M Y HEART WAS HAMMERING IN MY CHEST, AGAIN—AS it so often seemed to do around Baxter Badd.

This time, insanely, I was actually considering doing it.

Touching him.

This whole morning—afternoon, whatever—all I could think of was the way his...his manhood... had looked last night. Bare. Huge. It had looked as if it was straining. So engorged with blood it was near to bursting. I'd been imagining it like that, inside his plain black shorts. Enormous and thick and pink and straining.

Now he was standing in front of me, and I was sitting on the bed, feet on the floor, facing the door. His shorts were thin, almost like swim trunk material, but cut to look like regular shorts. His arousal was obvious, outlined behind the thin fabric. He looked… tense, all over. As if he was engaging in self-control, holding himself back. I may not have been a virgin, but I was totally inexperienced in things like this, so I may as well have been one for all I knew about what he was feeling, thinking, or going through. What he wanted.

Me, I knew that much.

To touch me. To hear me say things I could never say.

And…probably, for me to touch him. Do things to him I'd barely even dreamed of or fantasized about doing.

Like—I swallowed hard, staring up at him, and then letting my gaze travel down and down and down to his zipper, and the thick ridge bulging behind it—like unzipping his pants, taking out his *thing*, and touching it. Touching him, on purpose, until he reached orgasm.

Giving him what the online pornography videos would probably call a handjob. I'd watched…well… more than a few of those videos. It was my dirtiest, darkest secret: I watched porn. I had an account under a secret email address comprised of nonsense letters and numbers, which I paid for monthly with a pre-paid Visa card loaded with cash drawn from my secret bank account of money filtered from Father.

I watched porn regularly, habitually, almost obsessively.

I touched myself watching it. Made myself come, again and again, watching it.

I'd never, ever, *ever* come so hard or for so long touching myself, though, like I did when Baxter touched me. Not even close. The orgasms I gave myself were like paltry little sparks in comparison to the fireworks, the exploding-star supernova detonations he made me feel.

I'd watched a video, recently—the morning I left Yale for vacation, actually, mere hours before getting on the plane—in which a sultry blonde with massive fake tits had slowly, erotically and skillfully fondled a man to orgasm. The man hadn't been shown at all, except for his abs and his manhood, and the woman had frequently stared erotically and with great intensity into the camera, inviting the viewer to pretend it was him she was touching. I'd tried to pretend it was me touching him, and I'd come swiftly and hard. I'd never done that, had no reference for the fantasy, but it had been potent nonetheless.

Now, I was presented with an opportunity to live out that fantasy. With a man who, I was very certain, featured an even more incredibly impressive member than the man in the video had possessed.

Which...had been rather bogglingly enormous. Veined. Bulging at the head. Shiny. Smooth, yet hard looking, and also soft. Straining upward and away from his body.

I thought of Baxter, last night. Even taller, even thicker. Straight up, standing flat against his belly. The man in the video hadn't been circumcised, and Baxter, I was fairly certain, was. Not that it mattered. I could almost see myself wrapping a hand around him. What would it feel like? To touch him, to watch him have an orgasm I'd given him. The videos were obviously staged, the people in them actors. What would a real person, not acting, do?

I wanted to know.

When would I ever get this chance again? Never, probably. I'd never be in a position where I felt...safe enough, I supposed, free enough from the normal constraints of my life, even at Yale...to indulge in living out my many, many fantasies.

Baxter was watching me. He knew I was thinking hard.

"I want to do it," I said.

He frowned. "Do what?"

I swallowed, my throat dry, full and thick and burning with my throbbing heartbeat. "What...what you said."

His brows furrowed. "Gonna have to be a little more specific, honey."

I rubbed my palms on my thighs. Swallowed again. Breathed past my nerves. "Um. Touch you. Like you said."

"Like I said, huh?"

I nodded. Gathered up all the courage I had. "Make you—um..." I let out a breath and tried again, forcing the words out in a rush. "I-want-to-make-you-come."

He rocked back on his heels. "Evangeline, babe, I was just—"

"Pushing me, a little, to see what I'd do," I interrupted. "I know."

"I'm not sure you're ready for that, Eva."

I blinked, surprised, and then found anger boiling through me. "Do *not* presume to tell me what I'm ready for, Baxter. I can decide that for myself."

He held up his hands, palms out. "You're right, I'm sorry. I just didn't mean for you to—"

"Actually want something for myself?" I demanded. "You wanted me to just do things your way, on your time frame?"

He let out a breath. "You know what? You're right. That is sort of what I was assuming, I guess."

He let his hands fall to his sides. "I don't mean to think I can control you, or make you do things my way. This is about you. I want you to…" He shrugged. "Choose what you want for yourself. That's the whole point of this."

Mollified by the sincerity in his voice and in his expression, I pinched the fabric of his bright red polo and tugged him closer. "Then…take this off." I tugged on the shirt again.

He grabbed the polo by the back of the collar with one hand and hauled it off, tossed it onto the floor. "Okay."

"Now, just…" I felt my resolve wobbling, "don't laugh at me, and don't try to take control, okay?"

He frowned down at me. "Why would I laugh?"

I swallowed hard yet again. "I—because I've never…" I shrugged. "Done this. Any of this."

"You said you weren't a virgin."

"I'm not!" I shook my head and waved both hands in front of me. "Now shut up, you're distracting me. I *want* to do this, because it's…" I couldn't quite admit it out loud.

"It's what, Eva?" His voice was soft, kind, encouraging.

I looked up at him. Let out a breath, stared down at the floor, and released the truth from within me, where it had been caged for so long. "It's a fantasy of mine."

"To...touch me?"

I shrugged. "Not you specifically, no." I met his gaze. "Not until now, at least."

"Your fantasy is to...just...touch a man?" he clarified, sounding puzzled.

I nodded. "Yes. I don't want to talk about it."

"Later, maybe."

I shrugged, noncommittal. "Maybe." I reached for him, glancing up at him as I grasped the button of his shorts. "My point is, I've never done this before, so..." I shrugged. "I may not, um..."

He clasped his hands behind his back, to stop himself from touching me. "There's no right or wrong, Eva. All there is, is what you want. That's it."

I unbuttoned the fly of his shorts and then pinched the zipper between my index finger and thumb. Inhaled sharply, feeling a thrill shoot through me as I began to realize fully that this *was* real, that I *was* doing this. It wasn't a dream, or a fantasy. It may be simple to someone else, but to me, this was...a big deal. I pulled the zipper down, and the shorts sagged open. The bulge expanded, pushing apart the edges of the opened fly. A tug, and the shorts slid in a quiet plop to the floor around his ankles, and Baxter toed them aside.

I had to suck in a deep breath, and squeeze my

hands into fists and shake them out to try and stop the shaking.

"Eva, listen—"

I glanced up at him. "I know you're not about to try to talk me out of this."

"Hell no," he chuckled. "Just reminding you that this is real. Don't cheat yourself out of an experience by pretending it's not real."

"Oh." I nodded. "That is a good point."

It was, too. Thus far, I'd been sort of holding on to the idea that this was still all a very lucid dream. I knew better obviously, but it helped me cope. So much had happened, and I wasn't sure I'd be able to handle it all if I thought about it, so I chose not to dwell on any of it, and pretend it was all a lucid dream or a hallucination, or something.

But it wasn't.

This was my life.

I was in Ketchikan, Alaska. My father—and Thomas—had no idea where I was, for the moment, which meant they weren't monitoring me or my actions or my decisions. I was free to do what I wanted. No one had any expectations on me. Least of all Baxter.

I could do this. I wanted to touch this man, and I was going to. No one could tell me it was bad or wrong or not the behavior expected of a du Maurier.

I didn't know him, not at all. He was a virtual stranger. But he was a virtual stranger who had saved, if not my life, then saved me from an assault. Gotten me a shower, and clean clothes, and a drink or two. Introduced me to his family, who were really interesting and cool people, who had calmed me down and relaxed me and accepted me and gotten me to open up in a way I never had with anyone.

And then...he'd walked me to my B and B, and then he'd done...well...incredible things to me. Touched me. Made me feel wanted. Beautiful. Made me feel...*sexy*. In control, somehow, despite the fact that he'd pushed the situation from start to finish. But he'd given me the choice. Asked me if I wanted it, and forced me to admit that I did—forced me to admit it to myself. He'd never taken advantage of me, and was in fact being very careful with me, giving me every opportunity to demur, or change my mind.

Letting me dictate things.

Like now. I was just ruminating, staring, thinking, and he was in no hurry at all. Watching me, hands behind his back, brown eyes curious and patient. Heated, interested. Just waiting.

"I'm sorry," I said. "I'm just—"

"I got nowhere to be till tomorrow, babe. Take your time."

I wanted this. Just this, for now. I told myself to

open my mind, to let myself feel this and experience it and savor the moment. This was *my* moment. I was doing this because I wanted to, and for no other reason.

I just…had to actually do it.

I hooked my index fingers in the elastic waistband of his tight yellow boxer briefs, inhaled slowly, glanced at Baxter, and then at what I was about to expose. Slowly, I pulled the waistband away from his body and drew the undergarment down, careful to make sure the elastic didn't get caught. My heart was thundering, pounding wildly; Baxter looked calm and cool and composed, hands behind his back, one corner of his mouth tipped up in the tiniest hint of a smile. The muscles in his jaw were flexing nonstop, though, making a bit of a lie of his nonchalance.

In one smooth movement, then, I lowered his underwear until they fell free, and Baxter toed them aside with his shorts.

And now he was naked. Hands still clasped behind him, exposing himself to me, confidently, even a little arrogantly.

God…he was a work of art.

I looked him over, top to bottom, several times. Just soaking in the mammoth masculine perfection of him. Rugged, manly, powerful features. Sharp, chiseled, cliff-craggy jawline. Intelligent brown eyes.

Expressive mouth, one which I knew could kiss with power and gentility that could take my breath away. His neck was thick, corded. His shoulders were like mountain ranges, bulging with hard, rounded muscle. His chest, too, was carved as if from granite, and his abs were a study in raw brutal power, thick and blocky and hard as an anvil. He had a deeply-etched V leading down the line of his hip bones to his groin, and as my eyes wandered downward, my heart leapt into my throat and my pulse pounded in my ears and my hands shook, and my stomach did flip-flops. There, at the center of that V, was his manhood.

I had no way of knowing how many inches it was, nor would that have made any difference to me had I known, as I had no frame of reference. All I knew, was that it was beautiful. Nearly as thick as my wrist, and almost as long as my entire forearm, ridged and veiny, with a plump domed head. Heavy.

God, I should really learn to even *think* a few dirty words.

His...*cock*...was beautiful. And his balls looked at once heavy and soft.

His thighs were...I couldn't even come up with a metaphor or simile that was apt. A phrase from the golden age of science-fiction and fantasy rolled through my brain: might thews—Baxter had mighty thews. He was a football player, I remembered, and judging by the raw power of his legs, he could run down a freight train and tackle it.

I extended a trembling hand and touched his abs, slid my palm up to his chest, explored his pectoral muscles, and then back down. Traced the ridges and blocks of his abs. The lines delineating the muscles in his thighs. The carved angle of his waist, and his hips. I shifted forward a few inches, so I was closer to him, and palmed the cannonball hardness of his buttock, then again with both hands.

"I…" A laugh bubbled up out of me as I caressed his buttocks. "I like your butt."

He laughed. "Football scouts and agents actually look at players' asses. Big butts mean a lot of power."

"Then you must have…a *lot* of power," I said.

"Honey, you have *no* idea."

Oh geez. Oh boy. I gulped at the heat and the promise in his voice. "I can imagine," I murmured.

His chuckle managed to sound like he was teasing me. "You know, babe, somethin' tells me you probably couldn't. Not yet, anyway."

"Not yet?"

"I plan on showing you." His voice was a purr, now. Leonine. Thrilling. Seductive. "I plan on showing you my *power* and my *stamina*."

"Ohhh boy. Oh boy."

"Oh…boy," he repeated, monotone, sarcastic.

"You just said…oh boy."

"Cursing and vulgarity is not ladylike, nor is it elegant. It is the mark of an uneducated and decidedly unsophisticated mind," I said, instinctively quoting verbatim Mrs. Allison, the woman who had taught me comportment and decorum and proper social etiquette from the time I was eleven until I graduated high school.

Baxter's eyebrows arched. "Well fuck me, then, right?"

I felt my cheeks burning. "I—Baxter, I'm—I didn't mean—"

He laughed. "Relax, babe. It's fine. That's actually been proven to be untrue, but you can think what you want."

I eyed him. "What do you mean?"

He shrugged. "Well, just that several scientific studies have actually proven that a large vocabulary of curse words is a sign of greater intelligence, not less." He winked at me. "But I'll grant you that someone who swears a lot, like me for example, probably isn't very elegant or sophisticated."

I thought about it. "I suppose it's just been drummed into my head for my whole life that cursing is a sign of weakness and demonstrates a lack of decorum, and that there is no reason to engage in it. I don't curse as a matter of habit. It's not a…a religious or moral thing."

Baxter crossed his arms over his big chest, and quirked an eyebrow at me, with a wry, knowing smirk curving his lips. "You wouldn't be trying to distract yourself, now, would you? I ain't in any kind of hurry or nothin', but for someone who says she wants to experience this whole touching me and making me come thing, you sure are talking a lot."

I swallowed hard. "Yeah, I might be delaying a little." I met his eyes. "I *am* pretty nervous."

His smile was reassuring. "Nothin' to be nervous about, honey. Just reach out and grab it. I won't move, won't say a word."

I held his gaze. "No laughing at me, no teasing?"

"Some things I don't joke about, Eva. Gettin' my dick touched is right at the top of that list."

"I just…I don't want to—to do anything…I don't know. Wrong, I guess." I broke the gaze binding our eyes.

He chuckled, reaching out and lifting my chin so I was looking at him again. "Told you, there ain't no right or wrong. This ain't a test, or a game, or a competition. This is just two consenting adults, alone, doin' what feels good. Only advice I might give you is, to start out with, don't squeeze *too* hard, but I also ain't gonna break, so you don't have to act like I'm made of porcelain or some shit." He crossed his arms again. "This is about you, this time around. Don't worry about how I feel. You got your hands on me, I'm enjoying it. Promise."

"Okay." That actually did make me feel a little better. "I just…I don't want to hurt you or anything. I know you're…sensitive, down there."

He laughed again. "Honey, you plannin' on kneeing me in the sac or something?"

I glared up at him. "Of course not!"

"Then quit worrying. It don't bend when it's hard, and it only stretches so far, but…honestly, just…*do* it. Touch me. Quit thinkin', quit stallin', and just reach out and grab it. I don't bite." He glanced toward the ceiling with a shrug. "Well, I *do*, but not in this situation."

I laughed despite my hammering, jangling nerves. "Okay…okay. Here it goes."

He just stood still, arms crossed over his chest, like a living sculpture of an ancient god or a warrior from times of old, massive and hard and muscular and perfect, with a dauntingly enormous erection staring me in the face.

I started at his thighs, palms sliding upward from his knees. I couldn't help a detour back to his butt, because it really was incredible, taut and round and hard but yet the skin so soft, with a light dusting of dark hair. And then up to his abs, because what woman could resist touching that stomach, the hard marble blocks of muscle? I traced the V-shaped indents with my thumbs, and let my gaze fix on his erection. I sucked in a breath, blinked hard, let out the breath, and wrapped my right hand around him.

Oh…oh my. Oh my *god*. So *big*. Hard, yet silky soft. Springy, yet containing a core of steel. Smooth, and warm. I let my hand travel down, until my knuckles brushed his belly, and wrapped my other hand around him. I glanced up at him: his belly was tensed, and his jaw was ticking and pulsing, and his brows were drawn down, and his eyes were locked on me. He was stone-still, except for the gentle rise and fall of his breathing and the tick of his jaw.

One hand, again. I slid my fist up, slowly, marveling at the feel of him in my hand. I was amazed at myself, for doing this, inordinately pleased and proud, and wildly giddy. I pulled him away from his body, toward me, and then from side to side, testing the range of motion. Rubbed the rounded top part with my thumb, brushing the tiny little slit with my fingernail; he flinched when I did that.

"Crap, did I hurt you?" I asked, somewhat breathlessly, a little panicked, since he hadn't flinched even when getting punched during the fight or sliced along the arm in the alley.

He shook his head. "Nope. Exact opposite."

I flicked the little slit with my thumbnail again. "So this...? You like it?"

"Yep."

I kept my grip loose and light, and slid my fist up and down his length a few times, mimicking what I'd seen on the video. "And this? It feels good?"

His mouth quirked, as if he was restraining a laugh. "Hell yes. Crazy good."

I used both hands, and let myself enjoy the sensation of just stroking him and petting him, caressing his length, using all sorts of grips and touches and rhythms, experimenting and exploring.

I grinned up at him. "I really like this."

"You like what, exactly?" he asked, the furrowed ridge of his brows deepening, the ticking of his jaw becoming more rapid, his words coming through clenched teeth.

"Everything." I watched my hands, liking the contrast of my skin tone against his, the erotic view of his erection sliding between my fingers, the way he seemed to be struggling to contain his reactions. "Touching you. The way you feel. The way you look." I paused, just watching myself touching him. "I like that...that I can see you physically trying to...I don't know. Hold back your reactions."

He grunted wordlessly. "Not a reaction I'm holdin' back, sweetheart."

"Really? Then what are you struggling with?"

He made a sound that was part laugh, part grunt. "Everything. I wanna let you just touch me, and take as long as you want, but...it feels so fuckin' good, Eva. I'm goin' a bit crazy, here, watching you touch me. You're so far outta my league it ain't even funny, but here you are, gorgeous and incredible, and you're touching me like you're the one getting all the enjoyment outta this."

"Because I am."

He growled, literally growled. "You have no idea what this is like for me." He sucked in a deep breath, and I could see his abs tautening and hardening. "I'm a real bastard. I know that about myself. I'm a vulgar, violent, rotten son of a bitch, and I ain't ever gettin' into Heaven. So I figure this is as close as I'm ever gonna get, havin' a woman like you waste her time with a piece'a shit like me."

I frowned up at him. "You don't think very highly of yourself, do you?"

"Nah, I do." He inhaled sharply, held the breath, and let it out slowly as I stroked him with leisurely, lazy, slowness. "I'm a good-looking motherfucker. I'm built like a god. I can take a hell of a lot of pain, and I can dish out even more. I can run the hundred-yard dash in a damn near Olympic time. I'm smarter than most people would assume. I'm a good brother, a good friend, and damn good in bed. But am I a good person? Nah. Probably not, and I'm okay with it."

I caressed him with short, soft, sliding strokes, watching him breathe even more deeply as I did so. "I disagree. I think you *are* a good person. You've been nothing but kind to me."

"Maybe I'm just using you. Taking what I can get from you."

"I'm not expecting anything from you, Baxter. That's not what this is. I don't know what it is. Except that I'm getting as much from this as you are, if not more."

He was breathing heavily, now, inhaling and exhaling deeply through his nose, scowling at me in concentration. "You've got your sweet, sexy, innocent little hands all over my cock, Eva. I'm not quite seein' what you're getting."

"Something I've wanted to do for a long, long time," I said. "Experience this kind of...intimacy with a man. Something I've chosen, because it's what I want for myself. Choosing what I want, and who I want."

"I'm startin' to feel like whatever it was you experienced with that fuckface Thomas it wasn't anything like good fucking."

I squeezed, just a little, and glared up at him. "We are *not* talking about that jerk. Not here, not now. Not ever."

His lips quirked. "Noted. Sorry."

I smiled, to alleviate the tension of the moment. "I just…I'm enjoying this, a *lot*, and I don't want to ruin the moment talking about someone to whom I'm never giving another moment of my time, nor a single second of my attention."

I was stroking him rhythmically, with both hands, up and down and up and down, relishing the slide of all those hard, beautiful, veiny inches through my hands; his hips were flexing, ever so slightly, and he was breathing heavily, his jaw clenched hard, his eyes glinting and flashing, watching every movement of my hands, every once in a while flicking to my eyes, searching my face.

"You better stop soon, Eva," he murmured.

I frowned at him. "Why? I wanted to…I want you to…" I shrugged, looking at his erection instead of his face, now. "I want you to feel good. Like you made me, twice now. I want you to come."

He grimaced in concentration, every muscle taut and tensed, a deep growl rumbling in his chest. "And I'm gonna, any second now. But Eva, honey, it's gonna be a mess. You know that, right? I can't control that."

My eyes widened, and I gulped. "Oh. Right."

I thought back to the video—in that, the woman had used her hands for the whole video, and then, when the faceless male had gotten close to release, she'd aimed him at her breasts and he'd come all over them, and she'd moaned and whimpered and carried on like it had benefitted her somehow, sexually, when it obviously and clearly had not, and could not. In the video, that had seemed like an obvious conclusion to such an act. But sitting here, doing this, touching this man, a man with a name and a face and a heart and a soul and personality, *me* doing this, touching Baxter Badd intimately, bringing him to the cusp of orgasm, I just simply could not imagine doing...*that*. Letting him do that, *onto* me. Nor could I wrap my head around the other thing I'd seen in many videos: using my mouth. I'd never even touched a penis before now, in real life. I'd never touched—*him*; I barely even saw it. Nor had I seen a man orgasm. In my previous experiences, he'd grunted a few times, moved a little more vigorously, and then he'd rolled off and vanished. Assuming he'd come, any mess had been contained in the condom he'd worn.

This...with Baxter, this was a *whole* different experience. I wanted to watch him come. I wanted to be the one to bring him there, and I wanted to see what it looked like, the whole process. But to take it in my mouth or on my body? I wasn't quite there yet; I probably would *never* be there...but then I never thought I would be here, doing this. Who knew what I might do, in the future? Anything. I could do whatever I wanted. Maybe I *would* enjoy that, letting him—*making* him—do that to me.

Baxter …grunted again. "Eva?" He pulled out of my grip, growling with each breath. "Sorry, but I won't be able to hold out if you keep it up much longer."

"Could we move to the bathroom?" I suggested; the bathroom wasn't en suite, but was rather just outside the door, kitty corner.

"You go first, check that the coast is clear."

I moved past him, eased open the bedroom door, peered out to make sure no one was around. The hallway was empty, and I could hear the mower going outside, meaning John was out there, and I heard a blender whirring in the kitchen, meaning Beverly was in there. I snuck out, pushed open the bathroom door, waving at Baxter. He trotted into the bathroom after me, and I closed the door behind us, looking at him and suppressing a fit of giggles.

Baxter eyed me suspiciously. "What's funny?"

I breathed through the giggles. "I don't know. I'm sorry. Just…this is funny. You and me, sneaking around like teenagers doing something naughty." I bit my lip, trying unsuccessfully to keep another fit from washing over me. "Also, you running like—like *that*… it was just…it was funny."

"How so?"

I had to sit down on the closed toilet lid as I tried to suppress the laughter. "You were…your—your—" I waved in the direction of his crotch, and then tried the word out loud. "Your…*cock* was waving and wobbling all over the place, and it's just…it's funny."

He was standing with his back to the door, a smirk on his lips. "Say 'cock' again, Eva." The heat in his voice ensured any humor left in me disappeared immediately.

I stared at him. I had to take a fortifying breath. "Cock."

His eyes slid halfway closed, as if in some kind of rapture. "Hearing such a dirty word from such sweet lips, babe…it's—it's almost too much."

"Come over here," I said, and then realized it had come out sounding like an order. "Please."

A grin quirked his lips. "You can order me around all you want, Eva. Chances are, I'll probably listen." He winked as he swaggered over to stand in front of me, his back to the tub, only inches between us, now, in the small confines of the bathroom. "But only because I want to. Nobody tells me what to do." His tone of voice and the humor in his voice turned that last part into a joke. Preserving his macho attitude, but sort of…tongue-in-cheek.

"How…" I reached out and grasped him in one

hand, gave him a slow plunge of my hand from top to bottom. "How should I do this?"

He shrugged. "You could switch places with me. I'll sit on the tub, and you can get down here where I'm standing. Then, when I come, I'll come on myself instead'a on you or all over your room." A wink. "Pretty experienced at cleaning myself up, know what I mean?"

I blushed at the image. "You masturbate a lot?"

He grinned. "Hell yeah."

"Did you, since…since last night?" I asked, rising off the toilet lid and moving to the side so he could take my place.

He sat down, sinking low so he was perched on the very edge, his feet framing me on either side, braced on the tub, head tipped back to rest on the wall above the toilet's tank. He was relaxed, physically, but I could see the anticipation in the glint in his eyes and the tension in his muscles.

"Yeah," he murmured. "I did."

I knelt in front of him. I was thinking about all the videos I'd watched in which the actress went to her knees; usually, almost always, she ended up using her mouth. I wondered what it would taste like, feel like? To have him in my mouth? What does flesh taste like? I've kissed lips, but that's it. I shook the thought away, filed it away for later perusal.

"What did you...what did you think about?" I asked. "Is that too personal a question?"

He shook his head. "I'm an open book, babe. Ask me anything." His gaze was hot and hard. "What would you think if I told you I thought about you?"

I couldn't look away from his intense brown eyes. "I don't know. Partially I'd be flattered. Maybe a little embarrassed. And..." I shrugged and broke the stare. "Also, maybe a little...turned on." I forced my eyes to his again. "*Did* you?"

"Started to. This morning. I was in the shower, and I thought about you, last night. Making you come. Touching your hot wet little pussy. Kissing you. The glimpses of your tits I'd gotten. I started to imagine touching you. Kissing you. Getting my hands and mouth on those fuckin' amazing tits of yours, making you come a few more times."

"You started to," I prompted. "Is that how you...how you finished?"

He shook his head. "Nah. It felt...I didn't want to...I dunno how to put it. Cheapen you? Does that make any sense? Whacking off to you just felt... wrong, somehow. Dunno why."

"What did you...what did you think about to make yourself come?"

"Just...sex. Not anyone specific." He hesitated. "Although, now that I've seen more of you, I think maybe it was still you."

"It wouldn't feel cheap or wrong to me, if you thought about me. I wouldn't mind." I grasped him. Stroked him, staring into his eyes. "It would be...it would be erotic, knowing you were touching yourself and thinking about me. What would you think about, what would you imagine?"

"Jesus, Eva. Gettin' kinda bold, huh?"

"A little, maybe. Is that okay?"

His expression was fierce, wild. "Fuck yeah. Be bold, Eva. Take what you want. From me, from life, from everyone. I don't mean run roughshod over everyone, but...it's okay to get what you want. To live your life your way, to take what you want for yourself, as long as you're not hurting others in the process." He inhaled sharply as I started caressing his thick length in a quickening rhythm, one hand sliding tip to base, faster and faster. "You, being bold, talking dirty, it turns me on, Eva."

"Okay, then. Tell me, Baxter," I said, watching his face as I stroked him. "What would you imagine, if you masturbated while thinking about me?"

"Your tits, obviously. I would think about getting you naked. Touching you like I did in your room." He gritted his teeth, sucked in a breath, tensed, and then kept speaking, clearly struggling to hold on, now. "I'd...shit. I'd think about you riding my cock.

Fucking you. Making those sweet, lush titties of yours bounce all over the place. Watching you come all over my dick, screaming my name as I pounded into you."

I felt myself clench, and quake, my thighs pressing together. My core throbbed. The image was so potent, so powerful. I could almost—*almost*—see it: Baxter beneath me, his body huge and brutally beautiful and so powerful, and I would have him inside me, and I would be riding him like—well, like a porn star. *Fucking* him; oh god...that thought, that dirty phrase just flitted through my head so easily, so naturally, and it felt so good to think it.

"You want to...fuck me, Baxter?" I asked, and I didn't recognize the purr in my voice, the husky, aroused tone, the dirty words, even as I relished the knowledge that this *was* me, talking this way, doing these things.

I had Baxter's cock in my hands and because of *my* touch he was moments from having an orgasm. And maybe, later, he would do more dirty, delightful things to me.

He growled. "I swear to Christ, Evangeline, I've never wanted anything more in my entire goddamn life." He sucked in a breath, and his hips flexed, pivoting upward as I stroked him, tilting in time with my stroking hands. "Fuck, *fuck*, I'm close, Eva."

"Do you think I will like it, when you fuck me?" I asked.

He groaned deeply, through gritted teeth, and could only answer in gasps. "I'd...I'd make sure. I'd make you come so hard, so many times...and then... oh shit, shit—I think it would be the best...oh god, oh fuck—I think I might be creating a monster." His eyes flicked open, pierced mine. "I think you've got a wild side, Eva."

"What if I do?"

"Let it out, baby. Let that beast out to play." His fingers dug into his thighs, dimpling the muscle until his knuckles went white.

I used both hands, now. One on top of the other, sliding up and down in unison, and the faster I stroked him, the more violently his hips tilted.

"Fuck," he snarled, low, under his breath, eyes squeezing shut. "Gonna come in a second, Eva."

I breathed out shakily. "Good. Don't hold back, Baxter. Don't ever hold back with me."

"No?" He opened his eyes and stared at me. "Touch my sac. Gently. Just...play with 'em a little. It'll—oh...awww *shit*—it'll feel good for me. I'm so close now. You can jerk me hard, now. Harder, faster."

I slid one hand down to his testicles, and cupped them ever so gently. And they were so soft, so heavy. Exactly how they'd looked. I massaged a little, marveling at the feel of them. My other hand, around his cock…I did what he'd said. Moved my touch harder, faster. Top to bottom as fast as my hand would move, letting my fist slide loosely around him. He was bridged off the toilet, shoulders and neck braced against the wall, feet on the tub, buttocks clenched, hips thrusting.

So hot. *So* erotic. I was throbbing and tingling all over. My breasts ached, and my core was…I felt… *damp*, down there. So aroused. Watching him like this, it was…better than any fantasy, more erotic than any stupid, fake porn I'd ever watched. Because it was *me* doing it. Me making him like this.

He groaned again, and his butt slapped down on the lid and then he flexed so his erection speared through my sliding, jerking fist. "Now, Eva." His eyes flew open and met mine, and he looked down at my hand, around him. "Watch."

I watched. Oh, I was watching. There was no way I'd miss a single second of this.

"Slow, now." Baxter's hand touched mine, briefly, slowing my touching. "Slow and gentle, and don't stop."

I wanted to say something hot, say something dirty. Shock him—shock myself. "Come now, Baxter. I want to watch you come."

"Ohhhh—*FUCK!*" He grunted the last word.

I was stroking his erection like I had at the beginning, softly, slowly, just one hand. He was tensed, bridged upward, pivoting into my touch. My other hand, my left hand, was cupping his balls, massaging them, and I felt them tense, twitch. His whole erection throbbed in my hand, and he went still, hissing through clenched teeth as if barely able to restrain an animal, leonine roar.

And then he came.

A thick white stream squirted out of him and splattered in a stripe up his belly, over his navel nearly to his diaphragm, a violent release. Immediately, as I kept stroking him, unable to keep myself from speeding up my touch in excitement, he spurted again, and again, more and more of his semen pooling on his belly, some of it dripping hot and wet and sticky over my knuckles. He groaned, and I kept touching him, and he throbbed in my hand.

I watched, enraptured, as he kept coming, and then finally relaxed, collapsing abruptly, gasping.

"Ho…ly…SHIT," he gasped, breathless. "That was fuckin' intense as fuck."

I delicately and somewhat reluctantly set his penis down against his body, away from the mess. "I don't know what that means, when you say things like that."

"It means…" He seemed to have to force his eyes open. "It means, and I swear I'm not exaggerating, that *that* was the best orgasm of my life."

I felt pride and happiness and an erotic self-satisfied thrill shoot through me. "Really? Don't lie to me."

"I'll never lie to you, Eva." His gaze was fierce and genuine and open. "You touching me? Fuckin'… the hottest thing ever."

"It was hot for me too," I admitted.

"Yeah?" he asked, grinning widely.

"Yeah." I grinned back. "That was the most erotic thing I've ever experienced, too."

"There's more where that came from," he said, heat and promise rife in his voice.

I glanced at the mess, the viscous white pool of his come on his belly. "There is? When?"

He chuckled. "I mean erotic experiences, actually, not just my come."

"Yeah, well…I want more erotic experiences, especially if they feature your come."

He met my gaze, grinning mischievously now. "Taste it," he said.

I felt my heart stop. "What?"

"Taste it. Taste my come. Dip your finger in it, and taste it."

"Why?"

He shrugged. "So you know. You have to be curious."

Damn him. I was…I really was.

FIVE

Baxter

GODDAMN. I MEAN…GODDAMN. HOTTEST TEN MINUTES of my entire motherfuckin' life, and that's saying something serious. Immediately after orgasming, I wanted more. I wanted to strip her naked and make her come again. This time with my mouth, and then my cock. I wanted to lock us in that room and not leave until I'd had enough of her. Which…might be never.

She was still down there on her knees, staring at me intently, those wide green eyes innocent and horny all at once. Curious, too.

I reached down and grabbed her hand, taking her by the index finger. Brought the tip of that finger to the mess on my stomach. Hovered over it. She wiggled her hand out of my grip.

"I can do it," she said, somewhat snappish.

I couldn't help an amused grin; she had a fiercely independent streak a thousand miles wide hiding inside her. Hot as fuck, that was.

She hesitated, and then dipped her finger into the mess. I watched, my dick twitching, as she popped that finger into her mouth and licked the droplet of my come. Her eyes widened, and then she furrowed her brows.

"Not what I was expecting," she said.

"No? Better or worse?"

She shrugged. "Neither. I don't know what I was expecting, but that's..." She was blushing yet again, the innocent little thing. She hesitated, hunting for what to say. "It wasn't that bad."

"Not that bad, huh?"

She tilted her chin up, her expression hardening, going firm and determined. "No, not that bad at all." Her eyes sparkled and sparked, fierce. Eager. "In fact, I think I kind of liked it."

And then she dipped her finger back in, and licked it off, removing her finger from her mouth with a *pop*, then flicked her tongue over her knuckles, the tiny pink tip of her tongue licking away the stray droplets that had trickled onto her hand.

Oh boy, as she said. Oh boy.

I unspooled a wad of toilet paper and crumpled it up, but before I could do anything else, she took it from me. "Let me," she said.

I shrugged, and rested my hands on my thighs. "Be my guest."

Gently, with such a sweetly hesitant touch, she cleaned me, folding the toilet paper over and over again, wiping at me until I was totally clean, then she bent to peer at my dick, realizing that as I'd softened, some come had dripped free; she wiped that too, and then I lifted up so she could toss the wad into the toilet, and I hit the flush lever.

"We should go shopping, now," I said, standing up and offering my hands.

She grasped my hands and I pulled her to her feet. "We could stay here," she suggested.

I brushed her cheek with my palm. "Eager for more, huh?"

She nodded, a study of innocence and sweetness, yet her eyes betrayed fire and desire. "Yes, I am, actually."

I leaned in, kissed her, quickly and softly. "Plenty of time, babe. Let's get you some clothes."

"And something else to eat?" she said, leaning

against me to grab the doorknob. "I'm hungry."

I couldn't help sneaking a palmful of her ass as she leaned against me, and she went off-balance, giving me her weight for a moment, breathing softly in my ear.

"Orgasms make you hungry," I murmured.

"Then no wonder I'm so ravenous," she said, her voice warm and buzzing in my ear, close. "I've had three in the last…what? Ten, eleven hours? More than I've had in an entire month combined, I think."

"So you masturbate, do you?" I asked.

She pushed off me, tugged open the door, peeked out to make sure the coast was clear, and waved me back into her room. I went, and she followed, closing the bedroom door behind us. Evangeline scooped up my clothes and handed them to me.

"We're not talking about that," she said. "Get dressed. I'm hungry now."

I faked a snarky salute. "Yes ma'am. Getting dressed, pronto." I eyed her. "Why aren't we talking about whether or not you masturbate?"

She shrugged, slipping her feet into the borrowed flip-flops. "Because you'll make it all…*erotic*, and then we'll never leave, and I need food. And I really would like some different clothes. Not that I'm not grateful to Dru, but…I don't feel like myself in this."

"Maybe that's not a bad thing," I suggested

as I dressed, knowing I had to tread carefully, here. "Maybe...maybe it's time you explore different ways to feel like yourself."

She gazed at me steadily. "You may be right. But at the very least, I need underwear," she said, reaching for the door, "I feel so strange not wearing any."

I hissed. "Dammit, Eva, you can't say shit like that to me."

She paused, frowning, genuinely puzzled. "Why not? What did I say?"

"You, not wearin' any panties? Gets my head running down dirty paths, babe." I sidled up to her, her back pressed against the door, one hand behind her back on the doorknob. Snuck my fingers inside the elastic of the sweatpants. "Like how I could just..."

I held her gaze as I slid my fingers down, down, feeling the soft thatch of her trimmed but not sculpted or shaved pubic hair—which I found hot as fuck, for reasons I wasn't sure of.

"Just what, Baxter?" she prompted, staring back at me intently, almost daring me.

"Just slide my fingers inside you, whenever I wanted, and feel this...this tight, hot, wet little pussy of yours."

She gasped as I suited actions to words, sinking my middle finger inside her tight-as-a-drum channel. "Whenever you wanted, huh?"

"Whenever, wherever." Grinned hungrily at her. "I could sit beside you while we're eating, and I could just...do...*this*." I fingered her clit, got her writhing. "Drive you crazy. Knowing you're not wearin' any damn panties makes my horny-ass brain go haywire."

She thunked her head against the door and whined in her throat, pressing herself against my touch. "Baxter, god, how can you get me like this so fast?"

"Because you're eager and you're horny. You want it." I leaned in close as I touched her, knowing it would take only a moment or two more. I wanted to watch and smell and feel her come apart again— needing it like I needed to breathe, actually. "You like it when I touch your pussy. You want it so bad, don't you?"

She closed her eyes and writhed her hips. "Mmmm-hmmm."

"Say it, Eva. Let me hear you say you want me to touch your pussy until you come."

"This again?" she asked, opening her eyes to glare defiantly at me. "Fine. I want it, Baxter. I want to feel you touch my...my pussy. I want you to make me come."

God, the dirty words on her tongue, dropping from her lips...they seemed so much dirtier, so much more erotic. I talked this way all the time, but with

Eva, it felt…new, and hotter than it had ever been.

And then, within seconds, she was gasping against my neck, her breath hot, and then her teeth sank into the skin on the side of my neck and she was clinging to my shoulders, riding my finger for dear life, trying desperately to stifle her screams and moans of ecstasy.

"Damn, baby, you come *fast*," I murmured.

"Is that…bad?" she asked, gasping.

"Fuck no," I said. "It's good. It means you like it. You like being touched. You're ready to go, and it don't take much to get you there." I eyed her as I withdrew my touch. "You ever come more than once in a row?"

She eyed me in incredulity. "That's actually a thing? I thought it was just a myth."

I shook my head, choosing my words with care, this time around. "It's real. You come so fast, I'm guessing you could have multiple O's pretty easily."

"God, that would be…" She shuddered, eyes closing, shoulders lifting in a shiver. "That would be so intense, I'm not sure how I'd be able to handle it."

I opened the door, leaning close to whisper in her ear. "That could be a little experiment between us, then—to see how many times I can make you come."

She just blinked up at me. "I think I would enjoy being the subject of that experiment, Baxter."

"Yes, Eva, I think you will."

Shopping was fuckin' fun, actually. She would try on outfits and strut out wearing them, to get my approval. I approved everything, though, which only irritated her, discarding this shirt or that skirt as not fitting right or not the best pattern, or...so many different reasons. Yet somehow, as we left each store, she ended up with half the shit they had on the racks, despite discarding so many pieces. And we went to a dozen stores, all the clothing shops in Ketchikan. We'd climb into the Silverado my brothers and I shared, and we'd listen to country, a compromise between her taste for pop and my taste for heavy metal. Actually, I liked country, but I'd never admit it to anyone. We listened to music and the windows were down, and it was a gloriously gorgeous day, the sun shining brightly in a cloudless blue sky. The back seat of the truck was full of bags already, and she said she had a few items left she wanted to get. She had her phone out and a GPS app open, Googling which stores she wanted to go to and directing me to them. Now, she clearly had selected a store in mind, and was figuring out the directions to it.

When we got there, I quirked an eyebrow at her.

"Lingerie, huh?"

She shrugged. "I need underwear." A defiant stare met my gaze, when she looked at me. "And Hanes aren't really my thing. So yes, lingerie."

"Nothin' wrong with Hanes," I said, "but there also ain't nothin' wrong with some nice lingerie."

She climbed out of the truck, and then glanced back at me when I made no move to get out and go in with her. "Aren't you coming in?"

"You gonna let me watch?" I said with a smirk.

"Watch? No, I don't think so. That wouldn't be appropriate out in public."

"I figured I'd just make you and everyone else in there uncomfortable if I went in," I admitted.

She hesitated a bit more. "Just come in with me. Into the store," she clarified with an eye roll, as I started to open my mouth to make a comment, "*not* the changing room."

I closed the windows, shut off the truck, and followed her in. I stood near her as she discussed what she wanted with the saleslady, and then I followed her around as she perused the shelves. The saleslady came back with a handful of garments, all lacy and slinky and sexy.

As Eva moved toward the changing rooms, I remarked, "I didn't take you for the lacy lingerie type, honestly."

"I know. Most people probably wouldn't." She glanced back at me, lifting up the handful of bras and panties. "I started wearing this stuff when I was a teenager, because it was one of the few things I could choose for myself and no one was ever the wiser. Everything else was always very tightly controlled by my parents. Underwear? *That* I could choose for myself, at least. So I chose this kind of thing as an act of rebellion, and because underwear like this makes me feel…I don't know. Sexy. Like, if I'm wearing this stuff, just for me, I feel like I'm still someone a man would want, if he knew I was wearing it."

"Meaning you feel like no man would want you, otherwise?"

"Not really. Just that all the guys I've met are only interested in sex, politics, and money, and how they can get those three things out of me, rather than being interested in *me* for me."

"Can I just take this opportunity to remind you that while I *am* interested in sex, that's not *all* I'm interested in? And that I have zero interest in money or politics?"

She smirked at me. "I do appreciate the reminder, but I'm not in any danger of forgetting that you're in no way like any other man I've ever met." Her gaze raked over me. "In more than one regard."

I laughed, and jerked a thumb at the changing

rooms. "Go try that shit on so we can go eat."

She took a step away, and then paused, turned back to me, and held out her hand. "Let me see your cell phone."

Without hesitating, I slid it out of my pocket, unlocked it, and handed it to her. "Here ya go."

"Thanks. I'll give it back when I'm done."

"Done? With what?"

She shrugged a shoulder and turned away, her hair flipping in my face. "You'll see."

I'd said I was an open book, but I was a permanently single guy, and thus had a rather elaborate spank-bank stash of photos, videos, and websites in various places on my phone. I wasn't going to pretend like it wasn't mine if she happened to find it somehow, but it could also lead to a weird conversation, since I wasn't sure what she thought about porn. I figured she'd be horrified if she saw it, but seeing as I was wrong about the kind of underwear she liked, I could be wrong about that. A guy could hope, you know?

She was gone for a good ten minutes, and then emerged with the garments, strode directly to the cash register, paid for everything with a swipe of a card, and led the way out to the truck. I got in, started it up, and headed out.

"Where to?" I asked.

She shrugged. "The B and B real quick? We can drop off all the bags and I can change."

"You still using my phone?"

She smirked at me. "Yep." And that was all she said.

"Okayyyyy." I shrugged. "You're being awful mysterious all of a sudden."

She eyed me sidelong. "You got something on your phone you're worried about me seeing, Baxter?"

Uh-oh. She'd found something. I shrugged, nonchalant, even though I was feeling a little…nervous. "I don't have anything to hide, no. Nothing I'm ashamed of."

I just didn't want to alienate her this soon, since I really liked her. Like, not just because she had great tits, an incredible ass, and had given me the best handjob of my entire life—which, by the way, included every blowjob I've ever gotten. I genuinely liked her, as a person, aside from the raging inferno that was my sexual attraction to her. If she was anti-porn and had stumbled across some of my saved sites or the photos girls I'd hooked up with had sent me, it'd be over before it even got started.

She just gave me that odd little smirk again. "Okay, if you say so."

I eyed her suspiciously as I drove us to the B and B. "Eva, babe, you got somethin' to say, say it. You had my phone, and I'm a dude. A perpetually single dude with a high-rev libido, I might add. I ain't ashamed of anything on there. It is what it is."

She just laughed. "Baxter, relax. Trust me a little, okay?"

I let out a breath, because whatever she was up to, she didn't seem pissed, so…fine, whatever. Let her have her fun.

We reached the Kingsley's in a matter of minutes, and I helped her carry all the bags into her room. When all of her shopping was on her bed, she turned on me. "Okay, buster. Out. I need to try things on and change. I won't take *too* long."

I shrugged. "Like I said, I'm in no hurry. I can wait in the truck."

"Okay. I'll be out soon…ish."

I paused halfway out the door. "You still need my phone?"

She nodded. "Yep."

I shook my head and chuckled. "Okay then, little miss secretive." I told her my passcode, because like I said, I got nothin' to hide, and then I headed out to the truck and started it up, immediately switching the radio back to heavy metal.

Apparently to Eva, "soon…ish" and "won't take *too* long" meant upward of thirty minutes. Which, without my phone as a distraction, seemed a lot longer than it might have otherwise.

When she did emerge, she was dressed to fuckin' kill. A knee-length maroon skirt slit up the sides and a tight, V-neck, short sleeve, silver shirt in some shimmery material that hugged and emphasized her tits, which were lifted high by a bra with just enough cleavage showing to make my dick sit up and take notice, a pair of strappy silver gladiator sandals, and a small silver clutch purse.

She slid into the truck, smiling shyly at me.

"Damn, girl. We goin' somewhere fancy I don't know about?" I asked. "Because for real, you look... fuckin' incredible."

She ducked her head, tucking a strand of hair behind her ear. "Thank you. This is just how I dress. I'm not really a jeans and T-shirt sort of girl."

I shook my head. "Well you sure as hell won't hear me complaining, because I mean *damn*...you look *fine*."

"It's just a skirt and blouse. Nothing special."

I touched her chin and then brushed my thumb over her cheek, something I couldn't seem to resist doing, especially because when I did it, she tended to subtly nuzzle into the touch, which made something in my chest flutter and something in my stomach flip-flop. "Sweetheart, you're missing my point. It ain't the clothes, it's the woman *in* the clothes, and the way you look wearing them. You've got a way of making even just a skirt and blouse look like a million bucks."

She grinned at me. "Only a million? Don't short change me, now, Baxter."

I laughed. "Fine. A billion. A trillion." More seriously, then. "How about…you look absolutely priceless. Without peer."

"Thank you, Baxter," she said, primly. "Now… food?"

I laughed yet again, something I seemed to do a lot around her. "I love that you think with your stomach as much as I do."

And so we found ourselves sitting on the same side of a booth at my favorite burger joint, waiting for our burgers. Mine, of course, was a triple-patty number, no bun, with cheese, bacon, avocado, and a fried egg on top, sweet potato fries on the side. When it came, Evangeline eyed me, and then the burger, with incredulity.

"Wow, that's…a *lot* of food," she noted.

I nodded, digging in. "Yeah, well, you have noticed I ain't exactly Tiny Tim, here. I work out a lot, and need a lot of food to sustain my caloric output."

She tapped the fried egg and bacon topping the monster burger. "Isn't that a lot of cholesterol?"

I laughed. "Nutrition is actually a vastly misunderstood thing. Forget about BMI, forget about cholesterol, forget everything everybody told you about fat being bad. Eat good, nutritious, whole foods. Burn all that fuckin' processed, fake, chemical-laced, bleached white flour bullshit carb garbage, and get rid of any kind of sugar or sugar-substitute or sugar-derivative. That's the shit that'll kill ya."

She was staring at me. "Wow. You sound...passionate about this."

I shrugged. "Yeah, well, I've been an athlete my whole life. My body is my art, my profession, and my weapon. I want it to be in tip-top shape at all times, so I gotta put the right fuel into it. So yeah, I'm passionate about it. I don't see how everyone isn't, honestly. It's your fuckin' *body*, the thing you fuckin' *live in*, the only one you're gonna get, *ever*. How can you *not* take care of it? Yeah, donuts and bear claws and slushies and Twinkies, all that shit tastes good, but that shit is fuckin' killin' you, bro. Candy bars, soda, all that shit? It's fuckin' poison. Legit, poison. Might as well just mainline fuckin' drain cleaner as ingest that nasty-ass chemical bullshit."

"You use the F-word more than anyone I've ever met, you know that?" she asked, laughing. "But I take your point." She nudged the glass of diet cola in front of her. "So I shouldn't drink this?"

"Fuck is the most versatile word in the English language, and my favorite curse word." I lifted a shoulder. "And I mean, I sure as shit wouldn't drink that, even if it was the last beverage on earth. But you do you, babe. Ain't my place to tell you or anyone else what do with their bodies or their lives."

She slid the cola away and reached for the glass of water the waitress had set down when we'd arrived. "So what do you drink, if you don't drink soda?"

"Coffee, green tea, whiskey, beer, and water. Sometimes wine, but only dry red."

"Why?"

"White's full of sugar, that's why."

"Oh." She sounded forlorn, and I guessed she was sweet white kind of girl.

I laughed. "Babe, I'm not tryin' to tell you what do or what to eat. You wanna know what I think, I'll tell you. But don't feel like you have to change just because of what I think."

"I kind of want to change, though, and I *am* interested in what you have to say about this, since you're clearly very good at being healthy. I work out, do yoga, and run. I like being healthy, and I try to avoid junk food, but I do indulge sometimes." She finished her burger and started on the fries. "Bread is hard to give up. And so is my pinot grigio."

I nodded. "Dude, I get it. I was addicted to Mt. Dew in high school, and in college I ate like shit until my coach got on my ass about my belly. I went through withdrawals from that shit, I swear. Garlic bread and mozzarella sticks and loaded potato skins? That shit was my *jam*, man. I've always tended toward beer and whiskey so that part wasn't hard, but soda took a minute."

The conversation moved to our favorite movies as I finished eating and we sipped on coffee. I found it surprisingly easy to just talk to her. She was, obviously, wicked smart, but she was also very erudite, current on pop-culture and news, and had a wry, dry sense of humor that kept me constantly laughing and always guessing, never knowing what would come out of her mouth.

I was about to the pay the bill when a big, tattooed body slid into the booth opposite us.

I tensed. "Moss, what up, bro?"

I slid closer to Evangeline and wrapped my arm around her; felt her to be as tense as I was. Picking up on my tension, probably.

"I need to move up your fight," Moss said, without preamble.

I gave him the full-on death glare. "Dude, seriously? This is not the fuckin' place for that conversation, man. You know that. You have my phone number, fuckin' use it."

Moss was a massive man. Six-six and three hundred pounds easily, tattooed from fingertip to shoulders and all over his chest and neck, with a shaved head and a thick blond beard down to his chest, ears pierced from the lobes all the way up to the tips, fingers decorated with gold rings and platinum necklaces around his neck.

He lifted an eyebrow at me. "I *been* textin' you for an hour. You ain't replied, and I was walkin' past when I saw you, so I figured I'd deliver the message in person." His gaze went to Evangeline, raking her over several times, blatantly ogling. "And Basher, my man, you gotta introduce me to this fine-ass honey you got with you. Flavor of the week, amiright?"

"My phone died, forgot about that. Sorry." I tugged Evangeline closer. "And no, I don't have to introduce you to shit, Moss."

"Come on, bro. You can't keep a honey that tight all to yourself." He was leaning forward over the table, sliding his hands toward Evangeline's, making eyes at her. "Ditch this gorilla, babe. Come with me, I'll show you a *real* good time."

I leveled a glare at Moss that even he couldn't ignore. "Moss, listen to me. You got the fight connections and I respect that. We make each other money—*I* make *you* a shitload of money. But do *not* mistake me for your *buddy*, okay? I will fuck your shit up in ten seconds flat if you don't back the fuck off, right the fuck now. Feel me...*bro*? You know I don't play, so don't try me."

Moss stared me down, but he was the first to look away, leaning back in the booth and raising his hands palms out. "A'ight, a'ight. No harm, no foul. But I got you here; you gotta give me an answer. Can you fight tonight? The big money boys want to see you and Juarez ASAP."

"I thought it was Nagle? Since when is it Juarez?"

"Nagle lost to Rooster last night, got legit fucked up, so he's stuck in the hospital gettin' his forearm screwed back together. Juarez got tapped to fill in."

I sighed. "Nagle shoulda known better than to let Rooster get his paws on him. That big ugly fuck likes to break shit." I grimaced. "I gotta figure out my schedule before I can commit. I'll get back to you."

Moss shook his head, his beard waggling side to side. "Nah, bro. I gotta make the call in the next ten minutes."

I groaned. "You're killin' me, Smalls." I nodded my head sideways at Evangeline. "I'm busy, get me?"

Moss laughed, a deep belly laugh. "Bring the honey, then. I'll keep her safe," he said, winking at her.

"Yeah, sure. Dream on, Bullwinkle. I wouldn't trust you with a pet rock, Moss."

"You wound me, Basher. For real. I might cry."

I glanced at Evangeline. "You could hang back

with the girls, maybe?"

She shrugged, her expression carefully neutral. "Don't take me into account when making your plans, Baxter."

I sighed, not liking that answer, but knowing I had no choice. There was well over ten grand riding on this fight, and I would be getting a thirty percent cut of that. Plus, me versus Juarez would be a big draw, as we were both flashy, entertaining fighters, and I knew Juarez wouldn't fuck around, but also wouldn't go for serious injury, unlike some assholes.

I nodded, tapping the tabletop with my knuckles. "Fine. But I get fifteen percent of the on-site pool."

"Five," Moss countered.

"Fuck you, you stupid cow. Twelve."

"Fuck you back, you ignorant slut. Ten."

I held out my hand. "Original thirty percent, plus ten percent of the on-site pool."

Moss shook my hand. "Deal. I'll call you later with the location."

And then he was gone, ambling out the door, hands in the hip pockets of his sagging black jeans.

I blew out a breath and slumped down in the booth. "Shit. *Shit.*" I glanced at Evangeline. "I'm sorry about that. About him, and the whole scene. That's not normally how things get set up."

"So you're fighting? Tonight?"

I nodded. "Looks like it. There's a lot of money on this fight, even more now that there's been a last-minute lineup change."

She was carefully still. "You do what you have to do. Don't worry about me."

I sat up and pivoted in the booth to face her. "I really am sorry about Moss hitting on you like that."

She waved a hand. "That's of no consequence."

"Then what is? You seem upset. We met while I was fighting, remember?"

She shrugged. "I just...don't know where I fit in this. What *is* this?"

"You don't know what *what* is?"

Another shrug. "We messed around last night and then again this morning, which means what we're doing isn't a one-night stand. So then...what is it?"

I sighed. "Does it need a label?"

"Yeah, kind of. So I know what to expect."

"You need a label? Then call it... a tryst. Or a hookup. Hell, I don't know, Eva. This ain't like any other hookup I've had. Those are...cheap. Quick and easy, nothin' really to 'em but some sex and fun." I caught her gaze and held it. "You're not cheap, nor are you easy. This ain't just somethin' quick. I don't know how to label this, and maybe I don't want to try, you know? Let it be something different."

"I *am* easy, though...and cheap. If I'm doing something like this." She finally met my gaze, her expression apologetic. "I don't mean to insult you, it's just..."

"Hey, I'm not insulted. I'm all for cheap and easy sex, and frequently. My life hasn't really needed anything more. I was always focused on school and playing ball, and had no time or interest in anything serious. Don't mean I don't think there *can* be something more or something meaningful, if I wanted to look. I just wasn't interested." I touched her hand, covering hers with mine. "You're trying something new. That doesn't make this—or you—cheap or easy. Don't fall into that trap of self-judgment, Eva."

She shrugged. "Okay, so maybe that's true. But I still don't know what to expect, or where I fit."

"You can expect me to treat you right. I ain't gonna ghost on you, or decide I'm done once I get what I want. As for where you fit? You decide that, Eva. Like I said, you can hang at the apartment, or sit down in the family booth and pound some booze with the crew."

She blinked at me. "The family booth?"

I nodded. "Yeah. At Badd's, we have the booth closest to the kitchen and service bar that's permanently reserved for us brothers and their women.

There are always at least one or two people in the booth, reading, studying, or just hanging out and drinking. You got a permanent place in that booth whenever you want, regardless of what you may or may not expect from me. You can hang there, and you'll have good company. My brothers and the girls will treat you right. I think you discovered that last night. We may not have a lot of money and we may be crude sometimes, but if there's one thing we know, it's hospitality, okay?"

She tried a somewhat wobbly smile at me. "Your family is amazing."

"I don't get what happened with you, just now, though. What was it about Moss's visit that has you tripping?"

She shrugged. "I guess he just...reminded me that I don't fit into your life. He scares me."

I snorted. "Moss? He's a big ol' pussy. He organizes the fights because he doesn't have the balls to be in 'em. Lotta talk, not a lotta bite."

"He's still scary."

"I guess I can see that." I winked at her. "But when your older brother is a man like Zane, it becomes kinda hard for anyone else to seem scary."

She laughed. "You make a good point." She sobered, and met my eyes with a strangely serious expression. "I don't know why I'm so worried about fitting into your life. Though, I suppose it's not like that's what this is, anyway." A long, weighted pause. "Right?"

I shrugged, not liking the way that sounded, or my own viscerally emotional reaction to her words. "I mean, you got Yale, right?"

"Right. So whatever this is, it has an expiration date. Which is best for us both." She was looking at me intently.

I really didn't like the way my heart was hammering, as if protesting the truth in her words. "Right," I agreed, working hard to sound casual. "It's got a built-in expiration date. And until then, we can just enjoy whatever this is. Label, no label."

"Part of me does wish I could just hide out here forever, though," Evangeline said, after a moment of silence. "It would make avoiding Father and Thomas so much easier."

"Do you think they're looking for you?"

She nodded. "Oh, without a doubt. Father probably has an entire team of private investigators hunting me down as we speak."

"Even though you took off on your own, of your own free will?"

She nodded. "In my family, one does not simply vanish without a word. It's just not done. It's bad enough that I'm not interested in politics, but to run away like this? It's the height of embarrassment for my parents."

I shook my head. "I do not get that shit *at all.*" I eye her. "Why *did* you run away?"

"They expect things of me," she answered. "They pay for Yale. They bought my car. They would have bought me a condo near the school if I hadn't insisted on staying on campus, which was a whole big fight by itself. I should already be married to Thomas, according to them. There's no reason for me to even really need a degree in anything, when my breeding and pedigree is all about being a trophy wife for the great and mighty Thomas Haverton. He's planning to run for Senate soon, and it will look best, optics-wise, if he's married. My place, according to them, is at his side. Making him look good. Organizing his parties, having his perfect little children, decorating his perfect house in Georgetown—and *I'm* the decoration, by the way." A shrug. "I'm here because I just couldn't handle their expectations any longer. I needed a break. I had to…I just had to get away for a while, and hopefully figure out what to do next with my life."

She sighed bitterly. "They have my whole life arranged—it's all *been* arranged for years. He has the house already picked out. He's just waiting on me to come to my senses and finally agree to marry him. And my parents are putting ever more pressure on me to agree, no matter what I tell them. Next thing I know, they'll be using Yale as leverage."

"That's bullshit."

She nodded. "Yes, it is. But that's my life." She smiled at me, then. "That's why I'm here: I needed an escape from it all."

I thought about everything she'd said. "And I'm the escape, huh?"

She ducked her head, nodding. "Yes. I suppose that would be true." She met my eyes, yet again looking sorrowful and apologetic. "I'm using you, aren't I? God, that's horrible. I'm a horrible person."

I laughed. "Eva, babe. You're overthinking it. I don't mind being used. Not by you, not like this. I'm in this eyes-open, okay? You don't belong here, and I don't belong in Boston, or wherever the fuck Yale is. Like you said, this thing has a built-in expiration date. So quit vilifying yourself, yeah? You have my permission to use me, and then when you decide you're ready to go back to your life, you can wash your hands of me."

"Yale is in New Haven, Connecticut," she murmured, and then she stared at me, emotions I couldn't make sense of crossing her features too quickly to read. "I won't wash my hands of you, Baxter. I will cherish this time I have with you."

That caused something to pang, deep inside me;

I didn't dare look at it too closely. "Eva, babe—"

She gave me bright, happy smile. A little too bright, a little too happy, maybe. "Well...we've shopped and eaten. Now what do you want to do?"

"Aside from you, six different ways by midnight?"

She shuddered, goose bumps pebbling her skin. "Why does it have to be *aside* from that?"

I shrugged. "I dunno. Maybe it doesn't have to be."

Her eyes, locked on mine, were openly and blatantly curious. Heated. Daring me. Challenging. "No, maybe it doesn't." She nibbled on her lower lip. "But...why only six ways? Why stop there?"

I grinned, and slid my hand onto her knee, teasing up under her skirt. "That was just an expression. I'm sure I can think of a lot more than just six."

"A lot more?"

"A *lot* more."

"Because you mentioned a little...scientific inquiry, earlier." She placed her hand on mine, and urged my touch higher, the daring, darling girl.

"Ah, yes. The experiment. For science, of course."

"For science, of course." She hesitated a moment. "Um, but I have one question."

"What's that honey?"

"The B and B, while nice, doesn't exactly abound in privacy. And I'm assuming you probably live with your brothers…"

"I do," I affirmed.

"So…is there somewhere private we can go?" She licked her lips nervously. "Our little scientific inquiry might be best carried out in private, if you know what I mean."

I leaned close, whispered in her ear. "Meaning, you want somewhere you can scream, huh, Eva?"

She gulped as I traced the gusset of her underwear, under the table. "Yes, precisely."

"Precisely?"

She nodded. "Precisely."

I withdrew my touch and stood up, extended my hand to help her out of the booth, murmuring in her ear as I tossed enough cash on the table to cover our meal plus a generous tip. "I think I know just the place, actually."

"Lead the way, then," Evangeline said, and I didn't miss the fact that she was fairly buzzing with excitement.

Damn. The girl was *eager*.

The thought that floated through my head, then, scared the actual bejeezus out of me:

How am I supposed to give this chick up, when she decides to leave?

SIX

Evangeline

BAXTER HANDED ME UP INTO THE GIANT PICKUP TRUCK, gently closed the door after I was in, and then climbed behind the wheel. He thumbed the volume on the sound system a little louder, and then guided the truck out into traffic. I wasn't sure where he was headed, obviously, but I began to feel a little nervous when it became clear, after thirty-some minutes on a two-lane highway, that he was taking us well away from the city.

I glanced at him. "Um. Where are we going?"

He grinned at me. "Oh, just a little place I know

about. Why?" He glanced back at the road as he
turned off the tiny highway and onto a dirt track.
"Wondering if maybe I'm a chainsaw murderer?"

I rolled my eyes at him. "No, Baxter." But then as
the dirt track led deeper into the forest, I began to feel
the tiniest smidgen of doubt. "Maybe a little?"

He laughed. "Relax, princess. Trust me a little,
okay?"

"I'm trying. But you have to admit—this is starting to resemble the plot of a Lifetime movie where
the heroine gets kidnapped by the burly, good-looking villain. I mean, the woods, the dirt trail, the deliberate build-up of my…um…libido…?"

He laughed even harder, slapping the steering
wheel with one hand. "I mean not that I've ever seen
any of those movies, but I do see your point." He
let out another chuckle of amusement. "Listen…I
contracted for a handful of fights with this big-time
dude from the Bay area. That was a couple months
ago, now. Well, I won those fights I was contracted
for without even breaking a sweat, and he wanted to
book me for a whole bunch more. Sounded good to
me, since his money was nice and green and came in
handy dandy black duffel bags. Then after a few more
fights, he got into some tax trouble with the assholes
at the IRS and needed to offload some investments,
I guess. One of which was this cabin way up in the

woods. So then, a week or two ago my guy calls me up and asks if I'll do a fight for him in exchange for the deed to the cabin. I took the fight, cleaned up like a boss, and took ownership of a sweet little place in the forest some thirty minutes from Ketchikan. I've only been up here twice, once to check it out, and once to clean it up and stock it with some staples."

He gestured ahead of us as we crunched through dirt around another blind corner and then emerged into a clearing about a hundred yards in diameter. There was a patch of grass growing in a circle around which ran the dirt driveway, which butted up against the porch of an adorably quaint little log cabin. It looked old, but well maintained. There was an actual red well pump outside, near the porch, with a wooden bucket turned upside down beside it. A picture window with plate glass was situated beside the door, a red tin roof, a stone fireplace. Honestly, it looked like nothing so much as the setting for a Thomas Kincaid painting. All it needed was a gas lamp burning in the window and a trickle of smoke from the chimney. Behind the cabin, I could see hints of water from a lake or a pond.

"This is amazing, Baxter!"

He shrugged. "Wait till you check out the inside. I literally just got the place, and I'm not much of a decorator, as you can probably imagine, so it's how the guy had it, but he had good taste, I think. Not even my brothers know about this place, actually."

I glanced at him as we climbed the stairs up to the porch. "No? Why not? You seem close to them."

He laughed. "Oh we're close all right—*too* close. The second they know about this place it'll be 'Hey, Bax, can I use the cabin? Hey, Bax, can I get the cabin for the weekend? Hey, Bax, can Dru and I use the cabin?' I'll never get the place to myself again once they know about it, and I ain't even spent the night in it yet. So I'm keeping it to myself until I'm ready to share it. They'd all do the same thing, so it's not like it's... dishonest or anything."

He dug his keys out of his pocket and flipped through them until he found the right key, unlocked the front door, and led the way into the cabin. Which, as he said, was even more impressive than the exterior. It was tiny, maybe a two hundred or two hundred and fifty square feet at the most, but it was cozy. The walls were snug and the interior seemed nice and cool and dry, not at all drafty. There was a kitchenette in the back right corner, a stove-oven combo, a sink, an antique green refrigerator, a toaster, and a few cabinets. A door beside the kitchenette led into a bathroom, complete with a shower stall, and then the back left corner of the cabin contained a wooden four-poster bed that I suspected was handmade from trees felled right outside the door. The comforter and pillows were plain white, new looking, and neatly made. There was a little oil painting of a serene winter scene on one wall, and some old crossed snowshoes on another, and a mounted, stuffed rabbit head with some kind of antlers on the other.

I laughed and pointed at the rabbit. "Um. I didn't know bunnies had antlers."

Baxter snorted, trying to contain his laughter. "Seriously? You've never heard of a jackalope?"

I frowned at him, unable to tell if he was teasing me or not, and unwilling to admit I wasn't sure. "Jackalope? It's a real animal?"

He nodded, his expression serious now. "Yup. It's a very rare kinda thing. A real big jackrabbit mated with a kinda small antelope this one time, and they had these little baby jackalopes. They're super elusive and hard to hunt, so that mounted head up there is a real rare piece."

I stared hard at him, not wanting to look stupid in front of a man I was so attracted to, but also unsure if he was teasing or not. Because yes, I was a spoiled city girl through and through, and I knew it.

I thought back to my various biology classes. "I'm fairly certain one species cannot impregnate a totally different one."

He shrugged. "What about mules and hinnies?

And ligers?"

I frowned. "Yeah, but they're sterile. They can't reproduce. And those are similar and closely related species. A jackrabbit and an antelope are completely dissimilar."

He seemed to be struggling to contain laughter. "Nature is fickle, you know?"

I let out a distinctly unladylike growl. "Baxter Badd, if you're making fun of me, I swear I'll—"

He sidled closer to me, wrapped a big palm around the small of my back and tugging me up against him. "You'll what?"

I gasped at how close he suddenly was, how big his body felt against mine. How small and delicate he made me feel, which in turn made me feel just so... *safe*. My heart thumped and pitter-pattered as he buried his hands in my hair, tangling and tugging at the roots, pulling my face so close to his I could feel his breath on my lips.

I swallowed hard. "I'll...I'll make you take me back to my room in Ketchikan."

"I think I might just call your bluff, princess. You would do no such thing."

"Yes I would."

He bit down gently on my lower lip, licking it with his tongue, sending my heart rate through the roof. "You wouldn't. You know you're about to get fucked within an inch of your life, and you want it more than you've ever wanted anything." Keeping one hand firmly in my hair, gripping it roughly, just this side of painful, he slid his other hand down from the small of my back to clutch my bottom. "You've only gotten a little taste of what I can make you feel, Evangeline. You know you're not leaving until you've gotten the full Baxter Badd experience."

"You are! You're making fun of me!" I breathed, trying to sound irate and failing.

"Not making fun, babe. Just teasing." He glanced indicatively at the "jackalope" on the wall. "That's something taxidermists came up with way back when, to poke fun at city slickers. Turned into this running joke. Meanin', no, jackalopes ain't real." He grinned and squeezed my bottom. "But I had you goin' for a second, didn't I?"

I tried to glare sternly at him, which was rather difficult to do with his big, strong hand squeezing and kneading my buttock in a way that had me wanting to both groan in pleasure and grind up against him. "You had me doubting my knowledge of basic biology, I'll give you that." I let my hands drift up to slide over his broad shoulders. "You were laughing at me, though, and I don't like being laughed at."

He shook his head at me. "You're cute, honey. I wasn't laughing out of malice. I could just see your gears turning, trying to figure out if I was kidding but refusing to admit you weren't sure." He tapped me on the nose with a finger, and then slid his hand into my hair again, the other still on my backside. "Besides, you gotta laugh at yourself sometimes, you know? You can't always take everything seriously all the time, babe."

His hand slid to the other side of my bottom, kneading and caressing, and I wanted both his hands down there, touching and making me squirm and making me feel things I've never felt before, but I also really liked his hand in my hair, the way he was controlling my head, where I looked, where my mouth went, making sure I didn't try to escape any impending kisses.

"I don't like feeling stupid, either," I murmured.

"Ain't nothin' stupid about you, babe. You grew up in the city. Can't be expected to know things you weren't ever exposed to. I was just messin' with you a little, Eva. Relax. Just a little teasing. No big deal."

"People do not generally tease me, Baxter, so I'm a little..." I shrugged, unsure how to finish the thought.

"Uptight? Touchy?" He laughed as I huffed in indignation. "Teasing again, babe. Seriously, you need to get the stick outta your ass. Chill out, learn to take a joke, and maybe even give it back a little."

"I do not have a stick up my…" I huffed again, knowing if I avoided the word he'd used he'd teased me again, but also knowing I'd sound dumb if I tried to talk like him. "I'm *not* uptight."

He laughed even harder, burying his face against my throat. "You can't even say 'stick up the ass,' Eva."

I endeavored to retain the last of my dignity. "I just don't talk like that."

"No, but it'd be hot if you did."

"It would turn you on if I admitted that I have a stick up my ass?" I managed to say it without hesitating, and even felt a little burst of pride at myself, which was just embarrassingly stupid.

His hand squeezed my bottom again, his thumb teasing the seam between the globes of my buttocks, tracing it as if contemplating doing something I couldn't fathom, didn't dare conceive. "Yes, that turns me on." He pressed his hips against mine. "Can't you feel it?"

"I thought that was more to do with what you're doing to my bottom."

He nipped the side of my neck. "What…this?" He let go of my hair and grabbed my bottom with both hands now, and I gasped at the feel of both big hands on me, not quite able to fully clutch the entirety of my somewhat generous backside. "Yeah, gettin' a nice double handful of this big, beautiful ass of yours is definitely a fuckin' turn-on."

"Big?" I breathed, trying not to sound upset. "You think my ass is...*big*?"

He let go with one hand, and tipped my chin up so I was looking at him. "Evangeline. You are *not* for real right now, are you?"

I frowned up at him. "What? What do you mean?"

He jiggled one globe, and then the other. "Gonna give this to you straight, Eva. Yes, you got a big ass. Not huge, not like you need a whole zip code or anything, but it ain't exactly a dainty little thing either. It's big and juicy. And Eva, babe—that shit is a *damn* good thing. Maybe some assholes out there would say different, and I'd beat 'em to a drooling, bloody pulp. You got *curves*, honey. You got flesh to hold on to, curves to grab. You're a woman, a *real* woman. And this is just my opinion, but you got what a man wants on that goddamn gorgeous frame of yours... and that's *curve*. Okay? So don't take it as an insult—take what I said the way I meant it: as a compliment."

"It's hard to, though. I work myself ragged in the gym and doing yoga, trying to make my butt smaller, and then you come along and tell me it's *big*?—and I—it's hard to shrug off a lifetime of conditioning. Just because you say it is a compliment doesn't mean I can just snap my fingers and stop feeling the way I feel."

His hands resumed their double-handful massaging and petting and patting. "In that case I apologize, Eva. I didn't mean to upset you or hurt your feelings. I meant to compliment you, but if me sayin' shit like that is gonna upset you, I can find other ways to tell you you're sexy. Okay?"

I nodded, not quite trusting myself to talk, feeling far more upset and emotional than I should for such a relatively innocent exchange. "Okay."

He frowned down at me. "You're still upset."

I shrugged and nodded. "I guess so. Being hurt doesn't vanish just because you apologized."

He brushed my cheekbone like he did so often. "Hey, I didn't mean to hurt you, Eva, seriously."

I shrugged, trying to laugh and not quite managing it. "I know, and it's...it's complicated, and it's not entirely because of you. I don't want to talk about that right now, though." I gazed up at him, blinking through the emotions. "Can you just...can you kiss me?" I swallowed hard past the lump. "I need to be distracted."

His return stare was fierce and penetrating and hot. "I think I can manage that."

He brought both hands up to frame my face, and his palms were rough and sandpapery and enormous, and his thumbs brushed the ridges of my cheekbones in a soothing, comforting, yet arousing gesture of affection that made my heart thump and my stomach twist with flutters. His fingertips pressed into my hair at the back of my head, gently but firmly tugging my face closer to his.

And I went, so willingly I went, closing the space between his mouth and mine, desperate to feel, desperate to taste, frantic to devour every last scrap of this once-and-only-once experience. I pressed myself against his huge hard body, his hip bones bumping against mine, the thick bulge of his erection pressing into my lower belly and against the upper swell of my core. His biceps obscured my view to either side, and his shoulders rippled and swelled like mountain ranges. He breathed in slowly, a frown of concentration furrowing his forehead, and then he tilted his head to one side and slanted his lips across mine.

And this time, I was ready for it. Eager for it. I gasped at the first blush of the kiss, and my eyes fluttered closed as he softly feathered his lips over mine. It was a tease of a kiss at first, just lips ghosting against lips.

"Baxter," I murmured. "Stop teasing me."

He rumbled. "Teasing you? I'd never tease you." Yet he punctuated this ridiculous statement by escaping my attempt to deepen the kiss, evading my lips and then darting in to slide his lips on mine.

"It sure does feel like you're teasing me."

"I'm just...makin' sure you really want it," he said, a smile curving his mouth.

"I want it, Baxter. I really, *really* want it."

He backed away so our eyes met, his hands framing and clutching my face. "Then prove it. Take what you want."

Ah, so that was his game. Fine, then. He wanted me to prove my desire, to take what I wanted? I would. Oh, I would.

I reached up and wrapped my hands around his head, cupping the smooth-shaven skin of his scalp just beneath the tied-back hair. Pulled him down to me—no, not just pulled, I *yanked*. I jerked him down more roughly than I've ever handled anyone in my entire life. Our mouths clashed with such force our teeth clicked together and our lips mashed and I tasted the iron-sweet tang of blood. There was a pang of pain, but it only served to deepen my desire, and seemed to do the same for him. Indeed, I felt as much as heard the rumble of his laugh, a sound of amused heat.

I devoured his kiss. Took it from him and demanded more. I shoved my tongue into his mouth without finesse or gentility, and he met me fervor for fervor, clutching my face fiercely and growling in his chest, taking the fire of my kiss and returning it tenfold, kissing me harder than I'd ever been kissed. I moaned into the kiss and tasted his tongue and the tang of blood from a split lip—his or mine, I didn't know and didn't care.

But the kiss wasn't enough.

I wanted more.

I gasped as I broke the kiss, and my breathing was ragged and rough as our eyes met, intensity sparking between us. I wanted to say something bold, to make it abundantly clear what I wanted, but I had no words. So I used the only thing I had: my body, my hands, my mouth. I shoved at his polo, lifting up onto my toes to rip it over his head and throw it aside. I yanked at the fly of his shorts and tugged at them until they fell off, then wasted no time removing his boxer briefs. He was naked and grabbing at me.

I stepped back, out of his reach, gazing hungrily at his beautiful, naked body. I breathed deeply, gathering courage. I peeled off my shirt, tossed it on top of his polo, on the floor. I stared hard at him as I reached to my side and unzipped my skirt, letting it pool on the floor around my feet before toeing it aside, standing in front of him now in the lingerie I'd just purchased. And, indeed, I had purchased it *for* him. With him in mind. A deep, classic red, it was a sheer, see-through lace set, a bra that lifted and plumped my breasts and was sheer enough to tease him with hints of my areolae and nipples, and the underwear were… well, a whole lot of not much. A triangular wedge over my core, a strip of lace around my waist, and a thin string between my buttocks. I didn't typically wear thongs, but I was turned on wearing this, knowing how revealing it was, how erotic. Even if he hadn't seen it until now, I'd known I was wearing it for him, and I felt sexy and sultry.

And ready.

With his eyes on me, skating from my face to my breasts to my core and legs, I knew I'd chosen perfectly: his erection, prominently hard and thick and upright, hardened further at the sight of me in the lingerie. I could see a clear droplet of liquid beading at the very tip of his manhood, and for some reason, the sight of it made my core clench and my nipples tighten.

I twirled in a slow circle, pausing to show him my backside, posing for him. I felt a little silly posing, rising up on my toes so my butt would lift and tighten; I stopped feeling silly the moment I heard his feral snarl.

"God*damn*, Eva," he breathed. "Legit, I could come right here right now, just lookin' at your fine-ass body in that lingerie. You wouldn't even have to touch me, I'd just…pop."

"But…getting to touch you is half the fun," I said

over my shoulder, feeling bold, "and you touching me is the other half."

"Then get over here so I can get that sexy fuckin' lingerie off you and get to the fun part."

I shook my head. "No, I want to do it my way."

Facing away, I sucked in a deep breath. I reached up behind my back to pinch-and-release my bra, letting the straps slide down my shoulders so the cups sagged off my breasts, and then I let the bra fall to the floor in front of me. Then I hooked my thumbs in the strip of lace on my hips and slid it down, wiggling my hips side to side until the thong dropped off. Straightening, I resisted the impulse to hug my arms over myself to hide my breasts, and instead stood upright, hands at my sides, and kicked the lacy, racy thong away.

I pivoted to face him, and let him look at me.

And look he did. For several long moments Baxter just...stared at me. Drinking me in.

Eventually he breathed out a shaky breath. "No matter what happens, Eva, you gotta know one thing: you are, without any doubt, the single most beautiful woman I've ever known—and ever *will* know." He took a step toward me. "I gotta touch you now, babe. I *gotta*."

"Please," I breathed. *"Please* touch me."

He closed the space in a single step. His forehead

nudged against mine, and his hands circled my hips. I felt his breath on my lips, and I felt his erection against me, a velvety soft presence brushing against my lower belly and my mound. I couldn't breathe, I was dizzy and shaking all over with excitement and nerves and desire and, yes, even a little fear. I embraced it all, the fear especially. I used it all to remind myself that this was real, that I was choosing this, that this was something I wanted and was taking for myself, solely because I wanted it—*him*, because I wanted *him*.

It wasn't so much about the sex act as it was about the man. Yes, I was ferociously eager for the act, for the experience, but it was because of the wild, out-of-control need that Baxter Badd incited within me. I remembered all too well the decidedly lackluster experiences I'd had with Thomas, and I knew without a shadow of a doubt that whatever happened with Baxter tonight would be on a totally other plane of existence.

Baxter's hands slid up my waist and then rose to cup my breasts; I already wasn't breathing, but when his rough, callused palms closed over my breasts, I sucked in a sharp whimpering breath. Then, when his thumbs brushed over my nipples, I let out the breath in a whine.

I wanted to grasp his erection and make him come like I had before, but I also wanted to do...god,

I didn't know what. Dirty things. Dark, wild, forbidden things. Things I couldn't currently imagine.

So, instead, I started simple. I ran my hands over his biceps, and then his shoulders, relishing the hardness of the muscle and the softness of his skin. Indulging in the beauty of his statuesque, superhero's body. I slid my touch over his chest, flicked his nipples and delighted in the way he sucked in a sharp breath, and then traced the ridges and furrows of his powerful abs. Found my breath, finally, and then lost it again when his hands descended to my hips again, cupping their bell shape, and then I fought to breathe and managed only a whimper when a single finger traced the seam of my core.

He dipped that finger inside me, nudging the button of my clitoris just enough to make me jump and whimper. And then he backed away, dropping his hands to his sides. His gaze was fierce and serious as he stared at me.

"Go lay on the bed, Evangeline." His tone brooked no argument.

I swallowed hard. "Don't tell me what to do, Baxter."

His grin was quick and sudden and infectious, and he accompanied it with a wink. "Just play along, Eva. You think I'd tell you to do anything you won't enjoy?"

"I just…I've been ordered around my whole life. I've been obedient and submissive my whole life. I don't want to do that here, with you. I don't…I don't want us having sex to be about that."

"Then you take charge," he said. "Take what you want from me. Order me around. I'm serious. I can play the game, babe. I want you to have a night you'll never forget."

I stepped forward and let my fingertips trail down his belly, finally allowed myself to wrap one hand around his manhood. "Baxter, what I want is for you to…to not *tell* me what to do but instead to *show* me what to do. I'm not into power games, or any kind of games at all." I gathered my courage, dredged up my daring, let the deepest, darkest, dirtiest desires bubble up and emerge as words. "What I want, Baxter, is for you to *fuck* me, make love to me, have sex with me, whatever you want to call it. Give me a thousand orgasms. Show me what I've never had. Just…don't *talk* to me about it, don't tell me what to do—*show* me. I don't need words, I need action."

He rumbled a laugh. "Clear enough, babe. You want action, I'll give you action." He slid a finger deep inside me, curling it, making me weak in the knees. "I'm a talker, though, and that ain't somethin' I can just quit."

He withdrew his finger, scooped me up in his arms, and carried me a few steps, and physically threw me onto the bed. I hit the mattress on my back, bounced once, and then he was on the bed, prowling toward me on all fours like the wild beast he was. His grin was feral and ravenous.

"Know what I'm gonna do now, Eva?" he murmured, his voice rumbling from his chest.

I squirmed, rubbing my thighs together, unsure what to do with my hands. My breasts were pulled to either side by gravity, which wasn't a flattering look, in my opinion, so I hugged my arms around them on either side, propping them back up where they belonged.

"Um...make me come?" I suggested.

He was above me, his knees on either side of my calves, his fists braced in the mattress beside my shoulders. "Well, yes. But how do you think I'm gonna do that?"

I shrugged. "With your hands? Like before?"

He used one hand to grab both of my wrists, pinning them together in his one huge paw, and then brought them up over my head.

I squirmed against his hold. "Why are you holding my hands like this?"

"So you don't pose for me." He kept hold of my hands, dipping his upper body down to press his mouth against my throat, forcing me to tip my chin up.

"I wasn't posing, I just...I don't like the way my breasts look, hanging and saggy like this..." I twisted my torso so my breasts swayed.

He growled deep in his chest, bearlike. "I fuckin' love that look." He sucked my left nipple into his mouth, flicked it with his tongue, and then slid his mouth across to the right side, and repeated the movement. "I love seein' these fuckin' incredible tits of yours bare and natural. And babe, they ain't saggy. They're goddamn perfect, naturally perfect. Only way they'd stay upright when you're layin' down is if they're full of silicone, and while I don't mind that look, I like this one better."

He let go of my wrists and cradled a breast in his palm, bringing it to his mouth so he could twiddle the nipple with his tongue until I was gasping and writhing. "For real, the way you look, Eva? The body you got? You should be the most stuck-up, arrogant, snobby bitch in the world. You are literally the perfect woman. You could snap your fingers and point and have literally any man, *every man* in the whole fuckin' world at your feet, beggin' for ten seconds to just fuckin' *look* at you. Wars have been fought over women as perfect as you are."

"You're crazy," I breathed.

"Yeah, maybe. That ain't relevant to the fact that you're fuckin' perfect." He inched lower, kissing down to my diaphragm. "Back to the matter at hand. Yes, I'm gonna make you come. But no, I ain't gonna use my hands."

"You're—you're not?" I squeaked.

Lower yet, his tongue circling my navel. "Nope." His lips pressed a line of hot wet kisses down to the swell of my core. "You know what I'm gonna do, Eva?"

"What, Baxter? What are you going to do?" I breathed the question, desperate to hear him say it, and even more desperate for him to do what I thought he was about to do.

"I'm gonna lick your pussy until you scream my name. I'm gonna kneel between your thighs and I'm gonna worship at the altar of your sweet, beautiful, innocent pussy and I ain't gonna stop until you've come so hard so many times you won't know which fuckin' way is up."

"Oh god..." I gasped. "Please. Please, *please* Baxter. *Please* do that. Right now."

He slid backward off the bed, kneeling on the floor, and hauled me by my ankles down the mattress until my bottom was nearly hanging off the edge, and he gently, reverently parted my thighs, resting my feet on his shoulders. "Is that an order, Evangeline?"

I stared at him, my eyes wide, my breathing ragged. "Yes, Baxter. That's an order."

He laughed. "I love it when you beg me to do shit to you. And I love it even more when you order me to do shit to you."

"Then I'm both begging and ordering you to do…what you said."

"Say it, Eva. Please. Say it for me. Say what you want me to do. You know how horny it makes me when you talk dirty to me."

I swallowed as he kissed the inside of my left thigh, low, near my knee. "Baxter, will you please… oh—oh god, that feels good—will you please…lick my—my…my pussy?" That felt…amazing. Saying that. It felt almost as good as his mouth did, ascending the inside of my thigh, kissing upward closer and closer to my core…to my pussy. I wanted to say it again, to taste the words, to relish their dirtiness. "Lick my pussy, Baxter."

"Yes ma'am, Evangeline." I watched him, not daring to take my eyes off him as he began all over again, starting a line of hot, sucking kisses at my right knee upward, closer and closer to my core.

I propped myself up on my elbows so I could see better, watching raptly as his lips touched my flesh at mid thigh, then higher, and higher. I held my breath as he paused, my lungs frozen as his warm damp breath huffed over my vagina. I stared, unblinking, not breathing, waiting, waiting, wanting. And then it happened. His lips brushed against my core, pressing a literal kiss against me, lips to…well, lips. God, so hot. So erotic. His mouth was on my vagina. His lips were pressed against my pussy. I ached, just thinking the words. And then…ohhhhh, and then his tongue slid up the seam, ever so softly parting me. I whimpered, then, as he repeated the slide of his tongue up the seam, again and again. Every time his tongue ran wet and warm along the seam, I whimpered. And then his hands grazed up my thighs and his thumbs pressed against my outer labia and held them apart, and I ceased breathing entirely until the moment his tongue flicked, just once, against my clitoris. And then, at the moment of contact, a searing bolt of lightning blistered through me, shaking me, seizing me in a fierce, hot fist and squeezing me, from the core outward.

"Oh my *god!*" I shrieked, "Baxter! Oh god, Baxter. Do that again!"

He rumbled a laugh. "You like that, do you?"

"It's the best thing I've ever felt in my life!"

"Best thing you've ever felt, *ever?*"

"*Ever.*"

"Then by all means, my lady, allow me to continue." And continue he did.

Using the pads of his thumbs to separate the lips of my pussy, he ran his tongue over the opening of my channel and then to my clit, and then did it again. And then he flickered his tongue inside me, a strange, wet, warm, wriggling sensation that left me breathless, aching, unable to even gasp. Alien, bizarre, yet so so *so* amazing. I never wanted this to stop. I didn't even want to orgasm yet, I just wanted to feel his tongue and lips on my pussy, on my clit, inside me. Again and again, he licked against the opening and then my clit, and then slid his tongue in, withdrew it, flicked my clitoris, slid his tongue back in, then licked me top to bottom. There was no pattern, which was maddening and amazing at the same time. Because I'd partially lied to myself: I did want to orgasm. I wanted it so bad, now, that it was nearly physical pain. And I sensed that unless he gave me a pattern and rhythm I could sink into, I wouldn't be able to reach that plateau.

"Baxter…" I moaned. He hummed an interrogatory *mmm-hmmm?* without stopping what he was doing. "I need…"

He flicked my clitoris with his tongue, and then backed away to murmur, "Tell me what you need, Eva."

"I need to come."

"You want to come, huh?"

I gasped. "Yes, so bad. I don't just *want* to, I *need* to."

"In that case, Eva..." He slid a middle finger inside me and curled it, massaging a specific spot high and deep inside me that sent insanity blasting through me, wild and bashing heat that squeezed my core and my belly and my mind in a vise grip, "I think you should come. Right...*now*."

After he said the word *now*, he fluttered his tongue against my clit, and then sucked it between his teeth, his finger gliding in and out of my channel, and then he finally gave me a rhythm, his tongue circling around my clitoris in rapid circles, and the heat and the squeezing pressure exploded through me, took over, and I lost all control over my body, my mind, my mouth.

I felt myself screaming out loud as I came, an orgasm so powerful I was helplessly lost within the rippling tsunami of ecstasy. I was thrashing as I screamed, and I had Baxter's head in my hands and my hips were flexing; I was wantonly grinding my pussy against Baxter's mouth, taking every lick he gave me and demanding more.

But he didn't stop. Not when I came. He licked and slid that finger in and out, and then when the orgasm began to crest and fade, he added a second finger and used those two fingers to mimic sex and his flicking, circling tongue changed rhythms, patterns, and directions. Instead of circling, he flicked it side to side, occasionally using his lips to create suction. And with the change in tactics, I felt another wave begin to build inside me and I embraced it, accepted it, welcomed the onslaught of pleasure. Baxter fed the nascent orgasm, carefully and skillfully building it to a crescendo, and I tumbled over the edge a second time, screaming yet again, clutching his head as it shook side to side, his tongue flicking back and forth across my clitoris.

He still wasn't done.

He withdrew his fingers and just kissed my core, slowly, softly. He let the heat and pressure fade, just a little, and then began slowly building it back up again with a combination of circles and back-and-forth motions of his tongue, giving me one finger, and then two, and then one, mimicking sex and then massaging that spot inside me.

Again, I reached the crescendo and fell over the edge, screaming.

And this time, instead of wordless screams of bliss, I screamed his name. *"Baxter!* Oh god, Baxter! Yes, yes, yes!"

The orgasms had done me in, left me limp and gasping, and aching, and his touch, no matter how soft or gentle, was too much, too much, almost painful. I was so incredibly hypersensitive that I couldn't bear another touch.

"Bax, you have to stop. I can't take any more." I pulled at his head, tugging him up.

He crawled up my body, hovering over me. "Eva honey, I'm just getting started."

I stared up at him. "Y-you are?" The stammer should have been embarrassing, but somehow it wasn't.

"You on birth control?" he asked.

I shook my head. "No. It messes with my hormones and makes me moody, so I stopped. Plus, it's not like I have any reason to be on it, since I don't have sex."

He rose off me. "Be right back."

"Where are you going?" I asked, hating his absence from above me.

"Out to the truck. There are some condoms in the center console."

And just like that, he was out the door, still naked, still erect. He left the door wide open, letting the brilliant sunlight of early evening stream in to bathe me. I could see him, and the truck. He yanked open the driver's side door, leaned in, his taut buttocks flashing in the golden sunlight, rummaged around for a moment, and then withdrew and closed the door, trotting back in. He had a string of square, golden condom wrappers in one hand, and as he trotted his erection swayed side to side. Leaving the cabin door open, he swaggered over to stand at the foot of the bed. Ripping one packet free, he tossed the rest aside and climbed onto the bed.

"You keep condoms in the center console of your truck?" I asked.

He shrugged. "My brothers and I all share the truck, so it's a shared stash. We keep 'em there as a just-in-case precaution. Better to have 'em when you need 'em, you know?"

"So you guys are very…um, active?"

He laughed. "Babe. You met my brothers. What do you think?"

I wasn't sure how I felt about that. "I see your point." I eyed the one in his hand, and the other four or five he'd tossed aside. "How many do you plan on using, may I ask?"

He grinned at me. "As many as I can." He tossed the golden foil packet at me, and it landed on my belly. "Starting with that one."

I swallowed, realizing he wanted me to open the condom and put it on him. "I've never…" I lifted a shoulder, "done that before."

He inched closer. "Be a fun time to learn, then, yeah?"

I swallowed again, blinking. I took the packet

in my hands and sat up, then gingerly and carefully ripped it open and withdrew the latex ring.

Glancing at it, and then at him, I gestured with it. "Is there a right way to put it on?"

He nodded, taking it from me, pinching at a little bubble near the top. "See that? That's the part that goes on me. Then you just...roll it on."

I let out a shaky breath, moving to sit on my shins. "I did take sex ed in school, did the whole thing with the banana and all that...but it's been a long time since then and my only other experiences were—"

He reached out and touched my chin with a fingertip, interrupting me. "Eva, sweetheart, relax. You're nervous. Not your first time, but your first time in a long time. It's cool. Be nervous. Take your time. Ask questions. I'm not laughing at you, and I'll never tease you, not about this kinda thing."

He moved closer, lowering to sit on his shins like I was, and wrapped his other hand around the back of my neck, pulling me in, slanting his lips across mine. I sighed into the kiss and gave myself over to it. I knew what he was doing: distracting me, using the kiss to silence my doubts, using my libido to eradicate my nerves. I knew he was doing it, and I was grateful. I sank into the kiss, wrapped my hands around the back of his neck, traced the smoothness of the shaved sides of his head, and then tugged his hair free of the ponytail and ran my fingers through the thick, silky brown locks. His tongue explored my mouth, and mine explored his, and his hands found places to roam, and mine followed suit as well. He pressed the condom into my hands and played with my breasts, thumbing my nipples and hefting the weight of each breast in turn, and I palmed his pec and then his buttocks, and then finally I let my hand drift to his erection. I moaned in delight as the iron-hard, springy, velvety shaft filled my hand, and I stroked him, caressed him, re-familiarizing myself with the organ.

And then I broke the kiss. Met his gaze, and let him see that I was still nervous, but even more…well, horny. I wanted to come again. I wanted to feel his erection. I wanted to watch him orgasm, I wanted to be the one to make him feel that good, so good he was an animal, feral, wild, out of control. I wanted to give him what he'd given me.

I wanted to feel him inside me; I wanted to know how that felt. I wanted to be the thrashing, moaning, sweat-glistening, heaving-breasted, wantonly erotic woman in the pornography I watched, the one on her back as a muscular beast of a man with an enormous penis drove into her.

All this flashed through my head in the few seconds of eye contact, and then I shifted my gaze downward.

To Baxter's cock.

God, I loved that word. I decided I would use it more often. Cock. I loved the sight of Baxter's cock, almost as much as I loved the way it felt in my hands. I pinched the bubble at the center of the condom, placed it onto the top of Baxter's cock, and gingerly rolled the latex downward. Slowly, hesitantly. An inch or so of latex coated his shaft, and I grew bolder, using a caressing motion to roll it the rest of the way onto his massive manhood.

When it was all the way on, I admired my handiwork. Grinned up at him. "I liked doing that."

He palmed my buttocks with both hands and hauled me closer. "Then I'll let you do it next time, 'cause I sure as hell liked letting you do it."

He leaned into me, and his arms wrapped around me, and I felt myself tipping backward in his embrace. My thighs were wedged apart by his waist, and his weight pinned me against the bed, even though I knew he was bracing most of his weight on his arms. His lips brushed mine, and I immediately seized his mouth with mine, taking a wild, heated kiss from him as his fingers explored my pussy, brushing my clit, testing my channel.

He was above me, and I felt the tip of his cock nudging my entrance. "You ready, Eva?"

I swallowed, my heart hammering. Then I

nodded. "Yes."

He grinned down at me. "You sure?"

I clutched at his buttocks. "Totally sure. I need it, Baxter. Please."

Leaning backward and lifting up, he reached between us and gripped his erection in one hand. "Watch, Eva." He nudged the tip against me, pressing in ever so slightly. "Watch me put it in you."

"God, yes." I lifted up, craning my neck to watch. I glanced at him, and then back down to where we were seconds and mere millimeters from joining. "Now, Baxter."

His hips flexed gently, carefully, and he slid into me an inch or so. Only a tiny portion of his length, but I felt split apart, my eyes widening at the feel of him inside me. So...*much.* Yet it wasn't even a third of him.

"Touch yourself, Eva. I wanna watch you make yourself come while I put my cock inside you." He growled the words, and it was an order.

But this one time, I didn't mind—it was exactly what I wanted. My fingers flew to my core, and I touched myself with two fingers, like I did at home in my dorm, alone, watching porn. It took less than a minute for the orgasm to build, as I was primed by the previous three orgasms, and aroused to madness by the erotic vision of Baxter above me, a wall of solid, masculine muscle, his beautiful cock in his fist, that perfect organ splitting open my pussy. Filling it beyond bursting, to the point of pain. But the more I touched myself, the faster the pain of his enormous size inside my tight channel faded and became pleasure.

"More," I whispered. "Give me more of it."

He flexed his hips a little more, and my pussy swallowed another inch of him. I was nearing orgasm, now, and that wasn't enough.

"All of it, Baxter." I groaned, and then whimpered, and then I felt the orgasm trembling low, behind my core, and I met his gaze as my fingers flew around my clit, bringing me to climax. "NOW! God, Baxter, please...fuck me now!"

"Jesus Christ, Eva—" he snarled, and then...he gave it all to me.

I came.

Screaming his name, I came as he drove the entirety of his cock into me, and it felt perfect, more than perfect, beyond perfection. It was glorious pain, an ache, a burn, a sting, a fiery raging inferno of sensation I couldn't fathom. More and more, and more. He was fully inside me, and I was coming, his hips bumped against mine and I wrapped my legs around his waist and buried my face against the side of his neck.

Baxter fucked me, then.

He braced one fist in the pillow beside my face and stared at me, his gaze pinning mine. He slid one hand under my butt and lifted me off the bed, and his hips began pistoning. Slowly at first, then with increasing speed, until he reached a steady pace, hips bumping mine, thighs slapping against me. I felt him driving in and out of me, and I gasped and shrieked each time his cock slammed into me. My fingers clawed into his shoulders, and I refused to look away from him, refused to let him look away from me as he fucked me, and fucked me, and fucked me.

And I gloried in every single second of it. Every movement, every thrust. Each slap of our bodies meeting, I loved. I moved with him, lifting my hips to meet his thrusts, and then he began moving even faster and I felt an orgasm building up inside me, a fourth one. I wanted it, felt it coming, and I knew it would be the most potent and powerful one yet, and I needed it, and I knew the only way to get it was to fuck him back, to fuck him harder, to take it.

And that's what I did. I fucked him back, and I fucked him harder.

I got the orgasm. It hit me like an earthquake, ripping through me with the smashing intensity of a runaway freight train.

I screamed until I was hoarse, and that's when I felt Baxter reach his own climax.

He began to grunt and snarl, and his movement became frantic, and his eyes closed.

"No—look at me, Bax," I snapped. "I want to watch you."

He lifted up and grabbed my hips in both hands, and I palmed my breasts for him, offered them to him as he fucked me to his own orgasm. He accepted my offering, burying his face between my breasts as he snarled, and his hips slammed with furious, frenzied aggression that had me shouting *YES!* over and over again, in time with each thrust he gave me, because it felt so damn good and he was so beautiful, so rugged, so masculine, and him fucking me was the most incredible thing I'd ever seen, ever felt.

And then he came, and *that* was the most indelibly, unforgettably erotic moment of my entire existence.

He reared up, roared like a lion and pounded into my pussy, once, twice, three times, and then he faltered, gasping, and buried his face in my breasts once more, gasping. I threaded my fingers through his hair, and cradled the back of his head, hooking my feet around the backs of his thighs, and gasped with him.

When he lifted up, I framed his face with both hands. Emotions were running rampant through me, too many, too intense. "Bax, I—"

He didn't shy away from the emotions I knew he

saw in my eyes, on my face. "I know, Eva. Me too."

Flopping to his back, he tugged me over so I was cradled in his arms, listening to the thunder of his heartbeat, the rough sawing of his breath. His arms were around me and this was yet another moment burned into me, onto the fabric of my mind.

Every moment with Baxter, it seemed, was going to be burned into me.

I felt all the emotions, and didn't dare name them, because we'd agreed this had an expiration date, and those emotions didn't fit in with that.

SEVEN

Baxter

HOLY SHIT, HOLY SHIT, HOLY SHIT.

I am in so much fucking trouble.

That was…that wasn't just fucking. And I'm in full on freak-out mode inside, because she knew it and she knew I knew it. Same thing happened with Bast, and then it happened with Zane, and then it happened with Brock…like, in fuckin' chronological order or some shit, like this was a goddamned romance novel or something. So now, I'm supposed to believe it's happening to me, right? I'm gonna fall for the girl, and she's gonna fall for me, and some great mystical *deus ex machina*—yes, I do know what that is, thank you very fuckin' much—is gonna drop down from the sky to make it so we can be together in cute little happily ever after despite all the bullshit reasons our lives don't mix.

Yeah, fuck that.

Problem is, tell that to my heart. It's hammering away inside my chest like I just did a bunch of wind sprints and, let me tell you, my physical conditioning is fuckin' prime, okay? A little bit of nice hard fucking isn't going to make my heart pound like this. Nah son, this is straight up nerves and emotions. No way am I gonna sit and here be all introspective and turn each weird-ass fuckin' emotion over and look at it like it's a specimen on a lab table. No, nope, nuh-uh. Not doing that. What I'm gonna do is I'm gonna bury the emotions way down deep, and then I'm gonna strip the condom off my dick and throw it away, and I'm gonna dive back into the sweet and holy promised land that is Evangeline du Maurier, and her lush, eager body.

I mean *fuuuuck*, the girl is a rabid tiger in the sack, man. Legit, I have never been fucked like that. Never. She *wanted* that shit and she wanted it *hard*. She went after it like…well, like a woman who's been deprived of satisfying sex her whole life, who's finally encountered a man who can give it to her properly.

I swear on my mother's grave, if I ever come face to face with that slimy, useless, dickless, piece of shit, douchebag motherfucker Thomas Pussy-Boy Haverton, I'm going to knock his teeth so far down his skinny little neck he'll be shitting teeth for a solid week. And that, my friends, is a Baxter Badd promise.

Because to have a woman like Evangeline in your bed and not give her as many orgasms as possible? That's a sin. It's a mortal sin against sex, against manhood, against all of humanity. Like, how could he have this woman, this incredible, perfect, smart, gorgeous, eager, fierce, sexy woman in his bed, and just hump her and dump her? How? How is that shit even possible? I do *not* get it. I just don't.

I rolled off the bed, leaving Eva naked and—momentarily at least—sated, watching me curiously. I made sure to let her see what I was doing as I carefully pulled the rubber off, tied it up, and tossed it into the little garbage can under the sink in the kitchenette. Then I made a pit stop in the bathroom to take a leak, wash my hands, my face, and my cock, dry off, and then I went back to stand by the bed, staring down at Eva.

She blinked up at me, innocent and curious. "You wash up after each time?"

I shrugged. "Sure. Gotta stay fresh, you know? Nobody wants to be all sticky and stinky, so yeah, I wash up after each time."

Her gaze fell to my dick, which, for the first time since she'd met me, wasn't hard. "That's what it looks like when you're not erect?" She giggled. "It's kind of…"

I faked an angry expression. "You're laughing at my dick?"

She paled, thinking I was serious. "No! I just… I've never seen one—" she stammered, trying to find a way out of the laughter, but each time she tried, she would glance at my cock again and the giggles would start all over, and I was still holding the angry expression, and she would try to stifle it again. "I'm sorry, Baxter, I swear I'm not—it's not…" She breathed out shakily, caught between worry that I was really angry and hit by the giggles at the sight of my flaccid cock.

I couldn't hold on to the expression any longer, and I burst out laughing. "I'm teasing, Eva, relax. Limp dicks are inherently funny. They just are. As long as you don't laugh at me when I'm hard, we're good."

She glared at me. "You're a jerk. I thought you were actually upset."

"You really think I'm that sensitive?" I snorted, crossing my arms over my chest. "No way. I can take a joke. I grew up in locker rooms, remember? Lots of naked dudes, lots of teasing and giving each other shit about dick sizes and whatever."

She was eying my cock, again. Unable to stop herself, clearly, and I sure as hell didn't mind. Let the girl look. "It's just so different. So much…smaller. I had no idea."

"Well, I'm a grower, not a show-er."

She frowned up at me. "What does that mean?"

"Some guys, their cock is basically the same size all the time. When they get wood, it just gets harder. A little bigger, maybe it stands up a little straighter. They're what you call show-ers. Like, they show their actual size. Me, I'm a grower. It's like this, and then I get hard and it grows like triple the size."

Evangeline snickered, reaching out to touch the tip. "Triple? Try quadruple, at least. Quintuple. Sextuple. Septuple. Octuple, even."

"Octuple? You think my dick grows *eight* times bigger?"

"Maybe. I'd have to measure to be certain."

I laughed at that. "No measuring."

"No? I was always under the impression that all men have measured themselves at least once."

I shrugged. "I mean, maybe when we're like, thirteen and just discovering the wonder of a hard-on. Not as a grown-ass man."

Her eyes met mine, full of curiosity and humor and arousal. "So? Did you?"

I rolled my eyes, sighing in irritation. "Yeah, sure."

"And?"

"You want to know?"

She nodded, moving to sit cross-legged on the bed, facing me. "Yes. I really would like to know how many inches your penis is."

I laughed. "You really do?"

"Of course! It's part of the Baxter Badd experience. I want to be able to brag, even if just to myself, that I had sex with a man with a huge cock. And I want to be able to say how many inches it was."

"Keep in mind I was thirteen, and men keep growing until we're at least twenty-one. So it might be more, by now." I let out another breath, because it was weirdly embarrassing. "Eight and three-quarters inches." I laughed again. "I was so pissed it wasn't a full nine."

She blinked. "Eight and three-quarters inches? When I tell my girlfriends about this, can I just round up to nine inches?"

"Sure." I frowned at her. "Are you really going to tell your friends about this?"

"Would you mind?"

I shrugged. "Hell nah. Tell away. Just make me sound good, I guess."

Her gaze was serious, all humor gone. "It would

be impossible to make you sound anything except incredible, Baxter, because that's what you are. All I have to do is tell the truth, and even then I don't think most of my friends would really believe me. They'd think I made you up, because it just has to be impossible for a man like you to really exist. If it's too good to be true, it probably is."

I felt my heart flipping and twisting, and worked hard to keep that from showing. "You're full of shit, but thanks, babe. I appreciate the ego boost."

I wanted to touch her. I wanted to fuck her again, to see if it really was as amazing as it had felt last time. But I also wanted this to happen in a way that was best for her, and I didn't want to rush things. So I felt content to let Evangeline dictate the pace.

She uncrossed her legs and put her feet on the floor, reaching for me. Her palms slid up my waist, caressing my chest and my abs. "I want you to know, I wouldn't actually talk about you, for several reasons. First, I don't really consider any of the girls at Yale to be true friends. They're leeches and mooches and gossips and bitches, and I don't trust any of them, but they're fun enough to hang out with and study with and whatever, but they're not really true friends. Second, they really wouldn't believe me about you. You really are too good to be real. Third, I have a feeling I'll want to keep the memory of you all for myself.

I won't want to share that with anyone."

"And you should know, I won't be telling my brothers about this. They'll assume we banged, but I won't be giving out details, okay? I got too much respect for you to do that, even with my brothers."

"Respect?" She sounded honestly puzzled.

I nodded. "Yeah. I respect you. You're a strong, smart, successful woman. You have an independent soul, and a sharp mind. You're gonna go places, do important shit. You're not just some random chick from a bar or something, some slutty little sorority puffball. You have..." I hunted for the right word, and finally found it. "You've got substance, Evangeline. So, yeah, I respect you."

She seemed floored. "I—I don't know how to process that. No one has ever said that to me before."

"Well they should. And you should demand it."

She pulled me closer, so I was standing between her knees. "How long does it take for you to be ready again?"

"Done talking about that, huh?" I smirked down at her.

She nodded. "Yes. I am. I'm not here for deep, heavy, introspective, soul-searching, life-changing conversation, Baxter." Her eyes met mine, full of fire and desire.

"Then what are you here for, Evangeline?"

"The hot sex." She ran her hands down my hips, and then cupped my ass. "I'm here for your cock. And what you can do with it."

"The answer is, not long. Ten, fifteen minutes or so. Sometimes less."

"So…are you ready again now?"

I shrugged. "Why don't you find out?"

I kept my arms crossed over my chest, because the only thing I wanted to do right then was pin her to the bed and eat her sweet pussy for an hour or two. Or three. For real, I've never enjoyed eating pussy so much as I did hers. So sweet, such a delicate, complex flavor. Musk with a little tang, and a hint of sweetness. I wanted more. I wanted to make her scream again. Make her writhe and clutch at my head. Grind her pussy against me with that wild desperation I've only ever seen in her.

Instead, I kept my arms crossed over my chest and stood still and let Evangeline decide what happened next.

She gazed up at me, and then turned her eyes to my still-flaccid dick. She smiled to herself a little, but then when she touched me the smile faded. Especially when my cock twitched at her touch.

Evangeline spent the next few minutes playing with me. Just touching, cupping, stroking, tugging. Exploring. Her palms cradled my balls, and her fingers circled my shaft, measuring my girth as I grew. And then, when I was finally hard, she clutched my shaft with her hands, staring up at me as she caressed me with such reverence and such desire that I felt unworthy of the expression on her face. She couldn't really feel that way about *me* could she? Nah. But yet, it looked like she did.

I didn't know why, though. It was crazy. I mean, it was just me. Nothin' special.

She seemed to feel otherwise, though, as she gazed at my erection and stroked it and caressed it until I was actively holding back.

"There's so much I'm curious about, Baxter." Her voice was so quiet I had to strain to hear her.

"Yeah? Like what?"

She licked her lips. "What you taste like. What you would feel like, in my mouth. What it would feel like if you...if you came in my mouth." She sighed, and licked her lips again, and her hand gripped me softly, just beneath the head. "What you would feel like, inside me, bare. Without the condom. What it would feel like for you to come inside me, bare. What it would feel like to...to ride you. What it would feel like for you to—to fuck me from behind."

I groaned. "Holy motherfucking shit, Eva."

She blinked up at me. "What?"

"This is all about you, sweetheart." I struggled to

find words, because I was delirious, crazy, wanting all of that and possessing far too little restraint. "I want to satisfy your curiosity. Make every fantasy you've ever had come true."

"It kind of feels like there's a 'but' in there somewhere," she said.

"There is. I can't do some of those things right now. I'm not gonna go bareback with you if you're not on birth control—the last thing you need is to get pregnant, right?" I ground my teeth together, clenched my fists. "The rest of what you said you wanted? Babe, I'm all yours. Do what you want. Take what you want. You want to wrap that perfect mouth of yours around my cock? Do it. You want to ride me? Say the word. You want it from behind? Get on all fours on the bed and I'll show you exactly what that feels like."

She shivered. "The problem is, I don't know what I want more, or what I want first." She stroked me softly, gently. "It's like being at a buffet with all the best food in the world, but not having enough time to try everything, and not being able to try them all at once."

I stood and waited. She and I were in agreement on one thing at least: I didn't know which of those things I wanted with her more.

After a long, tense moment, Evangeline let out

a shaky breath and slid backward onto the bed. Her hand tangled into mine, fingers twining, lacing, making my heart thump crazily, stupidly, childishly. She pulled me toward her. I joined her on the bed, and we met in the middle, on our knees once again, kissing breathlessly. Wildly. With a passion I didn't know I possessed, didn't know existed.

Evangeline was the one to break the kiss, gasping. "I don't want to waste a single moment with you." She pressed her palms to my chest and pushed me, ever so gently, but with deliberate firmness, down onto the bed and onto my back. "This. I want this." She slid off the bed and retrieved a condom, ripping one free from the string. Kneeling beside me she said, "I want to ride you."

I stopped her before she opened it. "You want to feel me bare, just for a few seconds?" I met her eyes. "I'll make sure we stop and then you can put it on."

She shook her head. "No. I'm afraid it would be…too good. Neither of us would want to stop." She ripped open the foil packet. "Better to just not even go there."

I sucked in a sharp breath as she rolled the condom onto me. "Yeah, that's probably smart," I murmured.

I was lying on my back, arms at my sides, cock sheathed in a condom, staring at her as she sat beside me. And for a moment, we stayed like that. Eyes locked, feeling some kind of unspoken meaning in the moment, both of us knowing this was…different. Knowing it was time-stamped, with an expiration date neither of us could change. I don't know. There was just…a tension, an importance to it. It was scary, even for me. Intense.

And then Evangeline rose up onto her knees and slid one leg over mine to straddle my thighs. Her hair was loose, a shimmery fall of black. The cabin door was still open, letting in the sunset, a reddish-gold stream of light bathing her perfect skin, her perfect body. I felt my breath catch and my heart skip a beat at the vision of her, kneeling over me, astride me, sunset on her skin. I memorized the way she looked, in this moment. The way her skin glowed, the way the light glinted off her raven-black hair. The way her big, tear-drop shaped breasts hung heavy, nipples thick and erect at the center of her wide dark areolae. The swell of her hips, the delicate flower of her pussy, the neatly trimmed thatch of pubic hair that made her all the more womanly to me, unlike the shaved and waxed business of others I'd encountered. Her bright green eyes, fixed on me, taking in my body and my face and my cock with as much hunger and fierce emotion as I was feeling. Her exquisite face, each feature perfect. Those lips, her tongue sliding over them in anticipation.

And then she sucked in a breath, held it, and let it out slowly. She reached for me, grasping my cock in one hand. Then she shifted forward so her shins were beside my hips, so she was directly over me. Angling my cock away from my body, she leaned forward a little, so her breasts swayed pendulously, beautifully. I finally let myself touch her, sliding my hands from her hips to her ass—that ass, I loved that ass so fuckin' much it was crazy. I couldn't get enough of touching it, holding it, caressing it, squeezing it. I wanted to fuck that ass. I wouldn't—she was too new to this and too sweet and innocent and virginally clean for something so dirty, but I wanted to. Just because her ass was exactly that enticing, intoxicating. I cupped those tits, caressed them, thumbed the nipples. She inhaled sharply again as I did that, reminding me how sensitive she was, especially her nipples.

Another unforgettable tableau, then: Eva, leaning forward, her hand on my cock, guiding me to her slit, hair hanging over one shoulder. Her eyes going wide as I entered her. The whimpering, whining gasp as I filled her.

Her mouth fell open, trembling, her eyes wide, almost tearful. "God, Baxter..." She squeezed her eyes shut as she sank down onto me, her hands braced on my chest, seating me fully inside her achingly tight channel. "So...so *much*. You're so fucking *big*. It hurts, god, it hurts, but I love it."

"Give yourself a second to get used to me and it'll stop hurting."

She shook her head. "I don't want it to. I like it." When her ass squished against my hips, she leaned back, balanced. "You feel so good inside me, Bax."

It was hard to speak, hard to find words. "You feel fuckin' perfect, Eva. So tight, so wet, so hot."

She rose up, and I slid through her tightness with slick, wet slowness. "Don't do anything, Bax. Don't even touch me. Just...please, just let me have this all for myself, okay?"

"Anything you want, Eva." I put my hands under my head, which was the hardest thing to do, but I did it for her.

She kept her eyes on mine, and sank back down, filling herself with me again, exhaling as she did so. And then her fingers, the middle and ring fingers of her right hand, went to her clit, and she touched herself, flicked her clit in slow circles, keeping her hips still, just touching her clit until her eyes betrayed the heat and pressure building inside her.

And then she began moving.

She lifted up until I was almost out of her, and her fingers circled her clit faster and faster, and her other hand clutched at her tits, pinching her nipples and flicking them and cupping the heavy globes and letting them fall free to bounce, and then she sank down on me, impaling herself on my cock, moaning in her throat as I filled her.

I held utterly still, focusing on keeping the orgasm at bay for as long as I could, focusing as well on memorizing her, memorizing each moment, the way she moved, the way she looked, the way she sounded.

Again, she lifted up so I was nearly out of her, and then she sank down. Fingers circled her clit, pinched her nipples. Another lift and another lowering. Again, and again, slowly, each time deliberate. Moans escaped her constantly now, and her fingers slowed on her clit, and she stilled on me, fully impaled. Drawing it out.

"I don't want this to end," she gasped. "I want to make it last forever."

"I know," I growled. "Me too."

"But it feels so good, and I can't stop." She lifted up and sank down in one smooth movement, now, without pausing at the top. "I can't stop. I want it faster. Harder. *More*. But I want it to last."

"Shit, Eva," I snarled. "You're makin' it impossible for me to hold out."

"Are you close?"

"Not yet."

"Good." She rolled her hips while I was buried

deep, and a gasp escaped her. "Holy shit, that feels good."

I laughed. "I love hearing you swear."

"You're a wonderfully bad influence on me, Baxter."

"I know, that's me—sullying the innocence of a good girl like you."

She rolled her hips again, and again, her whimpering gasps becoming frantic. "It's perfect. The way you've sullied me is perfect. It's what I've wanted my whole life. You make me feel—I don't know. Maybe this will sound stupid, but...you make me feel... powerful."

I shook my head, staring up at her. "That ain't stupid, sweetheart. That's the truth. You *are* powerful. You're in control. You want me to come? You could make me shoot my load in thirty seconds flat. You want this to last another fuckin' hour? You can do that too."

"I *am* in control, aren't I?" she asked, rolling her hips on me yet again. "Like this. If I just kept doing this, I wouldn't have to touch myself, I would just come...so fast."

"Show me."

She flattened her palms on my belly to brace, to balance, and then began grinding on me, rolling her beautiful hips in ever-faster circles, and her mouth dropped open and her eyes went wide and gasps and moans fell from her nonstop, louder and louder. Moans became shrieks, and the grinding circles became frantic, and I had to clamp down hard to keep from coming as she rode me. God, did she ride me, then. She lost all control. She screamed as she came, her hips rolling wildly on me, grinding her clit against the base of my cock. She fell apart, her scream fading to moans and whimpers, and my cock was throbbing, aching, and my balls were heavy and taut and full, and I had to keep every muscle flexed to will back the orgasm as she rode me through the aftershocks, quaking and shivering and shuddering.

And then her eyes opened, and she breathed out shakily. "Your turn," she murmured.

"My turn?" I let a hungry grin curve across my mouth. "Can I fuck you however I want?"

"Oh please, please, Baxter. Please." There was no joke or tease in that plea, just raw honest need. She bent and kissed me, demanding my tongue, my cock seated deep inside her. Her lips moved against mine as she pleaded with me. "Please fuck me. I need to be fucked. I *need* it."

"Jesus, Eva. You talk like that I'm not gonna be able to hold it for long." I kissed her. "Seriously, that sweet mouth talking dirty is gonna be the death of me."

I lifted her off me, and she moved to lay on her back. I shook my head. "Not like that. Not this time." I decided to give her a little taste of rough, commanding, dominant Bax, the part of me I'd kept at bay for her sake.

"Then what—?" she began, but I interrupted her, grasping her by the hips and flipped her over to her belly. "Baxter, what are you—?"

I didn't give her a chance to finish. Once she was on her belly, I slid an arm beneath her and lifted her hips into the air, propping her on her knees with that glorious ass in the air and her tits smashed against the bed. "This, Eva. *This* is what I'm gonna do."

"Oh," she breathed.

"Yeah, oh." I reached between her thighs to finger her pussy, guiding my cock to her entrance. "You know what I'm gonna do?"

"Fuck me?"

"I'm gonna fuck you from behind." I drove into her, and she shrieked in surprised pleasure. "And I'm gonna fuck you hard. You ready for that, sweet thing?"

She whimpered as I filled her. "Yes, god, yes," she gasped. "I want that so bad. I want it more than I've ever wanted anything, Bax."

"Anything?"

She pushed back against me when I pulled back and began a thrust, so her ass slapped against my hips, jiggling in a way that made me throb and pulse. "Anything. I've literally had wet dreams about being fucked like this."

"For someone who never swears, you sure are dropping a lot of F-bombs."

"It's you. You make me filthy, dirty, and rebellious. You make me do crazy things. I'd never say that word outside of sex, or around anyone but you, but for some reason, you just...you bring it out of me."

"It's hot, so fuckin' hot, Eva. You're so sweet and innocent and perfect, and then you beg me to fuck you? God, babe. Legit, you're the hottest, most erotic thing in the whole goddamn universe."

I drove into her again, fucking deep, pulling out so just the tip of me was left inside her, and then slammed in again, the beautiful cushion of her perfect ass quaking and trembling with each thrust. She lifted up on her hands, so she was on all fours, and began meeting me thrust for thrust, grinding back into my thrusts, slamming her hips backward so my cock filled her and my hips slapped against her, encouraging the slap, making her ass shake even harder.

I couldn't help doing what I did next. I just...had to.

As I fucked her, I spanked her ass. "I fuckin' love your ass, Eva." Another spank. "Fuckin' you like this? This is every fantasy and every wet dream I've ever had. This ass of yours—" I caressed it, and then spanked it again, harder this time, and she gasped, shrieked, "it's just…fuck, you're perfect."

Another hard spank, accompanied by a hard thrust, and Evangeline screamed. "Keep going, Bax. Talk to me. Fuck me. Spank me."

"You like it when I spank you?" I asked, fucking her faster.

"Yes!"

I spanked. Fucked. "You like it when I spank your big beautiful ass, don't you? You like it when I fuck you from behind, fuck you so hard your ass shakes. Don't you, Eva?"

"Yes! I love it!"

"Say it."

"I love it when you spank my big, beautiful ass," she breathed, thrusting against me, using her fingers to bring herself to orgasm. "I love it when you fuck me from behind. I love it when you make my ass shake. I love it when you spank me while you're fucking me. I love the sting of your spanking. I want you to spank me harder, Bax. Fuck me harder. Come for me."

God, she was dirty. She'd embraced the dirty talk completely, and I was in fucking heaven. Correction: I was fucking Heaven. *She* was Heaven. Hearing her talk that way was…it was my undoing.

I lost all ability to hold back, to keep it under control, to be gentle. I went feral, went wild. I grabbed a fistful of her hip with one hand and spanked her hard, one cheek and then other, as I fucked her. So hard. I fucked her like a madman, and she screamed my name like a banshee and slammed into each thrust, fingering her pussy, and I felt her walls squeezing around me as she came, once, twice, three times, coming and coming and coming around me as I fucked her.

"Eva!" I shouted.

"Fuck me, Bax! Don't stop fucking me!"

Jesus. How was I supposed to—

Nope. Nope.

I canceled out that thought before it had a chance to even finish in my own head.

When the moment of my orgasm came, it was like unleashing everything within me. I came so hard I was dizzy, my vision tunneling, my body spasming. I was buried deep and grinding against the soft warm silk of her ass, trying to fuck deeper and deeper as I bellowed like a bear, both hands clawed into the meat of her ass, pulling those tan round cheeks apart so I could slide deeper, pounding and pounding and pounding, shaking her ass with each thrust, squeezing, jerking her where I wanted her: harder onto my cock.

Finally, after an eternity of ecstasy, I could come

no more, and my cock was going soft.

I let go of Eva, and she collapsed forward onto her belly, gasping raggedly, and I let myself collapse onto her.

"Holy…fucking…shit," I gasped, after a moment.

She laughed. "Yeah, exactly." She blew out a breath, trying to get her breathing under control. "Holy fucking shit."

"I love hearing you swear. Have I mentioned that?"

"I only swear for you, Bax." She pushed against me with her butt. "Lift up a second."

I immediately rolled off her, cursing. "Shit, I'm sorry, I'm probably crushing you."

She flipped to her back and caught me before I could go very far. "No, I just…I mean yeah, you were crushing me, but I wanted you to crush me like this."

She pulled at me, and I gingerly complied, lying down on top of her, front to front, following her guidance. She pressed my face into her pillowy breasts, and wrapped her arms around me, and I slid my arms to cradle her. I could hear her breathing, hear her heart beating.

Long moments of incredible silence followed, in which I felt more comfortable and happy and sated and blissful than I could ever remember feeling.

"Bax?" Her voice was querulous.

"Yeah, babe."

"That was the most incredible thing I've ever felt." She giggled. "I came six times. I counted."

"Six?" I laughed with her. "*Six*? Seriously?"

She laughed, nodding. "Yeah, seriously. Six! I didn't know that was possible." She sounded more sober, then. "I feel like I owe you more orgasms, like I ripped you off."

I let myself rest on her, my face pillowed in the most amazingly soft pair of breasts ever, my arms circled under her shoulders and neck, her fingers sliding through my hair.

"No way, babe. I got the better deal. That was the most intense orgasm of my life. Every time you make me come, it's more intense than the last."

"I still feel like I should give you one more, just to even it out a little."

I laughed. "Well, I'm certainly not gonna stop you, if you feel that way about it."

She giggled again. "I didn't figure you would." She pushed at my shoulder, and I rolled off her. "Go clean up and come back."

I did so, and then came back and lay down on the bed beside her. "What did you have in mind?"

She sat cross-legged beside me, and shrugged a shoulder, which did amazing things to her tits. "I dunno. Maybe just...like the first time I touched you? I enjoyed doing that."

"Whatever you want, babe."

And so she sat beside me, toying with my cock, fondling it. After a few minutes, when I finally started to feel her touch and respond to it, she met my eyes. "Am I...am I a freak? I mean, when you spanked me, it felt *so* good, and I—" she blushed, cutting off. "I just... it felt so amazing, and I wanted more."

I shook my head. "No labels, babe. I don't believe in shit like that. You like what you like, and you never apologize for it to anyone." I met her gaze, putting heat and hardness in my voice. "You got me, Eva?"

She nodded. "I got you." She stroked me, grinning. "I really liked it when you spanked me."

"That does make you a dirty girl, though. Which, in my book, is a damn good thing."

"I *am* a dirty girl." She stared at me as if coming to a decision. "I'm going to admit something to you now, something literally *no one* else knows."

I met her stare steadily. "Okay. Any secret of yours is safe with me."

"I know. That's why I'm telling you this." She sucked in a breath, broke the stare to watch her hand sliding up and down my shaft. "I watch porn. A lot. And I masturbate to it."

I literally choked on my shock. "You watch... porn?"

She nodded, cheeks flaming. "Yes. A lot of it. It's my dirty, shameful secret."

I wanted to laugh, but didn't. "That's the most amazing thing I've ever heard, Eva, for real. I respected you and was attracted to you before, but now? Knowing you get off watching porn? Seriously. That's fuckin' awesome."

"You really think so?"

"You're not ashamed of it, are you?"

She shrugged, and nodded. "Yes."

"Well...don't be." I sucked in a breath as she used both hands to caress me, bringing me closer to the edge. "Be proud of it. What do you watch?"

"All sorts. Blowjobs, anal, hardcore, all that stuff." She shrugged yet again. "It's so fake and so stupid, but I just...I can't stop. I can't get enough."

"So when you had my phone?"

She met my gaze, caressing the tip of my cock with her thumb. "I watched porn on it," she admitted. "I'd planned to just take a few pictures of myself for you to find later, but then I saw some of the nude pictures girls had sent you, and I wondered if you had porn, because I'm probably sort of an addict, honestly. And I found it."

"So when you took half an hour to get dressed, you were...?"

She nodded. "It only took me five minutes to

actually change. The rest of the time I was naked, on my bed, watching porn, and I masturbated. I watched it and I thought of your cock, and I made myself come. And *then* I got dressed."

"And you didn't *tell* me?" I faked outrage. "The hottest shit ever, and you keep it a secret till now?"

"Why is that so hot?"

I laughed. "I've always wished there was a girl out there who liked porn as much as me, but I figured that was a stupid idea."

She had me groaning, now, each slow stroke, hand-over-hand, bringing me closer and closer. "I never thought I'd tell anyone. I thought I'd be too embarrassed."

"Well, don't be embarrassed. It's not shameful. It's normal. You like what you like, and nobody gets any say in what you like or what you do, and nobody gets to tell you how to feel about what you like."

"I'm going to try to adopt that mentality from now on."

"You should. It's important. Your life is your business and no one else's." I growled. "I'm trying to be cool about this, but I'm so fuckin' close, Eva, you don't even know."

"You're about to come?" she asked, and I nodded. "Don't hold back. Don't hold it."

"I don't usually suggest this kind of thing, since

I like to leave it up to the person to decide, but...you mentioned wanting to use your mouth." I exhaled as my hips began to flex out of my control. "This might be a good time to try that."

"I might." She pumped at the base of my cock. "I've been thinking about it. I *am* curious."

"Totally up to you."

She met my eyes momentarily. "I know it is." She nodded. "Okay. I'm going to do it. Hold still, okay?"

"Okay. I will, best I can."

She wrapped both hands around me, angled my cock away from my body, and slowly leaned over me. Her tits brushed against me, and her hair tickled me, and then her lips were touching the crown of my dick.

And holy shit that felt amazing. Soft, wet, silky warmth. Just a kiss, at first. Her hands stroked me, pumping steadily. I felt her tongue, circling around the tip, and then her lips wrapped around the crown, delving the tiniest bit lower, and she suckled, and then backed away, kissing it again. God, so innocent, so clueless, and so amazing. So perfect.

I felt the orgasm bubbling up, and I buried my hands in her hair. "I'm about to come," I warned.

Her eyes lifted to mine, and the sight of her mouth wrapped around the head of my cock was all it took, with her eyes on mine, wide and aroused and pleased and surprised. I focused on holding still and letting her do everything instead of thrusting like I wanted to. Fuck, her mouth was so wet, so warm, and all she was doing was mouthing and kissing the head while stroking the shaft, and it was so perfect.

Heat blasted through me, and I couldn't hold it anymore. "I'm gonna come now, Eva." It hit me like a freight train, and I was helpless to stop it, her mouth sucking at me and her hands soft and slow as they caressed me root to tip, and then as I warned her she kissed the crown, making out with my cock, kissing it, licking with her tongue, bobbing just a little. "Now, Eva! Jesus fuck, I'm coming, god, I'm coming so hard—"

She backed away as I came, and she stroked me slowly through my orgasm, watching as I shot my come up my belly. When I finally finished coming, she licked the last droplet of come off the tip, and then kissed the head again once more, softly, lovingly.

Lifting up, she was a vision of erotic, sensual beauty. She had a drop of come sliding down the back of her hand, which she smeared away with her thumb, and then licked it clean.

"Oh...*wow*," she giggled breathily, eyes gleaming with excitement. "I...I *really* liked doing that."

"You did?"

She nodded. "So much." She eyed me. "Maybe

sometime you can teach me how to give a proper blowjob."

"You want a teacher, babe, I eagerly volunteer for the position. But, just sayin', you don't need teaching. What you just did was...unlike anything I've ever felt, and it was literally, once again, the best thing I've ever felt in my whole fuckin' life."

My phone rang, at that moment.

"That's probably your fight," Eva said.

And just like that, the moment was broken.

EIGHT

Evangeline

HIS PHONE RANG TWICE, THREE TIMES, AND BAXTER just sat on the bed, staring at it, a dark expression I couldn't read clouding his face.

"Aren't you going to answer it?" I asked.

He grumbled unintelligibly, a kind of wordless rumble of displeasure. "Don't wanna."

His phone rang and rang, and then finally stopped, a few seconds later it dinged with a voice-mail alert.

I couldn't help a laugh at the petulance in his voice. "Don't you sort of have to? I mean, you agreed to the fight, so you can't back out now."

"Yeah, but..." His eyes raked over my naked body, hungrily, appreciatively. "I got you here, alone, all to myself. Last thing I want now is to even talk to Moss, let alone head back into town to prep for a stupid fight."

He slid off the bed and went to clean up, then came back.

I felt thoughts and emotions, as yet unformed but still potent, bubbling up inside me as I watched him move across the cabin. "I don't want to leave here, either," I said when he sat back down on the bed.

His gaze met mine. "I hear a 'but' in there," he said, echoing his own words from a few minutes ago.

"But..." I shrugged, and forced the admission out. "But I also kind of want to watch you fight."

He was stunned, his jaw dropping out. "You... *what?*"

I ducked my head and wrapped a tendril of my hair around my index finger. "I want to watch you fight."

"You want to watch me fight?"

I frowned at him. "Is there an echo in here? What aren't you understanding, Baxter?"

He shook his head. "You. Why would you want to watch that shit?"

My stomach was twisting and my heart was

thumping as I forced yet more truth out. "I…I just do. It's—" I sucked in a breath, and then kept going, my words coming out in a rush. "It was kind of hot. A little scary, and kind of gross, but also…hot. I mean, you. You were hot. I didn't even want to admit it to myself then, but I was turned on watching you fight."

He just blinked at me. "You're for real, right now?"

I nodded. "Yes, I am. Is that a problem for you?"

He laughed. "Hell no! I'm just surprised is all. You…you have a way of constantly surprising me."

I crawled off the bed, retrieved his phone, and handed it to him. "Call him back."

Baxter sighed as he listened to the voicemail and then returned the call. "Fine." He put the phone to his ear. "Yo, Moss…a'ight, got it. Yeah, I know the place. See you in a few hours." He hung up and tossed the phone back on the pile of clothing. "Fight's at midnight in a clearing in the forest outside town a ways."

"So you have until midnight?" I asked.

He shook his head. "I gotta get there a little early, plus I have to do a warm-up workout and get a meal in, and it's a good thirty minutes from here to Ketchikan, and another thirty or so from Ketchikan to where the fight is." He reached for me. "But I've got another hour or so."

I squealed as he picked me up and tossed me

onto the bed, laughing helplessly in anticipation and excitement. "So, Mr. Badd. Whatever shall we do for the next hour?"

"I'm gonna eat your pussy again, is what I'm gonna do." He pushed my thighs apart and kissed up from my knee to my core. "And you're gonna scream as loud as you can, and then we're gonna fuck again. And then, maybe, we'll take a shower together and I'll fuck you in the shower." He flicked his tongue teasingly up my slit. "How's that sound to you, Miss du Maurier?"

"It sounds like you need to talk less and lick more, is what it sounds like, Mr. Badd."

He laughed as he buried his face against my core and brought me to a screaming, thrashing orgasm within a matter of minutes, and kept me writhing and screaming and grinding against his face for another orgasm, and a third, until I was trembling and limp and aching, and begging him to stop licking and start fucking.

Which was what he did, sliding a condom on so fast I didn't even see him do it, gliding into me on the cusp of a fourth orgasm.

But this time, instead of fucking me until we came, he stroked into me slowly, in lazy, measured thrusts, taking his time. I clung to him, explored the hard planes of muscle and the taut bubble of his butt and ran my fingers through his hair, and kissed him wherever I could reach, hooking my heels around the backs of his knees and letting him move with me as slowly as he wanted. Which was very, *very* slowly. Deliciously slowly. Achingly slowly. I lost track of time, losing myself in the wonderland of Baxter's cock filling me and stretching me and pleasing me over and over again.

Eventually, he began to move more quickly, grunting heavily as he began to thrust in earnest, and I touched myself as he moved, brought myself to orgasm in synch with his, and he bellowed and I screamed and we writhed in a sweaty tangle of limbs, and he kissed me as he shuddered to the end of his climax, and I couldn't even scream as my own faded, too breathless, too lost in the bliss of our union.

When he finally withdrew from me and discarded the condom, it was fully dark outside. He woke his phone and swore bitterly when he saw the time. "We gotta go, babe."

I moaned in disappointment. "We do?"

He nodded reluctantly. "That was a solid hour there, sweetheart. Gonna have to take a rain check on that shower sex."

And so we cleaned up and finally got dressed, and then Baxter locked up the cabin and we climbed into his truck and drove back toward town. Parking in the alley behind the bar, Baxter hopped out and circled the hood to open my door for me, handing me down. It was then that I discovered something new: an intense soreness between my thighs, requiring me to move gingerly.

Baxter noticed. "Sore, huh?"

I blushed, nodding. "Very."

"I suppose we might have overdone it a little, considering how long it's been for you." He frowned, massaging my lower back as we entered the bar through the kitchen door. "I'm sorry. I should have thought about that."

I shook my head, smiling up at him. "Don't apologize. It's a good sore. Like after a hard workout." I rubbed my thighs together as Baxter paused in the kitchen to steal a cup of french fries from the basket hanging over the fryer. "It's a reminder of...us." I'd been about to say something more explicit, but Xavier bustled into the kitchen at that moment, requiring a last second change in word choice.

Xavier growled as he saw Baxter raiding the fries. "Dude! I need those for an order!"

Baxter just grinned. "Aw come on, buddy, it's just a few fries."

"Which I need for an order that's supposed to go out, like now." With an irritated sigh, Xavier opened a freezer and pulled out a bag, tossing it to Baxter.

"Well, drop another basket for me, at the very least."
He grabbed a paper basket full of chicken tenders
off the warming counter and handed them to him.
"Might as well take these, you damn thief. I'll just
have to drop a whole new order and tell 'em I fucked
up."

After dropping a new basket of fries into the
grease, Baxter took the tenders and slapped Xavier on
the back. "You're the best, bro. And anyway, they're
drunk, so it's not like they'll even notice it took a few
minutes longer than usual."

I followed Baxter out of the kitchen and into
the bar, which was an utter madhouse. People were
packed in wall to wall, standing shoulder to shoulder,
drinks held up out of the way, jostling to get to the
bar to place orders, and dancing to the driving beat of
a song being played by Canaan and Corin.

I pressed my mouth to Baxter's ear. "Wow, it's
crazy in here!"

He laughed, twisting to speak directly into my
ear. "Weekend at Badd's, baby. The boys are crushing
it tonight."

He led me to a booth near the door to the kitch-
en, in view of the service bar, where Lucian was pulling beers and mixing drinks with such efficient speed
it boggled the mind. In the booth were Dru, Mara,
and Claire, a spread of food in front of them and a

bottle of whiskey. Mara, who was pregnant, was sipping sparkling water and munching on a celery stick, while the other two girls were downing a smorgasbord of fried food and sipping whiskey.

He pressed a hand to my lower back, indicating the booth with the others. "I gotta prep for the fight. You cool hanging here with the girls for a bit?"

"Sure, I'll be fine. Do your thing," I said, offering him a smile.

He gave my backside a squeeze and winked at me. "I'll grab you when it's time to go. You need anything or want anything, just ask. It's on the house."

And then he was gone, weaving through the crowd and out the front door. I slid into the booth beside Claire, who scooted over to make room for me.

"Hi," I said. "Hope you don't mind me crashing with you guys for a bit."

Claire quirked an eyebrow at me. "Of course we mind. We're a very snobby and exclusive clique, and you're just not our type, so go away."

I eyed her, trying to decide if she was kidding. "I can sit somewhere else."

Claire burst out laughing, elbowing me in the ribs. "I'm kidding. Jesus." Her eyes raked over me. "You need a drink."

"I do?"

She stood up on the bench, twisting around to

face the service bar. "LUCIAN!" Claire howled. "I NEED A ROCKS GLASS!"

Without missing a beat or even looking up, Lucian snagged a rocks glass, wiggled it in the air, and tossed it to Claire, who caught it and slid back down to her seat.

Claire poured a measure of whiskey into the glass and handed it to me. "You drink whiskey, right?"

I blinked at her. "Um, no?"

"Well, you do now. Drink up, hooker!" Claire raised her own glass and clinked it against mine.

"Hooker?" I asked, sniffing the whiskey. "Why am I a hooker?"

Mara tapped her glass of water against my glass. "It's Claire's favorite term of endearment. It means you're in the cool girls club. If she doesn't insult you, she doesn't like you. If she calls you a hooker and makes fun of you, it means she likes you and has accepted you as her friend."

"Oh."

Dru clinked me next. "Take a drink so you can spill about Bax."

I took a fortifying breath and then sipped at the whiskey gingerly. It burned in my mouth, and burned going down my throat, and burned in my stomach. "Oh my gosh. That's horrible!" I said, coughing and hissing.

Claire stared at me. "Gosh? Did you just...did you just say oh my *gosh?*"

I ducked my head and shrugged. "Yes?"

"Dude. Not okay. You're not six, and none of us are nuns." She lifted her glass to her mouth and threw back a huge gulp. "And you gotta slam it. Big gulps." She grinned at me. "You like to take big ol' swallows, don't you?"

I felt a blush creep over my face. "I...um..."

Mara laughed. "Take it easy on her, Claire, she's new. And she's obviously uncomfortable with your vulgarity."

"Yeah, I can tell. Little miss Eva is rather *proper*," Claire said, faking an arch British accent for the last word. She took the sting out of her words with a grin and an elbow to my ribs. "We can fix that *real* quick, can't we girls?"

"I'm not proper," I said. "I'm just..." All three women just stared at me. "Okay, fine. I'm proper. It's just the way I was raised."

Dru snickered. "Hang with us long enough and you'll forget all that bullshit."

"Baxter is already making inroads on that, I believe," I said. "He seems to take a sort of perverse pride in corrupting me, I think."

Claire snorted. "I'll bet he's making *inroads*. Big, long, hard *inroads*."

I couldn't help the giggle that escaped me. "You're ridiculous," I said.

She wiggled her eyebrows at me. "You didn't deny it, though, I notice."

"Deny what?"

"That you're taking Baxter's *inroads*." She leaned close to me and stage whispered. "By which I mean his dick."

I blinked at her. "Um. We…he and I—I mean." I sank lower in the booth, staring at my whiskey rather than the girls and their eager anticipation. "No, I'm not denying it."

Claire howled in laughter. "HOLY SHIT! She admits it!"

"Well *obviously* she and Bax are fucking," Dru said. "We all saw him honk her ass. He wouldn't honk the ass of a woman he's not fucking."

"He didn't…it wasn't a *honk*," I argued. "It was just a little…squeeze."

Claire reached out and gave my breast a slow, gentle squeeze. "*That's* a little squeeze." Before I could react to or even process the first time, she gave my breast a quick, rough squeeze. "*That* is a honk. He totally honked your ass."

Mara sniggered. "And by *honked her ass* you mean…" She finished the insinuation with a suggestive grin and a wiggle of her eyebrows

Claire choked, trying not to spew whiskey everywhere. "Might be a little soon for anal, even for Baxter, Mara. Little Miss Prim and Proper here probably doesn't go for that shit anyway."

"I'm *not* prim and proper!" I snapped. I took a deep breath and let it out slowly. "And no, we didn't do...*that*."

"If you're not prim and proper, then you'd say you didn't let him fuck you in the ass," Claire noted. "Which isn't what you said."

"Fine, I didn't let him fuck me in the ass," I said, keeping my voice pitched low, despite the volume in the bar. "Which I'm not sure is even possible anyway. He's so big I can barely walk as it is. If he did that, I'd..." I shuddered and shook my head aggressively. "No. No way."

"You gotta work up to anal," Claire said, matter of factly. "Start small. Just his pinky finger at first."

It didn't feel real, to be having this conversation with women I barely knew, to be saying these things out loud. It was a rush, though, exhilarating and fun.

"Have you *seen* the size of his hands?" I demanded.

Claire laughed. "He's a monster, all right. He's got those big ol' football player hands." She leaned into me. "He's a Badd brother, though, and none of them are exactly *small*, you may have noticed."

"I wouldn't know," I said, adopting a prim tone.

"I only just met Baxter, after all."

"Well I meant them as people, not their dicks in particular," Claire said. "Jesus, you are a filthy whore, ain't ya? Plannin' on baggin' more than one of the brothers, huh?"

"No!" I protested. "That's not what I meant!"

Mara shoved my glass into my hands. "Claire has actually probably seen more Badd brother dicks than any of us."

"That was an accident," Claire said.

I took a gulp of the whiskey, and once again it burned all the way down, but now I felt a nice little glow starting in the pit of my stomach. "What was an accident?" I asked.

"Oh, just that Claire has not only obviously gotten up close and personal with Brock's cock, but she's also gotten a nice little gander at Zane's," Mara explained.

"How does that happen by accident? Did you walk in on him in the shower or something?" I took another sip, and didn't even cough afterward.

"If it had been something like that, it would've just been an accidental glance at a soft dick," Mara said. "No, she got the whole shebang, erect and...*in situ*, as it were."

I stared at Claire. "Um. What?"

Claire rolled her eyes dramatically. "It was an

accident. By the time I realized what I was looking at, I was already hooked. I mean, it *is* a hot as fuck video, Mara. You have to admit that much."

Mara shrugged. "Of course it's hot as fuck video, the point is that it was a *private* video."

"Well excuse the hell out of me! We used to go in each other's phones all the time. I didn't know things were different." She shot me a look as she clarified for my sake. "Mara and I have been friends for a long time, and we used to be roommates. We'd check out each other's phones all the time, pull pranks and shit, you know, change each other's home screen photo to something stupid or whatever. Right after she and Zane hooked up for the first time, we met for breakfast and when Mara went to go pee, I thought I'd take a stupid selfie and make it her lock screen, like old times. Well. I took a bunch of selfies and then switched over to the photos app to see which one was best. I was swiping through them, and then *accidentally* swiped too far and this video popped up. It was just this blurry image, so, being curious and not realizing it would be a big deal to her since we used to share that kind of thing with each other anyway, I clicked on it.

"And what do you think I saw? This guy, a super *hot* guy, *by* the way—and a giant cock, hard as a rock, all nice and veiny and pink and lubed up. I mean, I'm a horny-ass bitch, so I watched the video. Which was fucking crazy intense, but the way he groaned her name and shit? And then when he came? Jesus! He shot this giant wet load all over himself, and I swear I nearly came right there in the booth just watching it, and I'd just gotten fucked a dozen ways to Sunday by Brock. Who, I might add, I didn't know was Zane's brother at the time."

"Wow." I squirmed in the bench. "So…wait. You two were both sleeping with Badd brothers at the same time, but you didn't know it?"

"Right. We didn't realize it until later," Mara said.

"When you walked in on me and Brock fucking on our couch." Claire squealed suddenly, pointing at Mara. "Which means you've seen Brock's cock too! We were reverse cowgirl, so there's no way you didn't see at least *part* of his dick."

Mara rolled her eyes. "I was sick as a dog and not really looking that closely."

"Admit it, bitch! You saw!" Claire shrieked.

"Fine! I saw!" Mara slammed her sparkling water as if wishing it was whiskey instead. "But only part of it, and only for a split second."

"But you saw, which means we're even." She wiggled her index finger at Mara. "So I'm not the only Badd brother dick aficionado in the family."

"I saw, like, a couple inches at most. What I really

saw was your stretched-out slut-pussy. Which, for the record, I don't need to see ever again."

Claire cupped her hands over her crotch defensively. "I am *not* stretched out. My shit is tight as a drum. I may have been a slut, but I kept my shit tight. Kegels, bitch. Do your Kegels and you won't get blown-out roast beef pussy even after taking a monster cock." She shot me a wink and a knowing grin. "Which means you better start doing Kegels if you're gonna keep fucking Baxter. Going by the size of his hands, I'm guessing he's got the biggest cock of all the brothers."

"What are Kegels?" I asked.

"Squeezing your PC muscles," Mara answered. "Like when you're holding your pee?"

"Oh. And doing that…" I hesitated a moment, trying out the exercise as I sat in the booth, "it…um, keeps your girl bits from getting stretched out?"

"Works for me, at least" Claire said. "Or maybe I'm just genetically lucky, and my pussy doesn't stretch out that much." She poured more whiskey for everyone and we all took another shot. "So. On a scale from Ballpark Frank to summer squash, with Johnsonville brats being in the middle, how big *is* Bax's dick?"

I took a bracing gulp of whiskey. "Um. I feel weird answering that question."

"None of them are shy, and neither are we. You're in the fucking-a-Badd-brother sisterhood now. I'm not saying you're *obliged* to answer, but it would be in the spirit of the sisterhood to give us at least a *hint*."

"But you're dating his brother," I argued. "Why would you want to know how big his penis is?"

"Because I'm still a dirty whore at heart, and I'm curious. He's a massive guy, so I'm imagining him having this colossal monster of a cock to match."

I bobbed my head side to side. "He's…proportionate all over, how about I just put it that way."

Claire laughed and clapped her hands. "Lucky you, in that case, because the scale of the man is absolutely absurd." She bumped her shoulder against mine. "You walking okay?"

I bit my lip. "Um. I'm…a little sore."

Dru laughed. "Ohhhhh honey, all of us can sympathize with *that*."

Mara nodded, joining in the laughter. "You should see us, some mornings. We're all hobbling around, half-crippled from a night of being plundered by a Badd brother cock."

"Especially when it's been a pounding-me-like-a-jackhammer kinda night," Claire said. "Was it a jackhammer kind of night? I know Brock can get a little carried away sometimes, and I suspect it probably runs in the family."

"It was a little bit of everything kind of night." I covered my face with my hands. "God, I can't believe I'm having this conversation!"

Dru eyed me. "What? You don't talk about sex with your girlfriends back home?"

I shrugged. "I mean, they talk, and I usually just listen." I took another drink. The whiskey was starting to go down more easily now, and I was starting to like it, as I got used to the burn. "It's not like I've ever had anything to add anyway."

Dru's gaze was speculative. "You never had anything to add...because you weren't having sex?"

I shrugged, nodded, and kept my gaze averted. "Pretty much."

"You weren't..." Mara paused to gasp dramatically, her eyes wide. "You weren't a virgin were you?"

"No, but..." I toyed with the glass and stared at the table. "I'm not exactly...very experienced."

Claire laughed, clapping her hands. "Oh man, oh man, oh *man*—you lucky, crazy, ballsy bitch! You go from 'inexperienced'"—she used air quotes, heavily emphasizing the word—"to fucking Baxter Badd? Damn, girl. I mean just...*damn*."

"It has been rather...eye opening," I admitted. "In a lot of ways."

Mara guffawed. "I bet it has! Eye opening...and

pussy opening too, probably!"

"Can we talk about something else, now?" I asked. "My capacity for shockingly blunt and personal conversation is kind of used up at this point."

And just like that, the conversation shifted to more innocuous topics, like which forthcoming movies we were excited to see, and favorite bands, and humorous personal anecdotes. The conversation was always funny, and always vulgar, always filled with jokes and good-natured insults, and the whiskey flowed freely and I ate more greasy fried food than I thought I was capable of, and had more fun than I've ever had with women who felt more like true friends than any of the girls I've known at Yale for three years, some of whom I've also known even longer than that.

I just...clicked with them. Which, in the back of my head and the pit of my heart, set off warning bells.

I ignored them, though, because I was having too much fun.

And then, before I knew it, Baxter was beside me, smelling like sweat and dressed in his fighter trunks and a baggy hoody, with a duffel bag in one hand. "Ready, Eva?"

I stood up, feeling a little wobbly. "Sure am!"

He eyed me, and the nearly empty bottle of whiskey on the table. "I take it the girls have been introducing you to our boy Jack Daniels, huh?" He took my hand and led me out of the bar through the kitchen door to the truck. "Have fun while I was gone?"

"So much fun! The girls are so great, *aaaaaand* I like whiskey." I realized, as I walked, that I was actually rather drunk. "Oh boy. I'm a little more unsteady than I thought I was."

"They are pretty great, and so is whiskey." He opened the passenger door for me. "What'd you talk about?"

"Oh, you know...this and that."

He laughed. "Which means they got the goods on us, I'm guessing?"

"Maybe a little of the goods?" Worry blasted through me. "You're not mad are you? I don't normally...I mean..." I sighed. "Ugh. I'm sorry, Baxter. I said I wouldn't talk about us, and I did anyway"

"It's all good, baby. No worries." Hopping into the driver's seat, Baxter shot me a reassuring grin. "I told you I'm fine with you talking about it if you want. Besides, each of those girls is impossible to resist once they decide they want something. And all together? Shit, you didn't stand a snowball's chance in hell of keeping the details to yourself."

"Only a little bit of the conversation was about that. And it wasn't just me talking, they were all...

rather forthcoming."

The rear passenger door opened, and Zane climbed in. "Hey, Eva. Ready for your first underground fight?"

Once Zane was in, Baxter backed out of the alley and headed for the highway.

"I don't know," I admitted, twisting in the front seat to smile at him. "You're coming too?"

"I'm his second, so to speak," He patted me on the shoulder. "I'll be with you the whole time, so nobody's gonna mess with you."

"Why would anyone mess with me?" I asked.

"Well, it's an illegal fight with illegal betting happening in the middle of nowhere. And, um, are you forgetting how you met Baxter?"

I felt a moment of shock. "Actually, yes, I had. So much has happened since then that I'd sort of blocked it out."

"You blocked it out?" Baxter asked, eyeing me as he drove.

I shrugged. "Yeah. You saved me from anything actually happening." I winked at him. "And you've had me sort of...um...preoccupied." Zane covered a laugh with a cough, and I pivoted to shoot him a look. "I was talking to Mara and Claire, and they shared a pretty interesting story about a certain...video."

He narrowed his eyes at me. "They did, huh?"

"So if you want to laugh at me, I can laugh back."

He chuckled. "I wasn't laughing at you, I was just a little surprised to hear you talking openly about it."

"Yeah, well, between Baxter and the girls, I seem to be doomed to be converted to the rife vulgarity you lot seem to relish so much."

Uncharacteristically for him, Baxter was silent for most of the thirty-minute drive, letting Zane carry the burden of conversation, in which I heard a few stories from Zane's days as a Navy SEAL, and some rather amusing anecdotes about growing up with eight boys in a three-bedroom apartment over a busy bar.

We pulled off the highway onto a narrow two-track road, which wound through the forest. After almost two miles, we started passing cars parked at the edge of a huge field in the middle of the forest, a space about a quarter of a mile wide and the same distance long. There were four huge trucks parked at the corners of a roped-off square, the ropes tied to the brush guards of the mammoth trucks, each of which had oversize knobby tires and LED light bars on their roofs, providing illumination for the makeshift arena.

There were at least five hundred people in attendance, at a rough guess, all milling around the ring. We parked, and Baxter and Zane pushed through the crowd, keeping me between their huge bodies, protecting me from the churn of humanity. There were several tables set up to one side of the ring, from which beer was being sold via several large kegs, frat party style. I also saw bottles of booze, and packs of cigarettes, and several handmade signs offering various strains of marijuana, as well as bags of cocaine and magic mushrooms. There was a long line of port-a-potties along one side of the field, and on the other side, a pair of tents stood in isolation.

Whereas the fight at which I'd first seen Baxter had felt more like an underground industrial rave, this setup felt more like a festival. Except, instead of bands playing music, men were going to beat each other up.

Why was I here, again?

Baxter led the way to the two tents, which as we approached I realized had signs affixed to them, with "Basher" printed on one, and "Juarez" on the other. Two huge, burly men stood to either side of each tent's doorway, and apart from their obvious size and tough, surly demeanor, each man had a gear belt strapped around his waist, equipped with a pistol and mace and other things I couldn't have named, plus earpieces connected to walkie-talkies; their gear made the "SECURITY" logo printed across their chests seem somewhat redundant.

"Armed security guards?" I asked Zane. "At an illegal boxing match?"

Baxter answered for Zane. "This fight in particular is a big deal. Lotta money on it, and some of the
heaviest hitters in the game are here to watch it and
bet on it. These guys are insurance that this shit ain't
gonna get out of hand."

"What would it look like, if things did get out of
hand?"

Baxter hesitated. "Nothing good. The kinda folks
who go to underground fights in remote fields in the
middle of the night ain't exactly the kinda folks who
are all about sunshine and roses, y'know?" He nodded
to one of the security guards. "Yo, Kevin. How are ya,
buddy?"

The guard, a massive black man with a stare like
ice, nodded back. "Bash, my man. Y'boy Moss is in
there, waitin' for you. Go on in."

Baxter indicated me with a jerk of his head.
"She's with me. Nobody gets within five feet of her,
you get me?"

Kevin tipped his head to one side. "And how many
reasons am I getting to keep my eye on your girl?"
Baxter unzipped his duffel bag, reached in, pulled out
a tight roll of money and handed it to Kevin, who
unrolled it and counted it. "That's about enough reasons, I figure. She can watch from one of the corner
trucks."

Which was how I found myself sitting alone in

the bed of a pickup truck. I'd been given a folding beach chair, a red Solo cup of beer, and instructions to stay put, no matter what. Kevin had positioned himself at the tail of the truck, close enough to obviously be there to deter people from approaching me, but still in a position to keep an eye on the crowd.

Zane had gone into the tent with Baxter, saying he'd be out to sit with me once the fights got started; apparently Baxter fighting Juarez was—like real, televised boxing or MMA matches—just the main event, and there would be a few other fights first, between lesser known fighters.

I sipped beer, and when I ran out, Kevin gestured at me and someone else scurried over with a refill.

The first fight was quick, two small, lithe men covered in tattoos bashing each other with fists and feet, one man clearly the superior fighter, making quick work of his opponent to win in a single round. The second fight lasted longer. After two minutes, someone rang a bell and the fighters separated, and a trio of bikini-clad women pranced around the ring, dancing provocatively to music blaring from speakers set up in one of the truck's beds. This went on for a couple minutes, and then the bell rang and the fighters approached each other, and started fighting again; if there was a referee, I never saw him. The second fight went through four rounds, and in between each round the dancing girls danced more and more provocatively, and after the fourth round, the girls started their dance by taking off their bikini tops, to the wild, howling approval of the gathered crowd, which was, obviously, predominantly men. The fight ended midway through the fifth round, with one man knocking the other out with a scything spin kick.

The winner was declared, and the fighters left the ring, and the dancers came back out and resumed their dancing, now topless.

I should have hated this. I should have been mortified, disgusted, and horrified. Not only at the brutality of the fighting, which had featured a lot of blood spraying, but also at the gratuitous nudity of the strippers, not to mention the fact that there clearly wasn't a permit for the alcohol being sold, much less the illegality of the drugs being sold so openly.

The whole business was sordid in the extreme.

And I loved it.

I got a thrill when the fights turned intense, and found myself cheering for one fighter or the other. I even felt an electrifying jolt of morbid fascination when the third and penultimate fight resulted in both fighters getting so gorily bloody that they had to be rinsed off and wiped down between rounds, leaving shimmery, slick, red patches of blood in the trampled grass.

When the third fight finally ended after six punishing, slogging rounds, the strippers/dancers made a lewd, gyrating, provocative show of removing their bikini bottoms—which meant they would be dancing completely nude between the rounds of Baxter's fight.

Which, strangely, didn't bother me...until I began picturing them rubbing themselves all over him, at which point jealousy blasted hot and sudden through me. I stamped it out quickly, refusing to let it gain traction, but it stuck stubbornly in the pit of my belly.

After their dance, the women exited the arena, only to return, as I feared, accompanying Baxter as he approached the ring through a wild, cheering, screaming path through the gathered crowd, which had doubled in size throughout the course of the previous three fights. He was a bona fide local celebrity, it seemed, at least in the underground fighting world, and these plastic-breasted, heavily made-up, spray-tanned strippers were hanging on his arms and bouncing along beside him at each step as he swaggered through the crowd.

He had earbuds in, connected to his cell phone, clutched in his hand. His hoodie was off now, leaving his torso bare, rippling with muscle and gleaming with a sheen of sweat. His hands and forearms were wrapped in white tape from knuckles to mid forearm, and his face was closed down, hardened, focused. He was no longer Baxter, the sweet, confident, crude, thoughtful, attentive, and wildly sexy man I'd spent the last two days with; no, he was Basher now, the primal, brutal fighter, with fists like concrete blocks and abs of marble. His hair was tied back into a small bun, and he'd shaved the sides of his head.

Despite the naked strippers hanging on him, he was utterly focused on his approach to the ring, not even seeming to notice the girls. And, when he got to the ropes, he shrugged them off brusquely, ripped his earbuds out of his ears and tossed them with the phone to Zane, who caught them and stuffed them into his pocket.

Baxter ducked between the ropes and swaggered arrogantly into the center of the ring, raising his taped fists above his head as the crowd began chanting—*Basher! Basher! Basher!* His eyes raked around the crowd, settling on me, perched in my chair in the bed of the pickup truck, and he made a beeline straight for me, ducking back out from beneath the ropes and stomping across the grass to me.

The milling crowd between us parted for him like the Red Sea for Moses, and he reached the side of the truck, palmed the edge of the bed, and vaulted in a single lithe bound into the truck, palmed my face in his big hands, rough and scratchy from the tape. His thumbs grazed my cheekbones, and his lips slanted across mine, claiming a quick, searing kiss from me before leaping back out of the truck as easily as he'd jumped in, returning through the crowd to the ring.

Juarez was waiting for him by then, having entered to little fanfare, without the strippers and without the wild howling and chanting of the crowd, making Baxter easily the favorite.

A man in a three-piece suit entered the ring and stood between the two fighters. "WELCOME TO THE MAIN EVENT!" he boomed in a voice that needed no amplification, silencing the wild audience as he prepared to introduce the fighters. "You all know the boys fighting tonight: Basher, the undefeated and unstoppable face-battering sensation, and Antonio Juarez, hardened veteran of the underground circuit and a tough, proven fighter." He turned to the fighters and addressed them. "We're fighting clean tonight, boys. No gouging, no biting, no bone-breaking, just good clean MMA brutality."

He paused for effect, surveying the crowd, which was growing restless.

"ARE YOU READY!" he bellowed.

To which the crowd promptly went berserk, screaming, some chanting *"Basher!"*, some chanting *"Juarez!"*, most just howling crazily.

The announcer pressed his palms to the chests of the two fighters, pushed them apart, then backed away and chopped his hand downward. "FIGHT!"

And then he exited the ring entirely, and the fight began.

I watched with my heart in my throat, my stomach twisting and fluttering, and excitement bubbling up inside me.

At least, until I felt a ripple of uneasiness flitter through me, prompting me to turn around to glance at the entrance to the field, where I saw four black SUVs and a black limousine enter at a barreling pace.

I didn't know for *sure* who was in that limousine, but the uneasiness in my gut gave me plenty of reason to have my suspicions.

Baxter saw them too, but Juarez was circling him by then, and he had to turn his focus to the fight.

Abruptly, Zane was squatting in the bed of the truck beside me. "Those newcomers look like trouble."

"I think it's my father. Although how they knew about this, or could even find this place I don't even want to know."

"What's the play, here, Evangeline?" Zane eyed me carefully. "Your call."

The crowd around the ring was manic and wild-eyed, pawing at the fighters whenever they inched too close to the ring's ropes. "The crowd looks... unpredictable."

Zane nodded. "Things look like they could get out of hand."

"You have to watch Baxter's back." I felt the heavy hand of loathing pressing in on me. "I always knew they would end up finding me. I have to go."

"Really? Doesn't sound like you want to, though," Zane remarked, eyeing me sidelong.

"I don't. But..." I shrugged.

"It's your life, your choice, Evangeline. Don't let others choose for you."

I sighed. "I wish it was that easy."

He stood up in the truck bed, watching with hawklike eyes as the intensity of the crowd surged, until the air fairly shook with the energy and the volume. "I have to get over to the ring. Kevin's got your back while you're in the truck."

I pushed at his meaty shoulder. "Go. He needs you. I'll be fine."

He eyed me. "You're sure?"

I wasn't, but I kept my doubts to myself. "I'm sure."

Zane hopped down and leaned close to Kevin. "Watch her, man. This shit is getting nuts."

Kevin nodded. "I got it."

And then Zane was gone, vanishing into the

crowd, and I was alone in the truck bed again, and now the SUVs, Mercedes-Benz G-Wagens like my father seemed to favor, were inching toward the back edge of the crowd in a line abreast, with the limousine behind them, pushing the milling, screaming crowd aside to approach me.

Teddy was in the driver's seat of the limousine, and I felt my gut sink the moment his eyes met mine.

My little escapade in Ketchikan, Alaska was over, it seemed.

And I was discovering that my head, my heart, and my body all had very different things to say about that.

Baxter

GODDAMN IT. I KNEW EXACTLY WHO WAS IN THAT LIMO, and judging by the expression on Evangeline's face, so did she. I couldn't do shit about it, though. Juarez was no slouch in the ring, and it was going to take every last ounce of skill and focus I possessed to pull the win out. I'd seen Juarez fight before, and he was one of the few fighters I was even remotely nervous to face. Add in the distraction of Eva and the approaching limo…this could spell trouble.

I had a lot of money riding on this fight, but I also had a lot of emotion invested in Eva. I'd known her, what…two days? Not even—just about twenty-four hours. But the thought of her getting into that stupid, fancy fuckin' limo, possibly to go back to that fuckin' tool Thomas…? That shit burned a hole in my gut.

I didn't want her to go.

I wanted her to stay. I wanted to kiss her again. Make her scream again. I wanted to just…chill with her at the bar, shooting the shit with the gang.

But her life was at Yale and her family was on the East Coast. She was way above my pay grade, destined to marry someone with a net worth I'd never make even if I fought in the big leagues with guys like McGregor, Silva, and Jones. She was destined to marry someone with an Ivy League pedigree, mansions in four states, and the attention of powerful people in Washington. She sure as fuck wasn't gonna spend any more of her time or attention slumming it with some no-name, no-neck brawler from a tiny cruise-ship town like Ketchikan.

I used the angst and anger those thoughts brought boiling up inside me to force my focus onto Juarez, who was testing me with a series of lightning-fast jabs and an even faster left front kick. His footwork was solid, and his defense was tight, and even his test jabs connecting with my shoulder and chest felt like being tapped by an anvil.

I couldn't spare another thought for Eva, not now.

A jab caught me on the chin, sending me backward and making my eyes smart, prompting me to retaliate with my own series of jabs and kicks, most of which Juarez easily turned aside or absorbed without flinching. The first round passed quickly, neither of us winded or bloodied, still testing each other's skills.

Zane was behind me as I rested in one corner, and I glared at him. "You're supposed to be with Eva, you fuckin' tool."

"This crowd is wild, man. Shit could turn in a split second. You need me to watch your back. Juarez has plenty of his own rabid supporters."

"Which is why you need to be with her, not me." I jerked my chin at the lights of the SUVs and the limo. "Especially with that shit about to go down."

"She told me to let her handle it."

"Meaning she's going back with 'em."

He shrugged. "Yep. Her choice, though, man."

I rolled my shoulders, ignoring the thudding bass of the music and the lewd show put on by the strippers. "I don't like it."

"You don't have to."

"I know. Fuck, man, I fuckin' know! But I still don't like it." I watched as the SUVs forced the crowd away so they could form a perimeter around the truck in which Eva was sitting, making way for the limo to approach. "It's bullshit."

"Her family, her life, her choice. She wants to stay, she'll stay. She's a grown-ass woman." He clapped me on the shoulder. "And she's too fucking good for you anyway, bro, and we both know it."

I glared at him. "Yeah, I fuckin' know, Zane, thanks for the reminder." The dancers exited the arena under the aggressive protection of the security team, and the bell rang. "I fuckin' know it, but that don't mean I have to fuckin' like it."

"Win the fight," Zane said, "then bitch about it."

I went out, and I fought Juarez. I forced my attention away from the scene unfolding beyond the crowd, and fended off Juarez's quick fists and quicker feet. He caught me with several lancing blows, making my cheek swell and splitting my lip, but I was the one to draw the first real blood, my left hook ripping open his cheek and a right cross bloodying his nose. He returned the favor almost immediately, though, with a scything, snakebite-fast sidekick I never saw coming, cracking my teeth together, followed by a wicked right jab to break my nose.

It was on, then. We bruised each other through the second round, and then I retreated to my corner to get cleaned up by Moss. By this point, each of the SUVs had disgorged four beefy-looking private bodyguards, the types that wore matching black suits, earpieces, and were armed for sure. They formed a semicircle around the truck, hands crossed in front of them, positioned to watch the curious crowd, which was starting to take notice of the unusual proceedings, distracting some of them from the fight.

"Stay focused, Bax," Moss rumbled to me as he dabbed at my nose. "That shit don't concern you."

"Yes, it fuckin' does."

"Ain't gonna get you your cut if you lose because you're distracted by pussy, even fancy-ass, high-class pussy like that."

"Watch your—" I started to growl.

He cut in impatiently. "Yeah, yeah, watch my fuckin' mouth, I get it. She's special, yada yada yada. Focus on the fight, Bax. Win the fight and then go chase the tail."

I snarled, prepared to curse him out, but the bell rang and I had to go face Juarez for the third round. I wasn't focused, though. Part of my attention kept drifting to Eva, standing in the bed of the truck, a red Solo cup in hand, still dressed in that fine-ass skirt and top she'd put on this morning, which she'd stripped off for me mere hours ago. She was facing the limo, back straight, head up, shoulders squared. Waiting.

Maybe I was reading things into her body language, but it seemed to me like she was preparing to face a firing squad, almost. Going into something she hated but had no control over. Which was fuckin' bullshit, if you asked me, but no one was asking.

I caught a sharp jab off Juarez, which brought my attention back to the fight, and I had to duck and weave and fend off a sudden flurrying onslaught of fast fists, which drove me back against the ropes and put me on the defensive in a way no fighter ever had before. I let the ropes catch me and warded off the punches, watching for an opening. Saw one, a slight hitch in his step as his foot caught a slippery patch of grass, giving me a split second to cut in with a messy but effective jab-cross combo. It put Juarez back on his heels just enough to let me get away from the ropes and the grabbing, pushing hands of the crowd pressed up against the edge of the ring, but then my gaze slipped, just for a second, to Eva.

A tall, stern, swarthy, black-haired man at the far end of middle age stood facing her in an expensive suit. He was speaking to her, and she was arguing back, gesturing angrily. Beside the older man was a younger version, blond hair swept backward, also wearing a full three-piece suit that probably cost more than the Silverado. The younger blond man stepped forward toward Eva, gesturing at the crowd, at the ring, at Juarez and me, and I could almost *taste* the derisive, bitter ridicule he was probably spouting, and

Eva pivoted to face the blond guy—Thomas, I would bet any money—her hands gesturing even more angrily, waving, chopping.

Good girl, Eva, stand up for yourself. Tell those fuckers who's boss.

But then, in the split-second between my gaze flicking back to Juarez and his onrushing left foot and back to Eva, she was hopping down from the truck, refusing her father's hand or Thomas's.

I caught Juarez's kick straight to my belly, knocking the wind out of me.

Eva was walking, shoulders hunched, toward the limo.

FUCK!—the sight of her walking away left me even more wounded than Juarez's kick.

Rage blistered through me, and I gasped through the breathless agony of a cracked rib, twisted aside to dodge a follow-up kick and block a one-two punch combo, accepting a third shot to the cheek in return for an opening, which I took.

One punch, the most brutal I'd ever thrown, with the full force of the red, seething rage boiling inside me.

It caught Juarez on the side of the jaw, spun him around, and he dropped to the ground, out cold.

I wasted no time sprinting across the ring, caught the upper rope and used it to vault myself over, landing on my feet at a dead run. The crowd parted, probably seeing the rage on my face.

As Eva stood waiting for one of the bodyguards to open the limo door for her, Thomas pressed up against her, pinning her to the side of the limo with his body; her father watched impassively as Eva squirmed and slapped at Thomas, trying to get away.

Oh, *hell* no.

The bodyguards saw me coming and formed a barrier between us, one of them reaching into his coat to withdraw a silver pistol. I halted a couple feet away from the line of bodyguards.

"EVA!" I shouted.

I felt a burst of pride when she finally shoved Thomas away with a violent curse, turning to look at me.

"Baxter," she breathed, and moved past Thomas, approaching the line of armed guards, stepping between them to stand inches from me. "Hi."

I was a bloody mess, my nose sluicing blood, my cheek split open, holding my rib cage with one hand. "Eva. You know these tools?"

She gave a half-hearted smile. "I know *that* tool, and *that* tool," she said, pointing at her father and Thomas.

"Evangeline du Maurier! This is unacceptable. Get in the limo, *now*," her father snapped. "No more of this nonsense. I've wasted far too much time and money trying to find you, and I'm not wasting any more."

"You didn't have to waste *any* time or money, Father," Eva said, without turning to look at him. "I came here by choice."

"You ran away like a wayward child, is what you did." Her father stalked over, pushing through the guards, eying me with distaste and disgust. "You're not…*friends*…with this—this *barbarian*, are you?"

"Yes, I ran away like a wayward child…except I'm an *adult*, in case you've forgotten," Eva bit out, her voice betraying her anger.

"We're not discussing this any further, Evangeline. The family vacation is already ruined. You are returning home immediately, and as for your future at Yale? Well…that remains to be seen."

Eva ignored him. "I'm sorry this is happening like this," she said to me.

I ignored the blood dripping off my chin. "Eva, babe. You gotta make your own way in the world. This bullshit?" I jerked my chin at her father. "You don't have to stand for it. You said it, sweetheart—you're not a kid. You don't have to go just because he says so."

She smiled at me sadly. "I always knew I'd be going back, Baxter. I just wanted to get away from it all for

a little bit. Experience a little bit of life away from"—
she waved a hand at the world behind us, broadly,
vaguely—"away from all of their expectations."

I sighed. "Well, I hope you experienced what you
came looking for."

Her smile was quick, hinting at a hidden leer.
"Oh, I certainly found what I...*came*...looking for,
and then some."

"She's got jokes after all," I said, with a sad smile.

"It always had an expiration date, Baxter."

"I know. But it just don't seem like you're the one
choosing when or how. It seems like you're letting
them choose for you."

"My life isn't here. I don't belong in this world."
Her eyes, man. They were...reluctant and hesitant
and confused, like she wasn't sure she was doing the
right thing. "I wish I did."

"Enough, Evangeline." Her father again, stepping between us.

"Back off, pops," I snarled. "The woman's talking
to *me*."

"Not anymore she's not," he said, unperturbed.
"Evangeline. Get in the limo, *now.*"

"Goodbye, Baxter."

"Bye, Eva."

"Thank you." She turned away, waving at me.
"For everything."

A wave? I got a fuckin' wave? Fuck that.

I slid my wrist and forearm under my nose, wiping away the blood, and stepped around her father, grabbed her by the waist and hauled her around. Jerked her up against me and palmed her juicy ass with possessive hands.

"A wave, princess? You think I'm gonna be satisfied with a *wave* goodbye?" I squeezed with both hands. "I do *not* motherfuckin' think so."

"I wish we had time for a...*proper* goodbye," she murmured, subtly pressing back into my touch.

"Me, too," I said, as I lifted a hand to brush my thumb across her delicate cheekbone.

She wiped at my upper lip with her palm, and then leaned in to kiss me, gently, softly, slowly.

I felt something cold touch my temple.

"Back away...*now*," a cold voice snapped, one of the bodyguards.

I lifted my hands, backing away. I twisted in place, and the barrel of the pistol touched the center of my forehead above my eyes. "You put that gun to my head, boy, you better be prepared to pull the fucking trigger." I met the eyes of the hired man, and saw someone who looked plenty willing to call my bluff.

Eva stepped up, pushing the bodyguard and his gun away. "Enough. Enough." She touched the side of my face, and I saw she had blood on her hands where she'd wiped it off me. "I'm going, Baxter. I have to go."

"All right, princess." I lifted my hands palms facing out. "You ever want to get away again, you know where to find me."

Off to one side, Zane was slinking through the crowd, a black semiautomatic pistol in his fist, inching toward me, one hand lifting to cup the bottom of the pistol in an easy, practiced weaver stance. I held my hand out to him, stopping him from rushing the scene and popping all these gorillas where they stood. Knowing Zane, he'd drop them all in ten seconds or less and not have a drop of blood on him, the smooth, deadly fucker.

I watched as Eva climbed into the limo.

The bodyguards remained in place as she slid in, followed by her father, and then Thomas last, who had the audacity to fucking smirk at me in triumph as he swung down into the vehicle. Bastard only had the balls to smirk at me because he had more than a dozen armed men between him and me. Pussy.

Then the bodyguards were climbing into their SUVs and pulling away one by one, leaving me standing alone, hands at my sides, as they drove away with Eva.

Zane appeared beside me. "Well *that* was fun," he said.

"No, it actually wasn't."

"You're just pissed because you didn't get a chance to pop that smarmy blond fucker in the nose."

I didn't feel the humor that normally defined most of my interactions with the world, and my brothers in particular. "No, Zane, I'm pissed because I feel like I just let a one in a million chance slip through my fingers."

His hand rested on my shoulders. "You said your piece, Bax. She chose her path."

"Yeah, well, I feel like she chose wrong."

"Not up to you, brother."

"I know."

"You'll get over her."

I sighed. "I don't know, Zane. This time, I really don't know."

He had no answer for that. All he could do was shrug, eventually, and shove me toward the truck. "Let's go, bro. I got a bottle of Johnny with our names on it." He laughed. "And I do mean that literally."

The black duffel bag full of cash Moss handed me didn't do a damn thing to soothe the ache in my chest, or the cold, heavy, squirm in my belly, which felt an awful lot like the burn of regret, and the sting of loss.

Which was stupid, right?

Zane drove us home, and I stared out the window, trying to figure this shit out.

I barely knew her. We had a little chemistry, had some seriously hot sex, but that was it. I'd had plenty of hot sex with plenty of hot chicks. When the time was up, I went my way, and never felt a single pang of anything as I put a door between me and the girl I'd just fucked. But this was different. Even when the girls had left me, ditching me for an early morning walk of shame out of my apartment in Calgary, I'd watched 'em go without a second thought, knowing there were countless more just like them, waiting for me to pick them up and take them home for a quick fuck and a quicker goodbye.

Somehow, I knew there wasn't anyone else like Evangeline, and that was what made this different.

She was what made this thing we'd shared so different; I didn't have to know her any better or any longer to know that was true.

Wasn't much I could do about it, though, was there? She had, as Zane had pointed out, chosen her path. She'd chosen her life, as I'd always known she would.

I just hadn't thought it would actually cause... you know...shit like feelings when she did.

I was starting to worry that what I meant by *feelings* was something awfully close to *pain*.

We got back to the bar, and I let Zane shove me up to the apartment, let him push a bottle of Johnny into my hand, and I tipped it back and wondered if it was even possible for me to drink enough to forget Evangeline.

I had a feeling it wasn't. I'd tried that once already, with someone else, and discovered, much to the regret of my liver, that it wasn't really possible. The fucking feelings always came back while I was sober, the sneaky little fuckers.

I was gonna try, though, and thank god I lived above a bar. I should warn Sebastian that he'd have to bump up his inventory of scotch until I was over Eva.

It was a week later, I'd won three fights, and had drunk my way through six shifts at the bar. I was currently being shaken into consciousness by Mara on the floor of the foyer of Zane's converted warehouse, seeing triple, and feeling a little pukey.

Mara was standing over me, a bucket in hand. "Baxter, you're a fucking dumpster fire. Why the hell did you have to pick *here* to pass out?"

I rolled onto my back and peered up at the six of her I was seeing. "Mara, heyyyyy." I was feeling strangely articulate considering how wasted as I was. "I'm not sure why I'm here. I don't remember walking here."

She bent awkwardly to set the bucket on the floor beside me, and then straightened slowly, one hand pressed to her swollen, about-to-pop belly. "If you're going to puke, puke in that, okay?"

I nodded sloppily, and grabbed the bucket. "Okay."

She stared down at me, one hand rubbing in a circle on her belly. "Zane says you've been a mess lately."

I nodded again. "I think I'm feeling what some people call regret."

"Eva?"

"She went away. Back to Yale. Buh-bye." I clutched the bucket as nausea pressed against my teeth. "I don't think I wanted her to, though."

"She was really cool."

"The coolest." I fought it back. "Too cool for me."

"That's bullshit. You just came from different worlds, and she had to go back to hers, and you have yours here." She hissed, pressing her hand more firmly against the side of her stomach.

I peered at her in consternation. "It's not time, is it?"

She shook her head, wincing. "I don't think so. Just Braxton-Hicks."

"Whassat?"

"False contractions."

"How d'you know if they're real, then?" The nausea wasn't going away, no matter how hard I tried to ignore it.

I probably shouldn't have had that second bottle of Johnny, but fuck, the stupid feelings wouldn't go away.

She didn't respond for a minute. "Real contractions…they get more intense and closer together with time, and they're evenly spaced. Braxton-Hicks are irregular, and eventually go away."

"Where's Zane?" I asked.

"The bar. Working. Covering for you, actually." Her words were clipped, and even through my drunkenness I could see that she was in serious pain.

"Yeah, I kind of got a little shitty toward the end of the night."

"It's eleven p.m., Baxter."

I laughed. "Oh. Um…oops?" I tried to sit up, and didn't quite manage it, and actually only managed to make myself more nauseous. "It's not every day you deal with heartbreak, after all."

She laughed through a wince. "Heartbreak, Bax? Really?"

I shrugged, which was a mistake, since it only made me more nauseous. "I think so. I'm pretty sure, at least. I mean, I've only felt this way once before, and it ended almost exactly like this. Only, this time it feels even worse. I dunno, I'm not really too...you know, in touch with my feelings and shit."

Oh god.

"And I'm gonna puke." I mumbled the warning, just in time.

I spent the next several minutes purging, which did actually make me feel a good bit better, more clearheaded. Still hammered, but better.

"Oh god, Bax, that's nasty." Mara backed away. "I am *not* dumping that for you."

"Nah, I got it." I made it to my feet, laboriously and unsteadily. "You sit."

I had to move slowly and carefully, using the wall for balance occasionally, but I managed to dump my mess into the toilet, wash my hands, rinse my mouth and make it back to the living room where Mara was sprawled on the couch, hands on her belly, a frown of pained concentration on her face.

She pointed at three bottled waters. "Drink."

"Yes ma'am." I sat at the opposite end of the couch and downed one of the waters, watching Mara fight through visible pain. Worry began to steal through me. "You okay, sis?"

She breathed out shakily. "I don't know, Bax. These aren't going away."

"Ain'tcha supposed to time them or some shit? I saw that on TV once."

She laughed, holding up her phone. "I am. They're every fifteen minutes."

"So…this is it, then, maybe?"

She nodded. "I think so."

"Shit."

"Yeah, shit."

I drank another bottle of water. "You call Zane?"

"Not yet. I want to be sure it's actual labor before I worry him with it. You know how he is."

"Yeah, regular ol' worrywart, that guy." I watched her as she hissed, leaning forward, legs splayed apart, hands clawed around her belly as she fought to breathe through it. "I think maybe you should call him, Mara. I ain't equipped for this shit."

She nodded. "Yeah," she clipped. "In a second."

After a few seconds, she breathed out in relief, and slumped back against the couch.

"This sucks," she said, through grated teeth. "Really, really sucks. I'm gonna kill Zane for putting me through this."

I laughed. "Now you sound like the chick from the TV show I watched."

She snorted. "Thanks." Mara eyed me speculatively. "You mentioned having gone through heartbreak before? Do tell."

I waved a hand. "Nothing interesting. Just some stupid chick I was into."

"Not sure I believe you, but I'll let it slide for the moment." She heaved herself forward, working herself to a position where she could lever herself to her feet, but couldn't quite make it. "I need help. I have to pee. Again."

I refrained from laughing and stumbled to stand in front of her, helping her to her feet. "We're quite a pair tonight, ain't we?"

She waddled to the bathroom, giving me the finger. "Yeah, well, I'm growing a human, you're just wallowing in your own sorrow. At least my excuse is legit."

I sank back down to the couch and let myself drift dizzily. It seemed like Mara was gone for a bit longer than I'd expected, but what do I know about what pregnant women do in the bathroom? Not much, that's for sure.

But then, when it felt like quite a few minutes had passed, I started to worry. "Yo, Mara! You alive in there?" I bellowed.

Silence, and then Mara's voice, thin and pained. "I need help."

I shot to my feet instantly, worry ramping up at the tone of her voice. I made it to the bathroom door in roughly three steps, knocking on it gently. "What's up?"

I heard the knob twist, and the door swung open

inward, revealing Mara on the toilet, a bath towel covering her lap, a puddle of something wet on the floor under her feet.

"Shit," I breathed. "What's going on? Couldn't make it in time?"

She gasped a laugh, despite obvious agonizing pain. "Fuck you, Bax." With one hand she was palming her stomach, and the other was grasping the edge of the bathroom counter in a white-knuckle grip. "My water broke."

"I don't know what that means, but it doesn't sound good."

"It's not." She nodded at her phone, on the counter near her hand. "Call Zane. Tell him."

I handed her the phone and she unlocked it, I dialed Zane, and waited for him to answer. It rang three times and then he answered, the bar ruckus loud in the background.

"What's up, baby?" he yelled. "Busy here."

"Zane, it's me, *baby*," I growled. "I'm at your place and your woman's water just broke."

"The fuck are you doing there, Bax?" he demanded.

"Fuck if I know. I showed up and passed out in your foyer, apparently." I tried a joke. "I go to you in my times of need, brother."

"Her water broke?"

"That's what she says. Looks to me like she pissed on the floor, but what the fuck do I know?"

"I DIDN'T PISS ON THE FLOOR!" Mara yelled. "Give me that, you asshole." She snatched the phone from me. "It's me, Zane. Yes, my water broke, and yes I'm sure. Yes, you need to come get me right the hell now and take me to the hospital…I don't know, he just showed up half an hour ago, hammered, knocking on the door, and then he fell into the foyer and passed out for a minute…yes, Zane, it's *time*, like right the fuck *now*. I need to go to the hospital *right now*, so get your ass home." She hung up, then, hitting the End button and tossing the phone onto the counter.

"What do I do?" I asked.

She reached for my hand. "Help me up." She grabbed at my hands as I held them out to her. "And if you look at me when my pants are down, I'll kill you, and then I'll have Zane kill you."

I stared at the ceiling as I hauled her to her feet. "Hold on to my shoulders if you need to. I won't look." I made a show of clapping my hand over my eyes.

Mara's grip was fierce as she clawed at my shoulder for balance as she struggled to bend enough to get her pants up, and when she was finished she was gasping for breath. "Okay, okay—I'm good." She pushed me out of the bathroom. "Now help me to the truck."

I walked backward, holding on to both of her hands, helping her make her way slowly toward the front door. A contraction hit her halfway there, and she rocked forward into my grip, keening through gritted teeth, her fingers digging into my hands with a force I wouldn't have thought her capable of.

"Fuck, fuck, fuck, this isn't good," she breathed, once it passed. "They're a lot closer together. I'm for real about to have this baby."

Panic rifled through me. "Can you try to at least wait till Zane gets here?"

She barked a bitter laugh. "Yeah, I'll just hold the baby in. No problem."

"Thanks, because that's not something I want to see, you know?"

"Anything for you, dear brother," she said, faking a simpering niceness. "Just help me to the goddamn truck."

We made it to the truck, and I helped her up into the passenger seat. She dug the keys out of her purse and tossed them to me before I closed the door.

"Drive," she barked. "Hospital. I have to—I have to get to the hospital."

"Hell, no," I snapped back. "I'm still drunk. I'm not drunk-driving my brother's pregnant wife fucking *any*where."

"Then get ready to help me deliver your nephew."

"It's a boy?"

"That's what they're telling me. Zane wanted it to be a surprise, though, so don't mention it." She eyed me. "You really can't drive right now?"

"Mara, this is me doing you a favor. I could *probably* make it safely, but I ain't taking that chance. If it was my life I was gambling with, maybe. This is you, and that baby you're baking." I shook my head and shrugged. "So, no, babe. I can't drive. Sorry."

She exhaled shakily. "Shit." She dialed Zane and held the phone to her ear for a minute, and then ended the call, cursing when he didn't pick up. "Must be driving." She twisted sideways and started sliding out of the truck. "Help me into the back seat. I need to lay down."

I helped her out and then into the back seat, laying her down across it. Her hands were on her belly, her head resting on her purse. "Think about holding that sucker in, Mara. No baby time until Zane gets here."

"Don't call my baby a fucker, you fucker!" she shrieked, as another contraction hit her, faster than the last one.

This shit was happening fucking *fast*.

"Sucker! I said SUCKER, with an S. Jesus. Chill."

She lifted up on her elbows to glare at me. "Do NOT tell a woman in fucking labor to fucking *chill*,

Baxter Badd."

"Sorry, sorry. This is just really intense, you know?"

Mara screamed incoherently in blind rage. "It's intense for *you*? *I'm* the one in labor!" She screamed again, in pain this time. "GODDAMMIT ZANE! WHERE THE FUCK ARE YOU?"

A motorcycle appeared at that moment down the street, approaching at a recklessly fast pace, squealing to a dramatic, skidding stop beside the truck. Zane hopped off, no helmet and windblown, panic on his features.

"Mara?" he called out, not even seeing either of us, as we were on the other side of the truck and he was jogging toward the front door.

"Over here, dipshit," I shouted. "In the truck."

He pivoted and ran for the open door of the truck, reaching for Mara. "Baby! You okay?"

'NO! I'm not fucking *okay!*" Mara screamed. "I'm about to have this baby *right now*, and your stupid brother is too drunk to drive me to the hospital and you weren't here!"

"I'm here now," he crooned, his voice calm. "I'm here now. Let's go, okay? I'll get you there." He shot a look at me. "Get in, Bax."

"Why me?" I asked, my drunk mouth running away from my brain or better sense.

"Because you're about to be an uncle and you should be there, fucker." He hopped into the driver's seat, twisted the ignition, and backed out the second the rest of the doors were closed. "And also because I'm about to be a daddy, and I'm scared out of my fucking mind, and I fucking need you, okay?"

I stared at him as he drove, both hands on the wheel, maneuvering aggressively toward the hospital. "You're *scared*? Haven't you, like, been in a billion firefights?"

"Yep, and that shit is nothing compared to this, Bax." He twisted the wheel in his fists. "Thanks for being there to help her."

"I didn't do much," I argued. "Just helped her move around."

"Well, still, good thing you stumbled your stupid drunk ass to my house, or she'd have been alone."

I grunted and waved a hand in dismissal. "She's family, bro."

We made it to the hospital in record time, got Mara checked into the labor and delivery ward and attended to by a physician—who determined that she'd have the baby relatively soon, but didn't elaborate on what that meant—and then Zane had me call Bast and the others, to spread the word about the impending arrival of the first Baby Badd.

Which, Jesus, that was weird to think about:

a baby. In a matter of something like hours, there would be a brand-new human being that hadn't existed before. Like, how did that make any damn sense? How could two people fucking create a new person? I got a little dizzy thinking about it, and turned to Zane as we sat in the room with Mara, who was connected to a shitload of wires and monitors, chomping on ice chips and glaring at everything that moved.

"Yo, Zane," I said, and he glanced at me with a grunt. "I been thinkin', and I think I sort of understand how you're scared about this."

He quirked an eyebrow at me. "How do you figure?"

I tipped my head to one side. "Well, I mean, until now it's been sort of a mental thing, Mara being pregnant. I mean, we all saw the ultrasound pictures and shit, and her belly has been getting bigger, but now that she's in labor, it's like...there's about to be a totally new fuckin' person in the world"—I gestured to him and then at Mara—"who you two created. Which is just...it makes me dizzy just thinkin' about it."

Zane clapped me on the shoulder. "Exactly. Now multiply that by a million, and add in the reality that *you* are personally responsible for that brand-new person. Like, it's your responsibility to not only make sure the little person doesn't like die or whatever, but also grows up to become a halfway decent person."

He let out a rough sigh. "Makes me wish Mom and Dad were around still, so I could let them know how much more I appreciate them."

I nodded. "Yeah, man. I hear that." I blinked hard against the weird bucket of emotions I was suddenly feeling. "Funny thing is, it's getting harder every year to even remember Mom."

"I know what you mean. I have a handful of memories, but even those are a little fuzzy, these days," Zane said.

"JESUS FUCK!" Mara howled. "You two have to pick fucking *now* to get all maudlin on me?"

I eyed her warily. "Wow. You're really in quite a mood, Mara."

Her eyes widened to unsafe dimensions, and she began physically trying to clamber out of the bed to get at me, screaming in what seemed to be equal parts demented, hormonal rage and vicious agony, requiring Zane to rush to her side and gentle her back to the bed.

"Bax," he said, glancing at me, "I think you best get a handle on that runaway mouth of yours, bub, or Mara might just actually murder you."

Mara hurled an ice chip at me, and it hit me on the forehead with such force I actually recoiled in surprise. "You're a fucking asshole, Baxter Badd! I fucking HATE YOU!" And then, confusingly, she immediately calmed, stuffed an ice chip into her mouth, and pointed at me with an index finger. "The heartbreak story. Spill. Now."

I thunked my head against the wall behind me, groaning. "Dude. It's nothing."

"Dude, humor the pregnant lady," Mara said. "I'm between contractions and I need a distraction."

Zane shifted his chair so he could hold Mara's hand and look at me at the same time.

I tipped back in the chair so I was balanced on the rear legs, my feet propped on the foot of Mara's hospital bed. "Fine. But this shit stays between us. I got a rep to uphold."

"That's why I'm so interested," Mara said. "Everything I've heard and seen about you says you are now and always have been a Hook-up Harry. I didn't think you'd ever had a real relationship."

"I'm your own fuckin' brother," Zane added, "and I've always been under the same impression. What heartbreak are we talking about here?"

I let out a breath, and spent a moment organizing my thoughts, which was a difficult process now that I was sobering up and entering the wicked headache stage of going directly from wasted into hangover, without the intervening sleep.

"It's not that complicated, or some big secret," I said. "Like you said, I've always been more into one-night stands and the occasional repeat hookup if the chick was bangin' enough and the sex was good enough. But once they got clingy or started wanting to, like, discuss feelings and what we are and shit, bam, that was it. I was always honest about that from the get-go, too. I was focused on my career, and had no interest in or time for bullshit like relationships, and I always, *always* made it clear from the start that it was gonna be no-strings sex. Which worked pretty damn well all through college and the first year I was in Calgary playing for the Stampeders.

"Then, during the off-season after that first year, I met this chick. A reporter, actually. Some minor local paper wanted to do a feature on me, since I'd made some pretty high-profile plays that season, and I was a new face in the town. Not a big deal, just a couple paragraphs about me and some photos on the front page of a Calgary paper. But the girl who did the interview was fuckin'…she was *hot*, man. Really cool, really chill, classy, easy to talk to. The interview should have been like twenty or thirty minutes, but we ended up having a two-hour lunch, just talking. She knew football, and there was something cool and hot about talking stats and plays and shit with a chick. She was the one who called me a week after the feature aired, actually, asking if I wanted to get lunch again, but on a personal level, not for an interview.

Like, a real date, she said. I was interested, since we'd hit it off without fucking first, which was weird, so I said yes."

Zane snorted. "You make it sound like talking to a woman outside the pursuit of sex is this weird, unheard of thing."

I laughed. "It kind of is, for me. Women were never much more than a distraction for me, you know? Like, I fuck because I'm a guy and I like to fuck, and women are fantastic and I love them, because tits and ass, and that's about it. And yeah, I know, that's macho, asshole, chauvinistic bullshit. But I do actually know women are more than just sex receptacles, okay? I do, I swear."

"Sure you do," Mara said, sarcasm dripping from her voice.

And then her hands tightened on Zane as another contraction hit her, and she grunted through it, and the grunt devolved into a forward-leaning, teeth-gritting scream, and Zane held her hand through it, murmuring something in a soothing voice, which I couldn't make out. After a few seconds, the contraction passed, and she flopped back against the pillows, sweating.

"I'm   seriously…fucking   pissed…my   water broke…before I could get…a fucking…epidural," she said, between gasps for breath. "Keep talking, Bax."

"Okay, so. We go to lunch, and it's cool, like the first time. We spend an hour and a half talking over coffee and croissants, and I'm super into the chick, and she seems to be super into me. Cool, right? Well, we do lunch a few more times over the next few weeks—and for the record, she's the only person I've ever actually truly dated, especially *before* we had sex. I've gone on a few single dates, and I take girls out if we're hooking up on a regular basis. Like, in college I had a roster of girls I was hooking up with, always no-strings, no commitments, no questions, and every once in a while we'd have dinner or see a flick together just for a change of pace from the fucking."

Zane chuckled. "What a gentleman."

I shrugged. "Eh, I've never claimed to be a gentleman." I felt uncomfortable and squirmy relating this story, especially as I got into the real meat of it. "So this girl, Lauren, was every bit as wicked awesome in bed as she was out of it. We had a seriously great time. I never had the talk with her about it being no-strings and we also never defined what it was, but we went out regularly and I just, without even thinking about it, kept sex confined to her. A week, two weeks, then suddenly it was three months and I'd kept it strict, only fucking her, and I only went out with her, and we were seeing each other a couple times a week, and I started to realize I was for real into her. Like with emotions and shit. We still hadn't talked about it, but it was pretty obvious this thing was...a *thing*."

Another contraction hit, and I paused as Mara growled through it, crushing Zane's hand and the bed railing. The physician came in at that moment, and I had to leave so he could check her. I'd only been in the waiting room a few minutes when Zane popped his head in.

"It's happening soon, bro." He scrubbed his hands over his head, his eyes wide. "Where's everyone else?"

All the brothers, Dru, and Claire all filed in right then.

"What's the word, Big Poppa?" This was Corin. "You got a baby yet or what?"

Zane was as close to a nervous breakdown as I'd ever seen him, pacing crazily, hands running obsessively through his hair. "She's about to have the baby, like any time now. He said she's fully dilated and almost fully effaced, so she should be ready to push any minute."

Claire headed for the door. "I need to see her."

Zane nodded. "Yeah, she's asking for you." He glanced at Dru. "You too. She wants you both there with her."

Dru just blinked. "She...she wants *me*? While she's having the baby?"

Zane pushed past Claire, leading the way to the room, addressing Dru over his shoulder. "Of course she does, dumbass. You're part of the family." He paused, popping back in to sweep his manic gaze across the rest of us. "Next time you see me, boys, I'm gonna be a daddy. So, like, say some prayers or whatever."

And so we waited, the seven of us taking up most of the waiting room, none of us really talking.

A hand shook me, waking me from a doze I hadn't realized I'd fallen into. "Wha—? Whassat?"

Zane was standing over me. And, for the first time since Mom's death, a Badd male had tears in his eyes. Even when Dad had died, none of us had openly cried, at least not around each other. I know I'd shed a couple tears in private, after a few bottles of Jack, but that had been literally alone in a dark closet at four in the morning in my Calgary apartment.

He wasn't bawling, but he had tear tracks on his cheeks, and more tears glinting in the corners of his eyes. "Bax, brother." He collapsed into the chair beside me. "I'm a father."

The others, all of whom had dozed off in the couple of hours we'd been waiting, all sat up.

"She had the baby?" Xavier lurched out of his seat. "Can we see him?"

Zane nodded. "Yeah. There's a lot of us, so the doctor said it would be best to do the visits in batches." He pointed as he named us, "Bast, Brock, Bax, you guys first. It's easiest to just go in order of age."

Xavier slumped back into the chair. "Being the youngest fucking sucks."

Zane jogged across the room and scooped Xavier into a playful headlock. "Xavier, buddy, you'll get a turn," he said, "I promise."

Xavier wriggled out of the hold with unexpected ease. "I know, I know. But we always do this shit in order from oldest to youngest, which means whatever it is, I'm always last."

Bast spoke up. "You go first, Xavier. I'll wait."

None of the others argued, so Brock, Xavier, and I followed Zane, who led us to the delivery room. Mara was in a chair, sniffling and crying what I assumed were happy tears, and Claire was on her feet, her arms curled around a blanket-swaddled bundle, bouncing her arms gently and rocking side to side. She glanced up as we entered, and she was crying too, which was almost as weird as Zane crying, because Claire was, in some ways, the toughest chick I knew.

Like a bunch of idiot kids, Brock and Xavier and I all crowded around Claire, jostling to get a look at our new nephew. Brock and I glanced at each other, an unspoken conversation passing between us, and we backed up a little to give Xavier space to be the first to hold him.

Claire, with the softest expression I'd ever seen on her face, smiled at Xavier. "Wanna hold him?" she glanced at Mara. "That okay?"

Mara was a goddamn disaster: her hair was a wild, greasy, sweaty mess, the makeup she'd put on the day before was smeared and running, and tears were dried on her face, but she'd never looked so... beautifully happy. I mean, you always hear about a new mother "glowing" which had always sounded stupid to me, but as I glanced at Mara, I finally understood it. She really was just...glowing. Not an actual literal glow, since she wasn't, like, radioactive, thank god, but just...glowing from the inside out. There really wasn't a better term for it, either. Just glowing.

"Of course," Mara said, sounding utterly exhausted but happy.

It was kind of weird to see her belly flat again, after so many months of watching it steadily grow.

Claire gingerly handed the bundle of baby over, and Xavier gathered him into his arms with an ease I would never have expected.

"You've held a baby before," Mara noted.

Xavier was bouncing much like Claire had been,

and nodded, glancing up at Mara with a brilliant grin on his face. "Yeah. My buddy Hajj's daughter had a baby last year. Hajj doesn't have a driver's license, so I drove him to the hospital, and I got to hold his grand-daughter." He cooed wordlessly at the baby, smiling goofily, making weird noises. "What's his name?"

Mara smiled. "Jackson. We've been calling him Jax."

"You're a couple hours old and you've already got a nickname, kid," Xavier said. "I've never had a nickname, since it's kind of hard to abbreviate or fore-shorten a name like Xavier."

He looked up at Mara and then Zane.

"Hey, it looks like he's got Mom's eyes!" he ex-claimed. "Another Badd with green eyes!"

"They could change over the next few months," Mara explained, "but they *do* look green to me too." She smiled. "Of course, it wouldn't be *that* weird for him to have green eyes, since I have them and you guys have green eyes as a recessive gene from your mom."

"That's true. But still, it's cool to see green eyes on another Badd." Xavier leaned close and did some-thing adorable and obnoxious with his nose to the baby, an Eskimo kiss or whatever it is you call it when you brush noses with someone. "Hey there, Jax. Welcome to life."

Xavier stared at Jackson Badd for a few more moments, just blinking and smiling and bouncing, and then he spoke again, but in the tone of voice of someone reciting poetry:

"When you were born, beloved, was your soul
New made by God to match your body's flower,
And were they both at one same precious hour
Sent forth from heaven as a perfect whole?
Or had your soul since dim creation burned,
A star in some still region of the sky,
That leaping earthward, left its place on high
And to your little new-born body yearned?
No words can tell in what celestial hour
God made your soul and gave it mortal birth,
Nor in the disarray of all the stars
Is any place so sweet that such a flower
Might linger there until thro heaven's bars,
It heard God's voice that bade it down to earth."

Everyone was staring at him again, as we had a tendency to do when he started spouting poetry.

He shrugged. "What? It's a poem by Sara Teasdale."

Brock chuckled. "And Sara Teasdale is…?"

"An American poet, born August eighth, 1884 and died January twenty-ninth, 1933. The poem is called 'Soul's Birth'."

"That's a very beautiful poem, Xavier," Mara said. "Thank you."

He didn't look up. "I didn't write it, I just quoted it. It seemed apropos for this momentous occasion."

I laughed. "Holy shit, Xavier. You are one of a kind, brother."

He blinked at me. "What? Why?"

I shook my head. "Never mind, kiddo."

The baby went to Brock next, who seemed fairly comfortable holding the baby, and spent a few minutes doing the bounce and rock thing, and making the stupid cooing noises everyone seemed unable to resist.

When it was my turn and Brock turned to me and moved to hand the bundle into my arms, I panicked. "Wait, wait, wait. What if I fuck it up somehow?" I backed away. "You probably shouldn't trust me with a baby, I might…I dunno, do something wrong."

Zane took Jax from Brock and moved to stand in front of me. "Bax, brother, you are an idiot. I love you, seriously, but you're an idiot."

I gaped at him. "I know, but…why are you reminding me of this?"

"Because you're not the fuck-up you seem to think you are." He pressed the child into my arms, and somehow my body seemed to take over on autopilot, immediately cradling the tiny, fragile, warm bundle. "You're a good person, a good brother, and you'll be a great uncle."

I stared down at the baby. He was...well, he looked kind of ugly to me. Squishy and wrinkled, and unhappy. His bright eyes were indeed green, staring back up at me like a freaky little alien. Cute, though. Irresistible.

I couldn't help the grin that stole over me. "Yo, Jax, buddy, what up?" I intentionally used a normal voice, even a little deeper and gruffer than usual, just to make a point. "I'm your favorite uncle, okay? Let's just get that squared away now, so there's no confusion later."

"Nah, man," Brock cut in. "*I'm* his favorite uncle."

Mara laughed. "I think he's bound to have seven favorite uncles." She let out an exhausted sigh. "Let's get the others in here so I can sleep."

Brock, Xavier, Claire, and Dru all filed out, and I finally handed Jax back to his mom.

"He's an ugly little shit right now," I quipped, "but I think he'll grow into his looks eventually."

Mara shook her head at me, laughing softly. "Asshole." Her eyes met mine. "Real quick, finish your story. What happened with Lauren?"

I groaned and rubbed my face with both hands. "Eh. We...dated, I guess you could call it, for four months. Then one day she came over after a date and sat me down and said she wanted to see other people. Which was really great timing because I was literally moments from telling her I liked her a lot and wanted to be clear about the fact that we were dating each other exclusively. I wasn't, like, about to profess love or some shit, but it was a big fuckin' deal to me to say even that much, and she beat me to the punch by dumping me."

"That sucks," Zane said.

I snorted. "Yeah. What was worse was when I asked her why."

"What was her answer?"

"That I didn't challenge her intellectually. She had fun with me and I was really great at sex, she said, but she wanted to date someone who provided more academic and creative stimuli—her words, there, not mine." I sighed, remembering how that had felt.

"Damn, dude, that's fucking harsh," Zane said.

"For real," Mara added. "What a bitch."

"I know, right?" I tried a grin, and mostly managed. "She got one more jab in before she left. She said, and I quote, 'We're just from different worlds, you and I, and you just don't fit into mine. I know it's not your fault, but it's just not something I can move past.'"

Zane and Mara exchanged meaningful glances.

"Thus the reason you let Eva go so easily," Mara said.

"That shit was *not* fuckin' easy," I snapped. "I let her go because I didn't have a fuckin' choice."

Zane nodded, and then shrugged, in a *yeah, but* sort of gesture. "And because you were scared she was gonna repeat history on you, with the shit about being from different worlds."

I chuckled bitterly. "No shit. Eva actually did say pretty much that more than once. Not in a mean way, just…stating the facts that we were from different worlds and had totally different lives, and thus the little tryst we were having came with a built-in expiration date."

"Oh," Mara said, "well that explains it."

"She never made me feel…stupid, not like Lauren did. But she made it pretty damn clear we weren't on the same level." I shrugged. "I was sexual education for her. A little walk on the wild side with a bad boy, and then she went back to her comfy little life on the East Coast with her Ivy League friends and her Ivy League wanna-be boyfriend."

Zane eyed me. "You're still hung up on her."

"Sure, maybe." I stood up and stretched, and then headed for the door. "Fat fuckin' lot of good it does me, though. Whatever. It's done."

"Bax—" Mara started.

"You just had a baby, sis, you don't need to worry about my bullshit. I'm a blockheaded caveman. I'll be fine." I grinned at them both. "Congrats, the both of you: you made a human! Now just don't fuck him up."

And with that, I left, letting the rest of my brothers have their turn.

TEN

Evangeline

Two weeks. It had only been two weeks, but it felt like it had been a year since I'd been brought back from Alaska...but then, at the same time, the two weeks had passed by so fast I'd barely had time to breathe.

Father had made it clear in no uncertain terms that I had to toe the line or he'd cut me off entirely. That meant focusing in on the poli-sci degree and abandoning my art studies. That meant taking the internship he set up for me. That meant, as well, agreeing to let Thomas "court" me, as Father put it. Meaning marry him, or else.

If I wanted to retain any semblance of my life, I had to do what he wanted. And what he wanted, more than anything, was for Thomas to take his place as Father's right-hand man in everything, be the son he'd always wanted and take over the company, for Thomas to get his seat in Congress so he could perform tactical political machinations behind the scenes on Father's behalf. My place in all that was to be the trophy wife. The arm candy. The perfect accessory to show around at parties and organize fund-raisers.

You bet your ass I was angry about all that…but my back was to the wall. I'd managed to put Father off for a while, saying I needed some time, but finally he'd sent Teddy to collect me from my dorm room, bringing me to his home office.

Which was where I stood at the current moment: outside his office door, nerves jangling—being summoned to Father's office wasn't a good sign. Not at all. I'd only been summoned there once before, when I'd totaled the first car he'd bought me, three months after my sixteenth birthday.

Teddy, towering beside me, knocked on the door, and then when Father called out a stern "Enter," Teddy pushed open the door and ushered me in.

Father tapped at his slim laptop as I approached his enormous battleship of a desk, and then when I remained standing instead of sitting in one of the leather armchairs, he closed the lid of the laptop and eyed me with dark-eyed scrutiny.

"Evangeline," he murmured. "Sit."

"I'm fine," I said. "I have things to do, so say what you want to say and be done with it."

"You'll sit, and you'll listen, and you'll obey," he barked.

I raised an eyebrow at him. "I'm neither an employee of yours, nor am I a child. You don't get to talk to me like that, Dad."

He quirked an eyebrow back at me: I'd never, *ever* called him "Dad" in my life. He liked to pretend we were haughty eighteenth-century aristocrats, and I'd just fallen into the habit of calling him "Father." Me using the more familiar term was a break in tradition, and one I hoped would put across the point that I wasn't going to stand for his nonsense any longer.

"I am your father, and I'll speak to you however I wish."

I crossed my arms over my breasts and glared at him. "If you want this to be…what's that term your idiotic politics people use…a productive dialogue… then you'll, you know, enter the fucking twenty-first century and realize you *don't* actually get to talk me like that. Speak respectfully or shut the fuck up."

He rocketed out of his chair, outrage on his face. "Evangeline du Maurier! What in the *world* has gotten into you?"

"You're trying to railroad me, and I won't have it."

"I'm forcing you to see sense."

"Maybe I don't *want* to see sense, though. What then?"

"I've tolerated your pigheadedness long enough," he bit out, leaning onto his desk, "and now it's high time you accept the instructions put in front of you by those who have your best interests in mind."

"The only person who has my best interests in mind is me," I shot back. "You have *your* best interests in mind, and Thomas's. You don't give a damn about what I want."

"You don't even know what you want, nor how to get it. You think you want to do *art,* and run off and have empty-headed little *adventures* with barbaric and unsavory roughnecks. You claim you're not a child, but your actions prove otherwise. I've given you rein this long, hoping you'd eventually grow up and see things with a more clear-minded and adult reasoning, but it seems I'm mistaken." He sat down again, reached into a drawer of his desk, and produced a manila folder. He opened it, spreading out several sheets of paper, twisted them to let me read them, and then let a smirk of triumph steal over his lips.

One glance was enough for me to know what he

was presenting me with a trump card, and I sank into the chair. "Dammit."

"Feeling rather vulgar, today, aren't you?" He tapped the topmost printout, a copy of my private bank account statement. "I've allowed this, thus far. No longer."

Allowed.

Allowed?

I glanced at him. "You knew?"

He snorted. "Of course I knew, idiot child. You think you can steal money from me and I won't notice? You weren't even very clever about it, honestly. It was money I gave you as an allowance, and for the most part you didn't really even *do* anything with it, so I let it be. And I kept my knowledge of it to myself, as kind of...ace in the hole, so to speak, in case you ever became rebellious." His smirk widened into a shit-eating grin. "You don't get to where I am by being naive or foolish, Evangeline."

I sighed, leaning back in the chair in defeat. "So... what now?"

He gathered the papers and rested his elbows on the desk, steepling his fingers. "I'm good friends with the president of this bank, so I've taken control of the account."

I sat forward, protesting. "I'm an adult and I opened that account myself! You can't do that!"

"You opened it with funds that were, technically, stolen."

"I didn't steal it! You gave it to me as an allowance, and I simply moved it to a different account."

He sighed. "Evangeline," he murmured condescendingly, "it's *my* money. *I* gave it to you, and I can take it back at my convenience. Arguing is futile." He slid one of the printouts to me, which showed that he'd shunted all the funds, except for five thousand dollars, into his own account, and named himself as the primary account holder, with me as a secondary account holder with only provisional access. "This is your new reality, my dear. That's what I leave you with, and it is all you will get. Unless…"

"Unless what?" I demanded.

He shrugged. "The same terms I laid out when I first retrieved you from the clutches of that…that *redneck,* in *Alaska,* of all places." He tapped his fingertip on the desk as he enumerated each item. "First, you finish your degree at Yale in political science, abdicating all pretension to your artistic frippery. Obviously, once you've gotten your degree and you've performed the second item I shall be naming shortly, you can pursue art all you wish, on your own time, as your husband allows.

"The second item, then, obviously, is to marry Thomas." He paused for effect. "Soon. All the arrangements have already been made. The church, the dress, the cake, the invitations to all the proper people, it's all been taken care of already. All you have to do is show up, say 'I do', and become Mrs. Evangeline Haverton, as has always been your destiny."

"My destiny." I went faint at his words. "And once I've done that, then what?"

"Then you receive your due portion of my estate."

"My...due portion?" I frowned at him, perplexed.

He nodded. "Yes, your due portion."

"I'm your only legitimate heir, Dad. Who else is there to receive a portion?"

"That is none of your concern."

I stared hard at him. "Thomas. You're giving most of it to Thomas, aren't you? You're just giving me a little...dowry, or whatever you want to call it."

"You're hardly being reasonable, Evangeline," he simpered. "You'll be living in the greatest of luxury. Thomas is wealthy in his own right, as well as being heir to a rather large fortune from Richard. And with some of the deals I have in process, Thomas is poised to become even more wealthy and even more influential. You'll want for nothing; you've *never* wanted for anything." He waved a hand in gesticulation. "Think of Thomas, of his looks, his charisma, and his current political influence, and he's only thirty! He could very well be president in a few years. Think of it! He could, feasibly, become the youngest president in history. Folks on the Hill are already talking about him for the next ticket. And you...*you* would be his wife. First Lady Evangeline Haverton. How does that sound?"

I sat back, never having realized the scope of Father's ambition. He wouldn't be president himself, but...that was never Father's way—he preferred to machinate in the background. Apply pressure subtly, wielding power from the shadows. He makes Thomas president, and then he's the puppet-master, with the power of the entire country at his fingertips.

But they needed me, for appearances. If I refused, they'd find someone else suitable, but still... they wanted me as their first and primary choice.

I was their pawn, a puppet. A tool.

I heard a certain gravelly, caustic voice in my head, then. *Nothin' but a tool, princess—that's all you ever will be to those fuckers.* He'd never actually said that, but it's what he would say, if given the chance.

Father chose a third printout from the folder, spun it around to face me, and tapped it with a fingertip. "In case you still have a little rebelliousness left in you, I think that may provide additional...impetus, shall we say, to concede. He seems to be the only thing you've ever shown any real interest in, besides your art."

It was part of a dossier on Baxter. Basically, it was a threat. Father could make one call, an email, even, if he was feeling lazy, and Baxter would be detained. Indefinitely. The underground fighting would be the way they picked him up, but then he would essentially just disappear into the system. At the very least, he would be arrested, and left with a permanent record.

I had nothing, no leverage, no choices. I could walk away from everything, but where would I go? What would I do? Go to Alaska? *Hi everyone. So um, I'm homeless and penniless—can I live with you guys, even though I only met you all once?* Right. They'd agree because that's the kind of people they were, but it would be charity. And what, I'd live with Baxter? A man I'd known for a matter of not even forty-eight hours, had sex with a handful of times, and then had walked away from? Idiocy to even consider it.

I felt tears pricking at my eyes, hot and stinging. "Fuck you. I hate you."

"It's for the best, Evangeline. And you'll thank me, eventually."

"No, I won't. Neither will I ever forgive you. Or even speak to you." I steeled myself. "Fine. I agree to your terms. But know this, *Dad*: I *will* escape. I will find a way to get out from under your control, away from Thomas, and I will live my life my way. I don't have any other options right now, but...someday?

Someday I will."

"You say *escape* as if I'm taking you prisoner, Evangeline."

"That's because you are."

He snorted. "Don't be dramatic, child," he said. "Besides, you *can* walk away, if you really feel that way. I've given you a little money. Enough to last you a while, if you're careful."

He was right. But…five thousand dollars? Would that even rent me an apartment? What would I do after that was gone? I had no work experience whatsoever, and currently didn't even have a degree. Without Father's money to finish the degree and his connections, I'd be utterly lost. I knew I was spoiled; I didn't know how to even go about getting a job, not really, and I knew if I tried to strike out on my own, I would…well, I would fail.

Better to plot long term. Get the degree. Cultivate my own connections. Plan. And then, someday, walk away from it all.

"You agree, then?" Father asked. "No more petulance or rebelliousness?"

I sighed, holding back tears. "You know I have no real options."

Father had the audacity to actually clap, laughing. "Very good, very good. I'll inform Thomas. The wedding should take place…let's see…" he consulted the calendar on his desk blotter, "in two weeks. That should give you plenty of time to trim down your figure a touch, which, let's be honest, has suffered some, as of late." He said this with unthinking ease, as if he hadn't just twisted the knife in my back, but added another and poured acid on the wounds.

I managed to hold back the tears until I was back at my dorm.

ELEVEN

Baxter

I WAS AT THE BOXING GYM I TRAINED AT, HAMMERING MY frustrations out on the heavy bag, when Corin walked in, his undercut ponytail tied up in a man-bun. He slouched against the wall near the heavy bag, tugging his earbuds out of his ear.

"Hey, tool, nice man-bun." I shot a grin at him as I grabbed the bag to stop its wobbling spin.

"Nice face, fucker," Corin threw back, stuffing his phone and earbuds in his pocket.

"Don't see you around here much," I said. "What's up?"

He shrugged. "Cane is busy, Xavier is building robots and reading quantum physics, Brock and Bast are both doing shit with their women, Zane is with his new kid, and Luce is tending the bar, which is deader than a graveyard. Leaves me with dick to do, so I figured I'd come see you."

I laughed. "Nice. I'm your last choice for something to do, huh? That's cool." I eyed him. "Canaan is busy, but you're not? That's new."

Corin followed me across the gym to the speed bag. "The Kingsley girls are in town. He's out with Tate."

"Where's Aerie, then?" I asked. "I thought that was how you four always paired off, Cane with Tate, you with Aerie."

He lifted a shoulder. "It's...complicated," he said, watching me roll the speed bag in a quick pattern of lefts and rights. "Aerie had some shit to take care of. We're catching Emolution together later."

"Emolution?"

"A local band. They're doing some cool stuff, I hear, and apparently Aerie is into indie music now, so we're gonna check 'em out."

"How long are the girls in town for?"

He shrugged. "I dunno. They were in school, but I guess they're taking some time off? I haven't really had a chance to catch up much; we've all been too busy. I literally just chatted with Aerie for like five minutes, and she was yammering on about her stupid East Coast gossip most of the time."

"East Coast gossip, huh?" I laughed. "Sounds awful."

He nodded, chuckling. "No shit. I literally could not care any less, but it's her world, so whatever."

Even the mention of the East Coast had my ears pricking up even as my heart twisted. It had been two weeks and four days—not that I was counting days or hours since I'd seen Eva—and I still couldn't quite squash the stubborn-ass feelings that kept cropping up whenever I thought of her.

Corin eyed me, an odd expression on his face. "You know, she did mention something that may or may not interest you."

I stopped the speed bag and cut away from Corin, unwrapping my hands as I headed for the dressing rooms. "If it's about Eva or whatever, I don't want to hear it."

"I think you do, asswipe."

"I think I don't, dick-knob."

He trotted to catch up to me, cut in front, and turned to face me. "Dude, this is me. I give zero fucks about pretty much everything. Yeah?"

I rolled my eyes. "So?"

"So if I'm saying I think you may be interested,

I'm not saying it idly." He twisted a heavy silver ring decorating one of his fingers. "Hear me out, and then do what you want with the info. Just don't be a petulant fucking child."

I crossed my arms over my chest and swelled up. "How the shit am I being petulant?"

"I didn't even say her name, *you* did, and you turned all ogre on me. And the fact that you had a hard time even saying her name tells me this information will interest you. You're storming off, acting all mental and shit. Like, get a grip, bro."

"I'll get a grip on your skinny fuckin' neck is what I'll get a grip on, pencil-dick."

He wasn't bothered by my threat. "Get a shirt on and meet me back at the bar. You'll wanna hear this, all right?"

"All right, all right." I waved him off. "Ten minutes."

"Ten minutes," he agreed.

It wasn't until I was back at the bar letting Lucian pour me a beer that I realized Corin may or may not have faked being bored just so he could worm this little talk out of me. The sneaky fucker.

He strolled in seconds after me, buds back in his ears, head bobbing to the beat of whatever he was listening to. He sat down and put his phone away as Luce poured him a beer, and we both took long drinks before he turned on the stool to face me.

"So, dick, what's this big news?" I started shredding a napkin, hating the nerves I felt, but not able to stop them.

"Aerie and Tate are big into the whole East Coast socialite thing, right? They keep up with the who's who, and who's dating who and what's big news and all that. They're actually pretty influential in that scene themselves, I guess. They have this blog they do, and Snapchat and Instagram and Twitter accounts with a shitload of followers, and they even have official sponsors and shit." He saw my warning glare, and took a sip to buy time. "Okay, okay. Whatever. They keep up with this shit, so the info is good, is my point."

"Just fucking say it, Corin."

"The talk of the entire coast, according to Aerie, is that Eva is marrying that tool Thomas Haverton. It was this big sudden announcement, and the real kicker is that it's supposedly happening next week, like... in four days."

Ice rolled through my veins, freezing me in place for several long seconds.

And then, without warning, the pint glass in my hand shattered. Pain sliced through my palm, and cold beer spilled everywhere. Corin yelped in surprise, and the ever-imperturbable Lucian appeared with a handful of bar towels and a napkin for my hand.

I stood up, soaked in beer and dripping blood from my hand. Corin helped clean up the spill and then brought one of the clean bar towels over to me, reaching for my hand.

"Touch me and I'll snap you in half, brother or not," I snarled. "Leave me the fuck alone."

Corin backed away, palms up and facing out. "Fine, dude, Jesus." He extended the towel toward me. "You're bleeding, though."

"Oh, for Christ's sake." Lucian sighed, sliding around from behind the bar. He snatched the towel from Corin and grabbed my hand, wrapping the towel around the cut and tightening it. "Calm down you big dumb oaf."

I growled a warning, but Luce just chuckled.

"I'm not scared of you, big brother, so quit growling at me. We are *people*, and we use *words*." He enunciated the last sentence slowly, and with exaggerated precision, as if I was either deaf or stupid or both.

"Luce, I swear to god—"

He tied the towel in place around my cut hand, and met my eyes. "She's marrying that guy, Bax, whether you like it or not." His voice was quiet, but his words cut through the haze of my rage. "So you have two choices: stop it, or let her go for real."

"I've *been* trying to let her go, goddammit," I snapped.

"No, you're drinking yourself into a stupor every night and trying to ignore it till it goes away. You haven't done the emotional work necessary to really move on. It's obvious"—he indicated my injured hand—"that you're very much *not* over her."

"It was *one day*, Luce. I shouldn't be this hung up on a girl I spent one day with. It doesn't make any sense."

"People don't make sense, Bax. Sometimes we just latch onto people and there's no rhyme or reason for it, and time has no real bearing on the intensity of it." He went back behind the bar and poured me a new beer. "You have to decide if you feel strongly enough to do something about your feelings. As you say, you spent a single day with her, so it could be nothing."

I drank half the beer, and then eyed him. "You don't think that's the right choice, though."

"It's not my life, not my choice."

"But?" I said, and finished the other half.

"But?" He tilted his head to one side as he poured me another. "But if two and half weeks later you're still hung up on someone you spent a few hours with, it stands to reason there might be something there."

"And you think I should go out to New York or wherever the fuck she lives—"

"Aerie said she heard it was happening at the

Wordsworth house or the Wadsworth house or some-thing like that," Corin put in. "It's in Connecticut, I know that much."

"So I go to Connecticut, then, or wherever the fuck the Wordsworth-Wadsworth fucking house is, and just crash the wedding?" I laughed and drained the beer as fast as I had the first two. "Yeah, that'd be cool. I'd be all like, hey there Eva, remember me? I'm the asshole from Alaska you fucked a couple times, and I don't think you should marry this rich, pow-erful, well-connected guy, because I have *feelings* for you."

Luce stared me down, his gaze steady and cool. "Pretty much, yes."

"I got pretty big fuckin' balls, Luce, but that shit would take stones I don't think even I have."

"Then that's your answer."

I growled. "I wouldn't know what to say."

"I dunno man," Corin said, "I know you meant it sarcastically, but I kinda feel like what you just said says it all. Maybe leave out the part about fucking her, though. A *tiny* bit of tact might go a long way in that situation."

I laughed in his face. "Yeah, ohhhhh-kay, good one, Cor."

He shrugged. "I was being serious, but whatever, man."

"You two are for real?" I gaped at them. "You saying I just pop down to fuckin' preppy-ass Connecticut and walk into their fancy shit wedding and tell her she shouldn't marry the guy?"

Corin nodded. "Yeah, that's what I'm saying." He raised a hand, two fingers extended. "Two questions, though. One, why do you call it Connecticut *preppy*? Weird way to describe an entire state. And two, were you actually even listening when she told us the story about Thomas?"

"Have you ever been to Connecticut?" I asked.

He shook his head. "Nah. All the gigs we did on the East Coast were in New York or Boston."

"I went to Penn State, remember? Some of us from the team went to parties in Connecticut a few times. The girls were hot enough, but they were these snooty-ass bitches, and the parties were all like…" I made a haughty face, and adopted a shitty fake English accent, "*mmmm, yes, quite*—that was the general tone of the parties, and the people. And those were just the *average* rich kids. The sense I get from Eva is that she's from, like, *heavy* fuckin' money. This shit is going to be bananas."

Right on cue, Corin started singing a Gwen Stefani song, until I threw a matchbook at his head to shut him up. "I call Connecticut preppy because there's not enough bad words in the English language for how I feel about those fuckers. Made me feel like I was shitting all over their Persian rugs just walking through their front door. I mean, yeah, I know statistically there have to be some cool people that come from Connecticut, but shit man, I never met any. And what's your point about the Thomas story? Yeah, I was there, and yeah I was listening. We think he's a tool, sure, but she's marrying him, man. Obviously she feels different."

"From what she said, and the way she said it..." Corin shrugged. "I really don't think she'd marry him willy-nilly like this. Not this suddenly. And especially not so soon after being here with you. Some other girl? Sure, it'd just be a hookup for anyone else, but—and correct me if I'm wrong, here—but I get the sense that she wasn't that type of girl—that's she's *not* that type of girl."

"So what, they're forcing her to marry him?"

"Situations can be more complex than we're able to see from the outside," Lucian said. "And you can't underestimate the influence family can exert on someone, nor the fear of the unknown. That's all she knows, that world, those people, that life. Who knows what factors are influencing her? You're not in her shoes, Baxter. Sure, it seems stupid to you, the idea that someone could force a person to marry someone else. But to her, it may not be so stupid or far-fetched."

Smart kid, for twenty years old.

I sighed. "Dammit. I hate logic."

"You'd rather sit around and wonder what could have happened? Live your life regretting not doing something?" Corin asked. "Maybe she's marrying him because she wants to. We could be wrong. Worst that happens, you waste a ticket to Connecticut and she turns you down, tells you to go the hell away. What do you have to lose?"

I twisted the empty glass on one of its bottom edges, shaking my head when Luce asked if I wanted another. "Fuck it. You're right. Fuck it. What do I have to lose?"

"Don't waste the time or money on a plane ticket, though," Lucian said. "Have Brock fly you down."

I shook my head. "Nah. I gotta do this myself, on my own. I'll drive down."

Corin boggled at me. "That's like...a sixty-hour drive, you goddamn lunatic."

"Just me, on Xavier's bike, hauling ass and not stopping except to pee and drink some coffee? I can make it in less." I stood up and headed for the door to pack a backpack and ask Xavier if I could borrow the Triumph for a few days. "Besides, the drive will give me time to sack up and figure out what I'm gonna say."

And what I'd do if she said no.

Shit…I'd have to figure out what I'd do if she said *yes*.

For that matter, I'd have to figure out what fuckin' question I was asking her in the first place.

TWELVE

Evangeline

I WASN'T READY FOR THIS. I WAS IN NO WAY, IN NO UNCERTAIN terms, ready for this. Not even close. I'd already puked twice, and had nothing else to puke up. My mother had offered me champagne, insisting it was just nerves.

It wasn't nerves—it was horror.

Dread.

Despair.

Resignation.

I was moments from going out that door and walking down the aisle to marry Thomas *fucking*

Haverton. The man I'd sworn I'd never marry.

God, you cannot imagine the triumph on his face when he'd swept into my dorm room as if he already owned me. I told him that there was literally no chance he'd ever lay a single finger on me, *ever*, even when we were married, so hopefully he had a mistress lined up already. He'd laughed and tried to grab me, and I'd slapped him, not once, but twice, forehand and then backhand, *bam-bam*, movie style. It was awesome—Baxter would have heartily approved.

"I'm marrying you against my will," I'd told Thomas, "but don't think I'll ever feel anything for you but hate."

He'd left without another word. He would still assume he'd be able to win me over, of course, but he'd find out how serious I was.

Maybe I'd find my own...what's the male version of a mistress? A mister? I don't know. Someone to please me sexually.

I despaired of that, though, because I knew I'd always compare anyone I ever tried to touch with Baxter, and any man would by virtue of simple reality fall *far* short.

No one could ever compare to Baxter.

Not to me.

That was over, though, wasn't it?

The door opened, and Father stood staring at me

coldly. "It's time, Evangeline." He held out his arm to me. "Are you ready?"

I only barely resisted the opportunity to spit on the floor at his feet, or in his face. Instead, I swept past him, ignoring him completely, and stomped—as best I could in a four hundred thousand dollar custom-made gown, complete with matching custom-made shoes, lingerie, and jewelry—down the hallway to the exit, which would take me outside to where the wedding was being held.

Yes, Father and Thomas had conspired so far as to have my entire outfit custom-made for me, right down to the underwear. It had all fit perfectly, too, irritatingly—but only because I'd stopped eating, basically, as my only of protest.

Also irritatingly, it was a clear, gorgeous, cloudless day, perfect for an outdoor wedding. Which was, of course, absolutely incredible. Beyond gorgeous. I literally could not have planned it more perfectly.

I hated it.

Every single thing, right down to the lilies and white roses, I hated it all.

I wanted to cry, but I refused to give them the satisfaction. I'd only cried once, the day my father dropped the hammer on me. Since then, I'd been stone-cold on the outside, and had spoken very literally not a single word to anyone. Even my old girlfriends from Yale, who had of course all been invited and swarmed me for information, got the silent treatment until they too went away.

Yes, I was being a petulant child about everything: thanks for the idea, Father.

I stood at the doorway, staring out at the rows of white chairs filled with the most wealthy and influential people, not just from the East Coast, but from the country. At the end of the aisle was an archway tastefully wreathed with white lace and several hundred perfect white roses, with a single red rose at the very top and center for punctuation.

The idea of white, of purity, made me laugh inside. If only they knew how dirty I'd gotten with Bax, only weeks ago. All the delightfully sinful things I'd done with him, and so desperately wanted to do again—and not with my imagination, my vibrator and porn on my iPad.

I wondered if he'd ever found the little surprise I left him. I let myself briefly think of how I'd watched my favorite video last night, masturbating while thinking of Bax, and wondering if he was doing the same.

Father appeared beside me, extending his arm to me. "You have to hold my arm as we walk down the aisle, at the very least."

I stared at him balefully, and kept both hands

firmly clutched around my bouquet of flowers, more white roses with a single red one in the middle.

At the start of the wedding march, I pushed open the door and stepped through, not even remotely caring how it looked that I preceded my father, walking alone, or that he had to trot to catch up to me, gamely trying to make it look like he was intentionally striding beside me, hands loose at his sides.

Tears pricked at my eyes when I saw Thomas standing there waiting for me, and I supposed everyone would guess it was out of happiness as opposed to the truth, but I really just didn't care.

Honestly, I'd have been happy if the earth would open up and swallow me whole, right then and there.

Baxter

I was camped out on the side of the highway somewhere in the countryside between Scranton and Middletown—I'd used my GPS app to detour along two-lane country roads so I could pull off to the side, pitch a tent, and hope for the best. I'd made crazy time down this way, at the cost of two speeding tickets and a third I'd talked my way out of. I had been driving for fifty hours straight, stopping only to top off the fuel tank, gulp down some coffee, and take a leak, and now I was only a handful of hours away from the wedding location, and the wedding was tomorrow afternoon at one in the afternoon.

And I had a plan.

I'd kept the tux I'd worn to Bast's wedding—it had been ruined because of the glass to my thigh, so I'd bought a new pair of trousers and now had a nice new tux. It was rolled up in my backpack, so all I'd have to do tomorrow would be change into it. Yeah, it'd be wrinkled to fuck, but I wasn't actually attending the wedding, just crashing it. And yeah, I planned to literally *crash* the wedding. It was gonna be epic. I'd installed a GoPro on my helmet, just so I could catch the fun on camera for the guys to laugh at later, regardless of how this turned out.

I was fucking lonely, now, though. It was four a.m., and everyone back home was sleeping, and I couldn't exactly call Evangeline, obviously, but I was just feeling...antsy and afraid and alone, I guess. Weird to feel fear, when I'd never felt it about anything in my life, even when I ran out onto the field for my first televised NCAA game at Penn State—nerves, anticipation, anxiety and excitement, yeah, but never fear.

This was legit fear. Real, actual fear.

What if she shot me down? What if she said yes and it turned out there wasn't anything between us except a couple good fucks? What if, what if, what if...

Laying in my little pup tent with my head on the grass outside the opening, staring up the stars, I decided to try my phone as a means of distraction. God knew I needed it, or all the bullshit jangling through my head would fry me to a crisp and I'd be useless tomorrow.

Shit, maybe I'd even rub one out.

Which was when I realized, with an actual shout of shocked laughter, that I hadn't so much as looked at a single picture since I'd met Eva, and hadn't jerked off since before I met her, either. Which was crazy.

Two and a half weeks, almost three, and I hadn't masturbated once; that was the longest I'd gone in my entire life, to the tune of...nineteen days, since today would be twenty, as I'd yanked it the morning I met Eva.

Crazy.

I unlocked my phone, and that was when I remembered Eva's little thing where she'd taken my phone and hadn't given it back for a few hours. I wondered what she'd gotten up to. I tried the photos, first.

And...holy hot *damn*.

She had taken a whole slew of selfies of her in

the various lingerie outfits she'd tried on, and each photo was sexier than the last. I was hard instantly, as I swiped slowly through the photos, perusing each one in detail, zooming in to get the full picture, as it were. I groaned out loud, laughing, when the lingerie selfies ended, and became full-on nudes.

The first few were awkward, weird and not quite flattering poses, but she hadn't deleted them, like most girls did with selfie fails. There was a short video, next.

Just her face, her hair loose, a close-up, and she was whispering. "You're right outside the dressing room, so I have to be quiet, because I don't want you to know I'm doing this. I can't believe I'm doing it at all, really, but it's the craziest rush I've ever felt! I've never taken a naked picture of myself, not ever. I barely even know what my own privates look like, so this is…it's crazy, crazy, *crazy*, and *so* much fun."

She swiped her hair out of the way, the camera tilting and panning to face the ceiling until she went almost out of the shot completely, and then down and to the side, showing the changing room and piles of discarded underwear and bras, and then the shot finally re-centered on her, giving me a tantalizing glimpse of her upper body and a hint of a nipple before focusing on her face again.

"Those first few shots are really bad, but they're

funny, and I almost laughed out loud when I looked at them. I'm leaving them, though, just because I feel if I'm doing this, I should be honest about the whole process. I think I've got the hang of the right angles and poses, now, though, so hopefully the next few selfies will be better. If not...? Well, it's not like you'll be able to complain to me, since you hopefully won't see this until after I'm gone."

The video ended then, and when I swiped next, I discovered that she really had figured the knack of taking a sexy nude. Because...*damn*. Holy shit, the girl was fucking fine. Beyond fine. I hadn't forgotten how beautiful she was, how sexy, how incredible, but this series of nudes she'd left on my phone were...

They were art.

And they were erotic as fuck.

The first few were from the changing room, and then the background changed to what was clearly her room at the B and B, and with the change in scenery, the hotness factor ramped up exponentially. In the changing room she'd been limited to standing up, using a mirror. In the bedroom, though...god. She could lay down, sit down, lay on her belly and take a butt-over-back shot, all sorts of creative poses, and ohhhhh man, did she get creative. Like, no lie, she could do this for a living. I'm a pretty damn good judge of this shit, too, being a connoisseur of pornography and all things erotic media. She was *good*. I remembered her saying something about wanting to do art instead of politics, and that made this click. She was seriously creative and talented, and she'd done this on a time constraint, using herself as a subject, with something she'd never done before in terms of posing nude herself. I couldn't even imagine what kind of amazing stuff she could create using familiar subject and techniques.

Back to the photographs of a gorgeous naked woman, though.

I kept swiping, scrutinizing each one thoroughly before going to the next, and my erection grew agonizingly hard in my jeans.

Next on my phone was a series of video clips, of her in the B and B bedroom; the first one set up what was going on in the series.

The clip opened to Eva on her bed, showing her from the neck up. "So, Baxter. I found your porno. And ohhhhhh *boy*, do you like porn. My, oh my, Baxter. You're a very...*bad*...boy, aren't you? A little secret I've never said out loud, even to myself is that I watch porn. I might tell you later, but for now it's a terrifying enough experience to even say it out loud, alone. I WATCH PORNOGRAPHY. A lot of it. Every day. And I masturbate to it."

The clip dissolved into shaking incoherency as

she lapsed into laughter. "Oh my gosh, oh my gosh, oh my gosh." It returned to her face, excitement making her lovely features glow as she fairly vibrated with animated energy; a low humming buzzing noise began, then, and a tiny vibrator slowly filled the screen in the foreground, and then vanished so the focus went back to her.

"You see that? That's my vibrator. My little tiny one, at least, the one I keep in my purse in case of emergencies. I've never used it, though, since I've never had the courage to actually masturbate anywhere except in my bedroom under the covers with the lights off and the door locked. I'm going to now, though. In broad daylight, with you right outside in the truck, waiting for me." She made a crazy, silly face. "I've never been this hyper about anything in my life, but you make me crazy, Baxter. So crazy. Crazy enough to do this. Swipe left, please." The clip ended, then.

So, obviously, I swiped as left as fast as I could and tapped the "Play" triangle. Eva was in the frame again, still from the neck up, this clip clearly taking place shortly after the first. She extended the camera to arm's length, giving me a mouth-watering, cock-destroying view of her naked body all spread out on her bed, legs parted, one knee bent and touching her opposite thigh to cover her pussy, her arm across her breasts to *almost* hide them as well—they were too big to completely be hidden behind her arm—her hair splayed out around her like an inky cloud. She had a mini silver bullet vibrator in her hand, and she stared up at the camera, biting one lip, a nervous, excited expression on her face.

"I just watched a video, right before I switched over to record this. It was this girl, on her knees, going down on a guy. The way she used her hands, and her mouth? God, I've wanted to do that. I want to be on my knees, naked, my hands and mouth around a man's...god, I'm so darn—so *damn*—conditioned to be good and proper that it's hard to talk dirty, it just feels bad and wrong and weird. I'm going to try, though, and maybe I'll teach myself to undo the conditioning."

She slid her knee away, giving me a view of her pussy, and her finger and thumb twisted to turn the vibrator to full power, and she slid her hand down her body, baring her tits and touching the vibrator to her clit. "I've always wanted to be that girl, naked and on my knees...sucking a man's cock. Oh...oh...*oh god*... even talking about it, using those dirty words makes me go crazy. Sliding my hand up and down his huge cock, and then using my mouth...god, what would that even feel like? To have a cock all the way in my mouth? Down my throat? I'm imagining you, Baxter. God, I'm getting close already."

Her eyes were closed and she was circling her clit with the vibrator, and her hips were gyrating up and down, making her huge, luscious tits shake all over the place. My cock was on fucking fire, now, leaking pre-cum, and I knew I had to get it out before I made a mess in the only pair of jeans I had with me. I yanked them open and shoved them off, kicking my boots off frantically in a tangled mess, tripping over myself in desperation. I scrambled out of the tent and got onto my knees a few feet away in the cold, dew-wet grass, ripping my T-shirt off to get it out of the way. I kept watching the video, hanging utterly on each millisecond.

"I hope you watch this and masturbate some-time, Bax. I doubt I'll have the courage to go through with it, to actually suck your cock, but I hope, when you watch this and masturbate, you imagine me like I'm imagining myself right now. Totally naked, on my knees in front of you. You're standing up. Hunched over me, with your huge hands in my hair. My breasts are shaking everywhere"—they actually were, in the video, so that wasn't something I had to imagine—"and I've got both hands around your cock. God, it's so big. So *fucking* big, Baxter, I can't even get my mouth all the way around it. I'm using both hands, and I still have so much space to jerk up and down—" She broke off, gasping, whining, thrusting wildly. "Oh my gosh, oh my gosh, Baxter. I'm gagging on your cock. Are you picturing it? Can you feel me? Can you hear me gagging? I know you've watched videos where the girl gets gagged, the one I watched was saved to your phone, probably a favorite of yours. Good choice, by the way. Short and hot and right to the point."

She moaned, her mouth falling open, and I could easily picture my cock sliding between those plump, biteable lips.

"I'm gagging on your cock, and you're grunting like crazy," she continued. "You're jerking me onto you, so I have no choice but to take all of you. Ohhhhhh!" This was a high-pitched whimper in the back of her throat as she stiffened, her hips thrust into the air, coming. "I'm coming, Baxter! Ohhhh! Oh god, oh god, oh god, oh god. You came in my mouth, shot your come all down my throat, and I choked on it. You came so much I couldn't even swallow it all, and it spilled all down my mouth and chin. Maybe it even dripped out onto my breasts. Or—or maybe I spit it out onto my breasts. I've seen that before, and it's kind of hot. Is that how it was in your fantasy, Baxter? Did I swallow it all, or did I spit it out onto myself? I wish I could know the answer."

She finished coming as she said that last sentence, and the frame closed in on her face, sweat dotting her upper lip, her eyes heavy-lidded and lazy with sex-fueled satisfaction. "I'm going to clean up, get dressed, put on makeup, and go out to the truck where you're waiting for me. And I'm going to pretend this never happened, and hope you don't find this until after I'm forced back to my horrible, stupid, meaningless life, controlled by my father and fucking *Thomas*. God, that ruined the mood, didn't it? Sorry. Maybe I'll record something after this to end my little experiment on a slightly sexier note than me complaining about my future." It ended then.

I rewound the video to the beginning, and watched it as I jerked myself off slowly. When she finished coming, I stopped it right before she ended it, and instead of going through it a third time, I closed my eyes and imagined her, as she'd described me—imagined *us* as she'd described us.

I shot a thick gout of come a good two feet across the grass, groaning and fighting to stay upright on my knees as I came, the intensity of it making me dizzy.

Reminding myself to remember in the morning that I'd come all over the grass right outside the tent, I set the phone aside and quickly re-dressed and slid back into the tent to watch the last video.

"Okay, here we go." She was dressed, walking as she spoke, her bedroom in the B and B retreating behind her as she moved to the door. "You probably noticed right away, since I have a feeling you masturbate rather frequently, but I logged out of your YouPorn account and logged into mine. So you can see what I watch. Maybe someday we'll be watching the same thing, masturbating at the same time. You won't know it, but I will." She smiled brightly, and did a finger-wiggle wave. "Goodbye to the Baxter watching this video, and…oh my gosh, you're so gorgeous…hello to the Baxter in your truck, waiting for me in real life."

The clip ended, and it was the last one.

I immediately flipped out of the photos app and opened my porn account, and sure enough, instead of my recent history, there was unfamiliar stuff, her history. There was one that was obviously watched a lot, so I clicked on it. It was one of those videos that tries to add some romance and emotion to it, supposedly catering to a female audience or whatever, I guess. It was hot, though, and became all the more hot when I imagined Eva watching it right now, at that exact moment, her fingers on her clit, a big vibrator in her pussy, moaning, thinking of me…

I jerked off again, a matter of minutes after the first time, thinking of Eva. Of us. Of what we'd done, of what I wanted to do. I didn't need porn, didn't need visuals, just needed my own imagination and memory, and the thought of Eva.

She was all it took for me, now.

I shoved the phone in the pocket of my leather jacket, which I tugged on against the coolness of the night, and fell asleep thinking of her, hoping and hoping and hoping I'd get a chance to even see her again, to kiss her again. To find out if there was something here, or if I was fucking nuts.

THIRTEEN

Evangeline

WITH THE BRIDAL MARCH PLAYING, AND THE GUESTS standing, I literally marched up the aisle and finally reached the archway, where Thomas and the minister were waiting. Father gave Thomas some kind of meaningful look, the way men can express a whole conversation with each other in a single manly stare, and then the minister was asking who was giving me away. Apropos, that—he really *was* giving me away, as if I were a possession, a prized mare.

I stood, trembling, fighting tears, and trying not to think about Baxter, ignoring the nattering, rambling bullshit of the minister. I think he'd been coached on my silence, and had tailored the ceremony to necessitate me saying as little as possible, it seemed, since when I finally I tuned back in he was in the middle of asking Thomas if he had rings to exchange.

At that moment, there was the snarling roar of a motorcycle from off in the distance. The minister stammered to a stop, glanced at Thomas and then Father for an explanation, but both just stared back in confusion and consternation.

Hope welled in the pit of my stomach, and I tried to not let it bloom too fully until I knew what was going on.

The minister tried to go back to the ceremony. "Thomas, do you have rings with which to pledge your eternal—"

The motorcycle engine roared again, cutting him off, and it was even louder now and approaching rapidly, and everyone was turning and twisting, trying to see anything, but there was nothing to see yet.

I stood in place, quietly slipping out of my heels in case I needed to jump out of the way or something—a silly precaution to take, making me think I had probably watched too many Lifetime movies. But then, with a third deafening roar, a black motorcycle rounded the side of the mansion and streaked toward us, ripping up the grass as the rear tire fishtailed.

I knew, immediately, who it was, despite the helmet obscuring his features.

The shoulders as broad as mountain ranges gave it away, the arms as thick as most men's legs, the trim waist, the powerful thighs gripping the snarling motorcycle. Father's bodyguards leapt to their feet and rushed toward him, but—obviously to me, not so obviously to them, I supposed—he had no interest in Father.

Bax only slowed a little bit as he carved across the lawn and straight down the aisle between the rows of chairs, scattering the people like bowling pins—they ran screaming as the bike approached. Hauling the bike to the side at the last second, he barked the throttle and squeezed the front brakes so the front tire locked in place and the rear tire ripped sideways in a dramatic arc, spraying sod and mud. He ended up less than three feet away from me, the motorcycle parallel to the archway, and his feet planted in the ground to prop himself up.

He was wearing a full-coverage helmet, which had a camera affixed to the top—his brothers would get a kick out of all this, I realized, and it was classic Baxter, to record this for them. I was grinning ear to ear as Baxter lifted the helmet off and tucked it under his arm so the camera would still record a level shot of what went on next.

I had eyes only for Bax, of course, but utter chaos ruled around us. Wedding guests were yelling and arguing, some were watching Bax and me, and others were taking videos with their cell phones. Mom was trying to do damage control, attempting to calm the guests. Thomas was freaking out, shouting at Dad, who was shouting back, and the venue security and management were hustling over, pointing at the damage to the lawn caused by the motorcycle, not to mention the broken chairs scattered by panicking guests.

It was chaos, and it was beautiful.

Not as beautiful as Bax, though.

He shot me an amused, cocky grin, wearing a rumpled but well-cut and insanely sexy tuxedo. "Hey, Eva. What up, babe?"

Father approached, his face stormy with rage. "YOU. Leave now or I shall have you arrested. I might anyway, you filthy redneck."

"You know people, I know people," Baxter answered, breezily. "Shut the fuck up a minute, though, I'm talkin' to the lady."

"Hi, Bax," I said, my voice bright and happy. "What a surprise."

"Yeah, well, I was in the area, thought I'd drop by."

I laughed, a genuine belly laugh. "In the area? Baxter...you live in *Alaska*."

He ran his hand over his head and squeezed his neck, and I realized then, with that gesture, that he was a nervous wreck despite his easy demeanor. "Yeah, got me there. Truth is, I drove sixty-some hours to get here."

"You did?"

He tilted his head to one side. "I stopped last night outside Scranton, so I could time my entrance. Gotta make a flashy entrance, you know? Folks love a good show."

"What is the meaning of this?" Thomas demanded, stomping forward with puffed-up bravado—but not before checking to make sure there were bodyguards nearby. "Seize him at once, Theodore."

Baxter's face hardened, taking on the ruthless, brutal, icy coldness of his Basher alter-ego. "You." He snapped his gaze to Thomas, who halted under that glare, visibly blanching. "You hold your fuckin' horses, pussy-boy. I'll get to you."

I couldn't help a snort. "Pussy-boy?"

"How I've always thought of him." He quirked an eyebrow. "And what'd I tell you about what it does to me when you talk like that, Eva? You're gonna make it hard for me to get off this motorcycle, and it looks like I got a bit of a tussle brewing."

I bit my lip, hesitating, and then let fly the joke running through my head. "I'm...making it *hard* to *get off*, huh?"

He guffawed. "Aww hell, Eva, you're killin' me here."

I laughed, but then sobered, stepping off the small dais to stand by the motorcycle, putting a hand on his arm. "Why are you really here, Bax?"

His expression went equally serious. "This ain't you, princess." He gestured at the archway with its three hundred hand-cut roses, and Thomas, and the Wadsworth mansion, and then at my dress with its four-foot-long train. "I know I don't belong in this world, Eva, but...are you sure *you* do?"

I swallowed hard, but couldn't speak. Which was fine, because he wasn't done.

"I know I'm just a dirty redneck from the shitend of Alaska—like your dad said—and basically a caveman, but I ain't gonna actually club you over the head and drag you off. What I *will* say, though, is that you should think really hard about this. Whether you really *have* to do this. I know I got no clue about your life, or what all these fuckers have on you to be forcin' you into this—or if they even are, because I mean, maybe you're marrying Tommy the Pussy-Boy because you want to. I dunno—"

"I'm not," I assured him.

"Well thank fuck: that means I'm not *totally* crazy," he said, playfully wiping imaginary sweat off his forehead and flinging it aside. "Point is, you don't want to do this, then don't do this. I ain't even sayin' you gotta be with me, I don't know if that's even... shit, if it's somethin' you could even consider in, like, a million years. I know we're different people from different worlds and all that, but...like I said, even if you don't wanna end up with me, or we try it and it doesn't work out, you deserve to live your life on your terms. Not *their* terms. You got class, and beauty, and talent, babe. You could *be* somethin' in this world. With me, without me, you oughta at least give yourself the gift of checkin' out what you got to offer the world, naw'm'sayin'?"

He was so scared, right now. I could tell by the way he was talking; by the way his eyes never wavered from mine. He was the kind of man who would ride directly toward whatever he was afraid of, and he would look it in the eyes and wouldn't look away, no matter what.

"Bax," I started.

He held up a hand. "One sec, babe. Lemme say one more thing." He sucked in a breath and let it out. "Evangeline, I just...shit—I dunno. I'm a way out for you, right here, right now. And I know you may not know how to navigate the world and shit, but you got friends out there, babe. I know you got pride, so you'd never ask, which is why I'm offering, not on my own behalf, but on the behalf my seven crazy fuckin' brothers, and on behalf of Claire, Dru, and Mara—and little Jackson Badd, who was just born about a week ago, by the way. I'm offerin' a place to crash, a chance to figure out yourself and your life on your terms. This part ain't got nothin' to do with me, okay? It's just…an open-ended offer of a place to crash with folks who think the world of you." He let out a breath, blinked hard a few times, clenched his hand into a fist, shook it out, and started again. "That's all I've got to say, Eva. So. Whaddya, say, babe? Wanna ditch this fancy shindig and go for a ride? It's only"—he checked his watch with a flick of his wrist—"sixty hours to Ketchikan, and there's whiskey waitin' when we get there. *With* me, or just with me…however you wanna play it, babe."

I blinked hard, sucked in a breath. It was, in a very real sense, a do-or-die decision. No do-overs, no going back, no time to have a long meandering think.

I had to *decide*, right then, what I wanted.

My father, Connecticut and the familiarity of the East Coast, the stuffy, stifling, stuck-up world I'd always known? Yale? Thomas…being Mrs. Haverton, the shiny trophy wife of the great and mighty Thomas Haverton?

Or Baxter Badd, who was so much I couldn't even mentally encompass all that he was.

His brothers, all seven of them, wild and vulgar and crazy and hysterical, but warm and friendly and so accepting, so giving, immediately willing to give you the shirts off their backs, willing to do battle for you, to bleed and risk death and even possibly end lives for you, willing to feed you, clothe you, and befriend you, willing take you in and shelter you, willing to listen to you and laugh and commiserate. And then there was Claire, and Dru, and Mara—she had her baby? OMG, I'd have to congratulate her, no matter what happened here—those crazy, amazing bitches. The bar. The twins and their kick-ass music. Even Alaska itself, the gorgeous scenery and the serenity and the drastically different pace and lifestyle and people...all of it.

Yeah, not much of a choice, was it?

Framed in this context, with Baxter in front of me, it was so blindingly obvious I felt almost stupid for not calling him the second I got back. But once I was dragged back here, it was just so easy to fall back into the role of the cowering, obedient good little girl I'd always been, even if that wasn't who I was inside anymore. I'd been changing steadily for a long time, realizing I wasn't happy and wasn't content to live up to their expectations and go along with their manipulative, controlling bullshit anymore, but it wasn't until I spent those magical, crazy hours in Ketchikan that I fully left the rest of my old self behind.

Evangeline, the East Coast socialite, the Good Girl…

She became Eva, the…

The version of myself I was suddenly ferociously eager to continue discovering.

I reached up and cupped his face, rubbing my thumb over his cheekbone, as he so often did to me. "Fuck this place, Bax."

"Hell yeah!" he crowed. Then, more quietly, a chagrined expression stealing over him, he tried it again more quietly. "I mean, are you sure? Not sure you'll ever be able to go back to the way things were."

I laughed. "I never *could* go back to the way things were, Bax. Not after you." I kissed him, softly, gently, quickly. "I'm with you."

"So…" He stared down at me, hope on his face. "You're with me, or you're *with* me? Just so I'm clear."

I tipped my head back and laughed. "Oh, Bax. Do I have to spell it out?"

He nodded. "Yep. Pretty much. I'm a dude, and I'm sometimes a little extra dense, even for a dude."

I snorted. "No, you're not. You graduated *cum laude* from Penn State. You're far from dense, Baxter." I crouched down, picked up my shoes, stuffed one each into the saddlebags of the motorcycle, grabbed his arm and stepped up onto the toe of one of his scuffed black boots—which he was wearing with his tuxedo—and swung up onto the back of the motorcycle behind him, clinging to his waist and snugging up as close to him as I could get, taking a moment to arrange the train of my dress so it wasn't in the way and wouldn't drag or catch on anything. "Does this spell it out for you?"

He rumbled a laugh. "Nope. Need it a little clearer."

I leaned forward bit his earlobe. "I'm coming with you," I murmured in his ear. "And later, I'm coming *on* you."

"Damn, girl. Now *that's* clear."

I laughed. "I'm curious—did you ever find my little surprise?"

He growled in his chest. "Last night. Came twice in a row, watching it."

"Wouldn't you know," I whispered to him, "I came twice last night, too."

"Maybe we can do some math, later, make two times two come to…" he bobbled his head back and forth as if calculating, "oh, eight or ten, maybe."

I laughed. "You're thinking a little too conservatively, Mr. Badd."

At that moment, the gathered crowd, which was now watching in stunned silent shock, and probably not a little fascination, began murmuring, as Bax and

I were very obviously whispering something dirty to each other as I straddled the back of a motorcycle.

"Now see here!" Thomas stomped forward angrily. "You can't just—and she can't—" He swiveled to face my father. "Lawrence, *do* something. Control your daughter!"

Baxter pivoted to glance at me over his shoulder, handing me his helmet. "Hold this?"

I took it, keeping the camera pointed at Thomas as Baxter toed out the kickstand, lowered the bike down onto it, and swung off. Baxter rolled his shoulders and shook out his hands, and Thomas backed up a few steps, holding out his hands.

"No, wait, *wait*—" He glanced at Teddy, head of security. "DO SOMETHING! He's going to attack me!"

Teddy quirked an eyebrow, glanced at me, and then gave a tiny shake of his head, and all the bodyguards—who had been tensed to move—stood down, watching impassively from behind mirrored sunglasses.

Baxter halted a few feet from Thomas, shrugging his shoulders, bouncing on the balls of his feet, and shaking his hands in preparation for a fight—it was all show, meant to intimidate and scare Thomas, and it was working.

"Want a free shot, pussy-boy?" Baxter tapped his

jaw. "Go for it, pop me one."

"What?" Thomas had no idea what was even going on. "What are you talking about? I'm not fighting you."

"No? Fine by me. But don't whine later on that I didn't give you a fair shot," Baxter said.

And then Baxter struck.

Bax's fist rocketed out, impacting Thomas's jaw with an audible, sickening *crunch*, and Thomas twisted and fell to the ground, out cold.

"Sorry, but I promised myself awhile ago that if I ever got the chance, I'd hit that fucker. Had to make good on it, y'know?"

I kissed his hand, tasting blood. "He's deserved that and more his whole life."

Bax thumbed my lips. "Ready?"

I lifted up on the footrests of the bike to kiss him. "Ready."

He kissed me, a long, slow, deep, erotic, private kiss, and then swung on in front of me, bringing the bike to life. "Put that helmet on, princess."

I ripped off the veil and tossed it aside so I could shove the helmet on, and then clutched Bax with a squeal as we tore away from the ruins of my wedding, turf spitting out from the rear wheel.

We rode for a little over an hour, and I felt exhilarated in every second of it, clinging to him, laughing as we crested hills and rounded bends, leaning into it—he had given me some basic instructions when we left the venue about how to safely ride behind him, leaning into turns and all that, and I took to it like a fish to water.

We were in the middle of nowhere, surrounded by rolling fields, trees to either side about a mile or so away, no traffic in either direction for at least twenty minutes.

As we rode, I thought of the videos I'd left him. The things I'd talked about in that video, the fantasies I'd conjured up for us, and how many times I'd made myself come over the last few weeks, thinking of Bax, of doing those things to him.

I tugged at his sleeve. "Stop a minute!" I shouted.

He hauled the bike over to the shoulder and into the grass. "What's up, babe?" he asked, twisting to glance at me.

I removed the helmet, slipped off the bike—careful to avoid anything that might be hot—and strode into the tall grass beside the shoulder, stretching my muscles. "I just need a break."

Which was true, as I was cramping and chafing from the unfamiliar position, and rattled numb from the vibration of the engine beneath me.

"First time on a bike can leave you a bit sore," he conceded.

He still had the motor running, so I approached and twisted the key to turn it off. "Mind if we just... take a quick break?"

Baxter caught some note in my voice. "Yeah? What are you thinkin', sweetheart?"

He put out the kickstand and swung off, standing in front of me, pressing his body up against mine, framing my face with his hands. I kissed him—god, did I kiss him. All I did was kiss at first, circling my arms around his neck and pressing up against him, but that was all it took. He hardened against my belly immediately, and kept hardening the longer I kissed him, more deeply with each second, kissing him until there was absolutely no doubt left as to how I felt.

When I finally broke away, he breathed out with a shudder. "*Damn*, Eva."

"I needed that," I said.

"Me too," Bax rumbled. "Me fuckin' too."

"I've been so alone, I was going crazy." I rubbed his chest, feeling his hard muscles under my hands, my libido a boiling cauldron inside me. "I missed you."

"Missed you too, babe."

Curiosity ruled me, for a moment. "You did?"

He chuckled. "No, babe, I did not so much as look at another person the last few weeks." He laughed again, rubbing the side of my arm. "Shit, honey, I didn't even find what you'd left for me until last night."

"You didn't?"

He shook his head. "I was too upset from missing you and hating that I'd let you leave to even think about that. Didn't even touch myself the whole time."

"But you saw the photos and videos last night, though?" I gazed up at him, letting myself sound every bit as breathy and sultry as I felt.

"Stopped for the night way out in the middle of nowhere, pitched a little tent, and camped out under the stars. Got lonely, thought about checkin' my phone to distract myself." His voice darkened to a sexy, thrilling purr. "Found your little cache of hotness."

"And?"

"And babe...that shit was *incredible*. The photos? Jesus, Eva. You could be a bikini model. Could also be a bikini model photographer. That shit was gold, man." He shook his head in amazement. "Wicked hot. The nudes, though? Holy fuck, honey, I could look at every nude photograph ever taken, and those of you would be the hottest I've ever seen."

"And the videos?" I prompted. "What did you think about those?"

"Can't even, Eva," he bit out, grinding against me. "Just thinkin' about 'em is dangerous. Might pop, right in my fuckin' pants, just thinkin' about the one where you got yourself off."

"I thought about that every single night," I told him. "What I said in that video? About you, about what I wanted to do? I thought about that video every single night since I left you, thought about doing that stuff, and I came so hard so many times."

He growled. "Jesus, really?"

"Really." I lifted up and kissed him. "And now…" I let go and backed away a step.

"And now…what, Eva?" he asked, heated suspicion in his voice.

"And now I make that fantasy a reality."

"Oh my good god*damn*, Eva. You for real right now?"

"Hell yes, I'm for real," I said. "Every last bit of it, I want to do it, right now, right here."

"On a road in the middle of the day?"

"I haven't seen a single car this entire time."

"It *is* a pretty remote road…not exactly the fastest route," he mused.

I laughed. "Something tells me you chose this route on purpose, hoping for something like this."

He tipped his head to one side. "Might've considered the possibility in the back of my head."

"Good considering," I said, and dropped to my knees.

"You're fuckin' gorgeous, Eva," he murmured.

I reached for his pants, undoing the button and lowering the zipper. "Don't compliment me, don't ask me if I'm sure, don't tell me this about me or anything like that. Just go along with the fantasy, okay?"

"This ain't fantasy, Eva. This is reality."

"I know," I said. "That's the best part."

With his trousers undone, his cock bulged out. I reached up behind myself and tugged down the zipper of my dress and pulled it forward and off, so I was naked from the waist up—for him, but also for me, because I got a thrill from the daring of it.

"Ho-*ly* fuck."

I grinned, and yanked his trousers down, and his underwear. "Take off your shirt. I want to see more of you."

He ripped off the coat and tie, unbuttoned a few shirt buttons and tugged it up over his head. "That better?"

His trousers and underwear were around his ankles, and he was naked the rest of the way up, all on display for me. "Perfect."

And then…

I grabbed his cock.

Slid both hands around him and spent a while just touching him, re-familiarizing myself with the glorious magnificence of his cock. Stroked and caressed him, the head, the shaft, his heavy balls, all over, until he was moaning in his throat. I gazed up at him, nerves jangling through me. I licked my lips, opened my mouth, sighing nervously as I lowered my face toward him.

"Eva—" he murmured. I took him into my mouth, and he groaned, a long, low rolling sound. "Goddamn, Eva. *Goddamn.*"

I smiled, or tried to, in pride at the raggedness of his voice. I say I *tried* to smile, but with his dick in my mouth, smiling was impossible, because my jaw was levered open to the max, lips stretched to accommodate his massiveness.

I spent a long, long time, then, reenacting everything I'd visualized and fantasized about sucking this incredible man's incredible cock. I knew he'd make me scream later, and I knew he'd show me sweetness and roughness and everything in between.

This wasn't about that.

This was about me.

Taking what I wanted for myself.

I went slow, learning the feel of him, learning how to keep my teeth off him, how to angle to take more of him—learning that the feel of him sliding down my throat was a thrillingly frightening rush as I fought the urge to gag, opening my throat and breathing through my nose. I used my hands, stroking him.

I used my mouth all over him, along the sides, on his balls. I used my tongue, licking every delicious inch.

I gloried in his cock.

Drowned myself in it.

Felt the wind on my breasts, stole glances up at him, and at the blue sky and the road, and shuddered in excitement at the thought that someone might drive by at any moment.

I learned the erotic thrill of the way he responded, the grunts when I took him into my throat, the soft moans when I licked him, the breathy inhalations when I tongued the slit at the top, the long snarl when I bobbed, slowly taking more and more and more.

I felt his stomach tighten, felt his hips flexing. His hands buried in my hair, gathered it up on the top of my head.

He was close.

Eagerness zinged through me, but I resisted the urge to hurry him to the end. I kept dragging it out, switching from one thing to another until he was groaning and grunting and all those other yummy, erotic noises nonstop, and his hips were flexing, shoving his cock at me.

"Fuck—*fuck*," he grumbled. "Can't...can't hold out any longer, babe. Been tryin' to hold it, to feel this for as long as you're willin' to do it. But I gotta come, honey. I fuckin'—I *gotta* come soon."

I was willing to do this as long as he could hold out, and longer. I *enjoyed* this. I'd heard a lot of girls at school talking about doing this, and how they did it for various reasons. Some because they knew the guy liked it, some only if they had to, some because he'd go down on them if they went down on him, some blatantly said it was to get him into a receptive mindset so he'd do things for them, and other said they flat out hated it—I understood all of that except the last one—and only a very few said they genuinely *enjoyed* doing it.

I guess I'm in that minority, then.

When he said he just *had* to come, I backed away and let him fall out of my mouth, giving my jaw and throat a quick break before the big show. I just gazed up at him, stroking him to keep him on the edge. Smiled at him. Kissed the tip of his cock, and he grunted, thumbed my cheekbone, shaking his head at me with a grin that was...

Loving, maybe.

"Killin' me, Eva."

"Not yet," I breathed. "But I'm about to."

"Fuck."

I grinned at him. "Remember everything I talked about? Give it all to me. Don't hold back. I can take it." I demonstrated, by taking his cock into my mouth and down my throat until I gagged, held there, bobbed shallowly, gagging, and backed away. "I *like* taking it."

"Fucking holy goddamn shit."

I laughed. "Are you ready, Bax?"

He shook his head. "*Fuck* no."

"Good."

I kissed the head of his cock again—because I loved his cock and because he seemed to find amusement when I did so—and then I slid him between my lips, deep, deep, deeper. Changed angles so I could look up at him, and then leaned forward, breasts swaying as I began to truly go down on him in earnest. Thrills raced through me, pebbling my skin, as he began grunting and even making soft, high-pitched noises—those were my favorite. I went after those high-pitched moans, sliding him deep and backing away, and I got them from him, noises I don't think he'd ever made before.

No hands, now.

I wrapped them around his ass, clawed my fingers in, a subtle encouragement. Pulled at him…a not so subtle encouragement.

His hands gripped my hair tightly, and he hunched over me and started thrusting.

I adjusted to accommodate this, backing away so he could thrust as deeply as he wanted.

Fuck, this was hot.

He fucked my throat, then, and I let out a moan as he did so, bobbing into his thrusts.

God, yes.

I gagged on him, clawing at his ass until I was sure he'd have marks.

"Now, Jesus, Jesus—Eva—fuck, *now!*"

There was a loud honk right then, the blare of an air horn from a semi, and I started. I glanced up to see Bax giving the driver a middle finger, and there was another blare of the horn and the roar of an engine as he pulled away, leaving us alone.

The thrill of having been seen blasted through me, and I felt myself aching, throbbing, and turned on to the point of desperation.

And then Bax came.

The truck had thrown off the timing, and I'd lost the preparedness of his warning, so when he unleashed, I wasn't expecting it. It made it even hotter, even more erotic, even more thrilling. He came with a roar, thrusting into my throat and then backing away, and my mouth was filled with thick hot tangy musky salty come. I swallowed it, but he was coming even more and I swallowed that, but then, just as I'd fantasized, it was too much and so unexpected that I couldn't keep up, and what I couldn't swallow spilled out around his cock, dripping down my chin. I was gagging on it, my mouth forced open by the need to breathe and swallow, and he thrust right then, into my throat, so I clutched at his cock with both hands, gazing up at him with his come trickling down my mouth, swallowing and letting even more spill out. He was still spurting, and it hit my chin, and then I took him back into my mouth and sucked, licked, swallowed as he spurted the last little bit, and I jerked his length eagerly, hard and fast, sucking it all out of him, pumping him until he sagged, and his cock was sucked dry of every last bit of his come.

I stood up, my knees creaking and aching, and he clung to me, burying his forehead against mine.

I laughed, and tried to kiss his forehead, but got his eye instead. "Hi."

He groaned raggedly. "Um. Hi?" He held on to my shoulders for balance. "Eva, that was…"

"My fantasy come true?"

"Yours and mine both, babe." He wiped at my chin and the corners of my mouth, and I laughed when he stared at his hands as if wondering what to do next, since there was…um, a *lot* of come on his hands.

I guided his hands to my dress, and he wiped his hands on the expensive material.

"I hope you liked that fantasy—I mean, *reality*," I said, "because with as much as I liked doing that to you, I think it's going to be happening kind of a lot."

He laughed deliriously. "I think I can handle that."

I lifted a shoulder delicately. "I mean, I liked it…a *lot*." I ran a hand down my front, lifting the front of my dress to bare my core. "A *lot*, a lot."

"That much a lot?"

"So much I'm crazy horny." I slid a hand into my underwear, and then slid them off and stepped out of them. "I think I need help with it. I don't have a vibrator anymore. I left everything I own, and I have zero dollars." I gazed up at him, touching myself. "Whatever will I do?

"I dunno, lady," he drawled. "I think I might know a couple things."

"Think you could show me some of them?"

He hiked up his pants, zipped them but didn't button them, and then lifted me into the air and set me on the bike, side-saddle style. Spread my legs apart, and leaned in; the motor was cool by now, so I could rest against the pipes. He draped my feet over his shoulder and made me scream…oh, I don't know how many times: I didn't bother counting.

We were honked at twice while he ate me out, and I came all the harder for it.

"I think I got a little exhibitionist on my hands," Bax said, as we finished re-dressing.

"Maybe so," I agreed. "We'll find out together."

"Guess we will, love, guess we will."

That was a new one. In the time I'd known him, he'd called me sweetheart, sweet thing, babe, baby, honey, girl, lady, woman, all kinds of different terms... but never once had he called me *love*.

A quick, sharp glance at his face told me it hadn't been a slip.

"Yeah, love," I echoed, "I guess we will."

It was the first time I'd used a term of endearment for anyone in my life, and I liked the way it tasted on my lips, almost as much as I liked the lingering musk of his come on my lips.

"Take me home," I told him.

"Home?"

"Yeah. Home...to Ketchikan, Alaska."

EPILOGUE

Corin

CANE AND I HAVE KNOWN TATE AND AERIE KINGSLEY our whole lives. They went to school with us all the way from kindergarten to middle school, at which point their pretentious dingbat of a mother, Rachel, moved them to New York in search of better things than what Ketchikan had to offer. Well, actually, she left them in Ketchikan first, for a while, letting her folks raise the girls. Then, when she met Bob the investment banker, she popped back up here long enough to pack 'em up and move 'em out.

That was the year we started high school. By

junior year, Canaan and I were already on our fourth band, Bishop's Pawn, the one that took us into the big time. We'd started out gigging locally, and then as far as Anchorage, and then Vancouver and Seattle, and then down the West Coast to LA and San Francisco and San Diego. We barely graduated high school, since we were too busy gigging to bother with petty boring bullshit like grades or attendance. We worked out a deal with the principal, who was a former drummer in a successful band himself, whereby we would turn in assignments remotely and check in with him regularly via email, and he'd pass us. It worked out, and we even got those diplomas early, which freed us up to start taking gigs across the country, in places like New York.

On our first gig in New York, the first thing we did was look up the Kingsley twins.

I mean, you can imagine we were close, being two different sets of identical twins, a boy set and a girl set. Lots of talk, lots of gossip. But, strangely enough, that's all it has ever been: gossip. All the four of us ever were was friends. We chilled together, went to the mall and to movies, got stoned together, that kinda thing. I think we all thought of trying to hook up, but we just…never did. Not with each other. The girls hooked up with the popular guys and the jocks, and Cane and I hooked up with…well, anyone we could, honestly, and we even talked about our various hookups. But it never led to anything between us. Which is just…funny, isn't it?

I mean, those girls are fuckin' fine as fuck, man. And cool, funny, sophisticated, and a little crazy. Canaan and I, obviously, are somewhat less than normal, too, being tattooed, bona fide rock stars by sixteen, rarely actually *at* school. popping in for a week or two here and there. It's a match made in heaven. Right?

Wrong.

It just never happened. Damned if I know why, and damned if Cane knows why, seeing as we've discussed this ad nauseam. *Why haven't we hooked up with Tate and Aerie?* One of us would ask, and the other would answer with *damn if I know, bro,* and we'd start in on how cool the girls are, how hot they are, or we'd talk about the various projects the girls had worked on, the girls being crazy creative themselves. Photography, painting, performance art, graffiti, weird avant-garde music, you name it, the girls had tried it. And every damn thing they did was fucking amazing: *Brilliant, stunning, a tour de force,* as the critics might say.

They never tried to monetize it into a career, though, and seemed weirdly content to go along with their nutty-as-a-fruitcake mother's plan to turn them into New York socialites, paragons of virtue and sophistication.

Those girls are a lot of shit, but paragons of virtue, they ain't. We know this, and we know it for a fact, from their own mouths, having discussed—as mentioned—in detail, the various sexual arts we'd all gotten up to.

Wait, you're confused.

They moved to New York, I'd said.

See, we always just connected, and on a personal level. We got each other in a way no one else did. Twins understand twins, and artists understand artists. But to have twins who are artists? Finding that? That's a one in a trillion to the third power kind of rarity. So when Rachel The Fruit Loop moved the girls to New York, we stayed in touch. We emailed in giant CC chains, and texted in a constantly-buzzing group text thread, we FaceTimed and Skyped, and we even wrote actual, stupid, wrist-cramping letters, and we chilled for old time's sake whenever all four of us happened to be in Ketchikan in the summers— anything to retain that mystical, golden connection to the only pair of people on the goddamn planet who understood us.

It got harder as Cane and I got bigger in the music world, and as Tate and Aerie got bigger in the hoity-toity world of upper crust New York City. We kept in contact, but it got nearly impossible to keep the connection as strong as it had once been, especially when we started touring overseas and they did semesters in Paris and London and Rome.

Then, we got the call that Dad had died—the awful, unthinkable horror.

We kicked free of the tour, which had sucked mightily, since we'd been touring with bands we'd grown up idolizing, but our fucking dad had just died so obviously we had to go, and may the consequences get fucked like a cheap hooker.

The connection almost snapped, then.

We got sucked into the whirlwind that was eight Badd brothers all grown up and in one place, each of us with wild hairs up our asses, and the girls were just everywhere at once doing I don't even know fucking what, posting on Insta from Rome and then Tahiti and then New York, and then Dubai, all within a month.

Now, they were back in Ketchikan, indefinitely.

Or, sort of. They were *going* to be back. I'd kind of lied to Bax: the girls weren't actually *in* Ketchikan yet, but we'd had a group video chat in which the girls informed us that they'd decided they needed an indefinite break from being world famous social media darlings—their words—and in which I'd learned, via Aerie's babblesome rambling, about the announcement that Eva was marrying Thomas, a wedding which had been speculated about for years but had never quite materialized. Aerie had said, blah blah blah, an off again on again relationship blah blah blah, all the rumor mills were that Thomas was a horrible sot and a philandering womanizer and just a real jerk blah blah blah.

That long rambling train of thought? That's what it's like to talk to the girls. So yeah, buckle up, ya'll.

This here gon' be *fuuun*.

The girls are back in town; the boys are back in town...

And though Cane and I haven't outright discussed it, we've decided we want to figure out once and for all why we haven't hooked up with those fine-ass Kingsley twins, and do something about it.

Tate for Cane, Aerie for me.

Right?

Ehhhh...it might be a little more complicated than that, methinks.

This is two sets of identical twins we're talking about here, and ain't not a one of us any kind of normal, ya'll.

Meaning—translating my *Corin is a crazy lunatic* nonsense—

I have no idea what that means, actually.

Just that whatever happens, it probably won't be like any of us are expecting.

See…when we had the group video chat, the girls were whispering a lot to each other in little private asides, which was normal. What wasn't normal was the weird gleam in their eyes, or the way the camera angles had somehow worked in our favor, meaning we were getting "accidental" down-blouse looks at their fine-ass titties.

Them's just might be into us, Brother Cane, I'd said to him.

Yessir, they rather do seem to be, Brother Corin, he'd replied.

Heh. We're so funny.

You ever tie a sparkler to a cat's tail, and then try to hold on to it?

That's kind of like the Kingsley twins.

Like I said…this here is gonna be fun.

Crazy, but fun.

I hope.

Visit me at my website: **www.jasindawilder.com**
Email me: **jasindawilder@gmail.com**

If you enjoyed this book, you can help others enjoy it as well by recommending it to friends and family, or by mentioning it in reading and discussion groups and online forums. You can also review it on the site from which you purchased it. But, whether you recommend it to anyone else or not, thank you *so much* for taking the time to read my book! Your support means the world to me!

My other titles:

The Preacher's Son:
Unbound
Unleashed
Unbroken

Biker Billionaire:
Wild Ride

Big Girls Do It:
Better (#1), Wetter (#2), Wilder (#3), On Top (#4)
Married (#5)
On Christmas (#5.5)
Pregnant (#6)
Boxed Set

Rock Stars Do It:
Harder
Dirty
Forever
Boxed Set

From the world of *Big Girls* and *Rock Stars*:
Big Love Abroad

Delilah's Diary:
A Sexy Journey
La Vita Sexy
A Sexy Surrender

The Falling Series:
Falling Into You
Falling Into Us
Falling Under
Falling Away
Falling for Colton

The Ever Trilogy:
Forever & Always
After Forever
Saving Forever

Badd Brothers:
Badd Motherf*cker
Badd Ass
Bass to the Bone

The Black Room
(With Jade London):
Door One
Door Two
Door Three
Door Four
Door Five
Door Six
Door Seven
Door Eight
Deleted Door

Standalone titles:
Yours
The Long Way Home

Non-Fiction titles:
Big Girls Do It Running
Big Girls Do It Stronger

Jack Wilder Titles:
The Missionary

To be informed of new releases and special offers, sign up for
Jasinda's email newsletter.

Made in the USA
Lexington, KY
10 August 2017